WIDOW'S PEAK

CELIA HARWOOD

NEUF NEZNOIRS LIMITED

Published by Neuf Neznoirs Limited
Unit 10, 91-93 Liverpool Road, Castlefield, Manchester, M3 4JN.
e-mail: gemggirg@gmail.com

ISBN 978-0-9933261-0-3

Revised and reprinted 2018

British Library Cataloguing in Publication Data.
A catalogue record for this book is available from the British Library.

Printed and bound in England by 4edge Ltd. Hockley, Essex
Tel: 01702 200243

For
BETTY ALLEN
of Buxton.

Chapter One

The whole of the spa town of Buxton turned out for the Sale of Work in aid of the Returned Soldiers' and Sailors' Convalescent Fund. Or, more accurately, the ladies and gentlemen who, in their own estimation, were the town turned out for the occasion. Most of the ordinary folk of Buxton took no part in the event because, in these difficult financial times, they either had little idle time in which to create items for sale, or no spare money with which to purchase things they did not need, no matter how good the cause.

This particular charity event, ordained at the highest level of the town's society, was taking place at Top Trees, the largest mansion in that part of the town known as The Park. At the beginning of the War, Lady Caroline Carleton-West the chatelaine of Top Trees, had rallied support from the ladies of the town and, for four years, they had knitted socks, wound bandages, and assembled parcels to send to the troops recruited from the Peak District, and anxiously scanned the lists of killed or wounded for names they knew. That same group of ladies had now organised the Sale of Work. Although the War had ended eighteen months ago, there were still quite a few returned soldiers in the town, undergoing hydrotherapy treatments or convalescing, so the need to raise funds was self-evident.

The Sale of Work was due to begin at three o'clock. At a quarter to the hour, Lady Carleton-West was in command of the small drawing room at Top Trees ready to welcome the Deputy Mayor and other distinguished guests. Those of lesser consequence would be ushered by one of the servants straight to the garden marquee where they would be greeted by the organisers.

Lady Carleton-West was a large, solidly built woman, in her late fifties, and of striking appearance. Tall and with very strong facial features, she was never destined to be either a beauty or the shy violet type. However, she was very astute and from an early age had understood that, with the right advice and a generous dress allowance, any woman can aspire to elegance, no matter what size or awkward shape she has been endowed with. At the age of twenty-one, for the first season after her marriage, she had put herself into the hands of Monsieur Raymond, the head couturier at that famous London fashion house, Maison Christophe. He had created evening gowns and day wear specifically for her, unique designs and, therefore, very costly; but where money is no object, creativity can flourish unfettered. Maison Christophe still supplied Lady Carleton-West with individual creations at the beginning of every season.

Lady Carleton-West had no patience with women who were too weak to resist the latest fashion, even when the style was unflattering for their figure. She remained firmly corseted despite the more relaxed dress rules which had been gaining favour with the younger ladies since the War. She had recently eschewed the fashionable blouse dress which, as she said forthrightly, would only make her look like a sack of coal even if it was the very latest style. Lady Carleton-West's milliner was just as skilful in designing her hats which emphasised her best features and her hairdresser, who came daily, was a genius. Consequently, Lady Carleton-West always appeared to advantage wherever she went. She was much admired and much feared by the ladies of The Park.

Lady Carleton-West's self-appointed lieutenant, Mrs Mary Giffard, was in the marquee at Top Trees inspecting the arrangements and giving orders to the ladies who were putting the final touches to the stalls.

'Decorated plates. How original,' said Mrs Giffard, as she passed Mrs Patterson who was timidly arranging her own contribution at the end of one of the tables. 'I'm sure someone will find them attractive.' Mrs Giffard moved on, eyes glinting, lips pursed, like a sergeant major inspecting a platoon notorious for its sloppiness. 'Mrs Hampson, I think those aprons would be better over there next to the pot holders. They are more likely to interest someone who is looking for plain, practical items.' She whirled around and glared at a maid who was almost invisible behind a large potted palm. 'Ah, Beryl, there you are. At last! Bring that over here. Put it next to the easel. That watercolour needs something to draw the eye. No, not there,' she added, impatiently. 'More to the right. No, my right, not yours!'

Mrs Giffard had an income to match Lady Carleton-West's and, unlike that lady, she was blessed with a face and figure that complemented any fashion currently in vogue. She ordered her clothes each season from a couturier in Paris. Although she was in her late forties, she was still very good looking and must have been stunningly beautiful as a young girl. Thick, dark hair twisted into shining coils and secured at the back of her head with jewelled combs, a heart-shaped face, perfectly proportioned and accentuated by a little dip in her centre of her hairline, large dark eyes, long eyelashes, high cheekbones, and a straight, elegant nose. A sculptor could have used her face as a model for Helen of Troy. There was nothing that needed correction. The same, unfortunately, could not be said of her personality.

Very little was known about Mrs Giffard other than that she was a very rich widow recently returned to England, having lived for many years in the Far East. Mr Giffard was never mentioned. During her first weeks in Buxton, Mrs Giffard had been forced to remind her new acquaintances and the tradespeople that her name was pronounced Jiffard.

She had to repeat this instruction so frequently that people began to refer to her as "Mrs Giffard-pronounced-Jiffard" as though that was her name. It had started as a joke but had soon become a widespread habit.

♣♣♣

At Hall Bank, separated from The Park by the Pavilion Gardens, an elderly clerk pushed open the door of one of the upstairs offices at Harriman & Talbot, Solicitors, Notaries and Commissioners for Oaths. He said, quietly: 'It's a quarter to three, Miss Eleanor. You did ask me to remind you.'

Eleanor Harriman looked up from her desk. 'Thank you, James,' she said and paused. 'Although, I wish it wasn't. I wish it was six o'clock. Then the wretched Sale of Work would be over and I would be strolling peacefully in the Gardens with Napoleon.' She put down her pen and stretched her arms out in front of her. At the sound of his name, Napoleon, a large Boxer, sat up, anticipating activity and hoping that it included him.

Napoleon had been given to Eleanor by her father on her birthday the second year after her brother Edgar had been killed in France. Eleanor had named him Napoleon because of his habit, as a puppy, of tucking one front paw under his chest when he was asleep. The name had proved appropriate for other reasons because, like his namesake, he was also very good at conquering and occupying other people's territory. He was her constant companion. When she was at work in the office he would snooze on the floor beside her desk, or sit and look out of the window at the people promenading on the Slopes. If a client arrived, he would be ordered to move to the living quarters on the floor above but he would make only a tactical retreat and position himself at the top of the stairs so that he could eaves-drop.

'Oh, how I hate these charity events. It would be so much easier just to send money.'

'Yes, Miss Eleanor, it would, but it's expected,' said James. 'Not all of the people in The Park go to Manchester when they want a solicitor and if we do not support them, they will not patronise us. It is unfortunate that Mr Harriman has been called away to that creditors' meeting in Manchester today, else he would have gone. But he will not be back until five, and Mr Talbot is still at Court, so there's nothing for it, I'm afraid. You will have to go in their stead.'

He spoke with the familiarity of a long acquaintance. James Wildgoose had been Harriman & Talbot's confidential clerk for over thirty years and had known her when she was a little girl and not the solicitor she now was.

'Mother would have enjoyed it. She loved that sort of thing.'

'Her passing was a great loss,' said James, gently.

'Very well, James,' said Eleanor, sighing as she reached for her coat. 'I'm resigned to my fate. But I shall bring back a pair of very prickly knitted socks for you to wear.'

James merely smiled and retreated to his desk on the ground floor, leaving her to tidy her hair and put on her hat and gloves. Eleanor went in search of their housekeeper. 'I'm off now, Mrs Clayton. Will you keep an eye on Napoleon for me?'

'Of course, Miss Harriman. He's no trouble.'

'That's because he admires your cooking. Oh, Lord! Speaking of cooking. I've just remembered. Those cakes Mrs Giffard wanted you to make for the afternoon teas. Do you want me to take them with me?'

'No, that's all right,' Mrs Clayton said. 'Mr Wildgoose had young Eric deliver them this morning.'

'Bless you both. That's wonderfully efficient of you and I shall be able to face her with a clear conscience. I'll have to buy a few things at the sale. Is there anything particular you need for the kitchen?'

'No, Miss Harriman, I don't think so, thank you… although, now you mention it. This pot holder has seen better days so a new one would not go amiss.'

'Right you are. I'll get going then,' said Eleanor.

Eleanor went downstairs leaving Napoleon with Mrs Clayton. James, who was waiting for her in the outer office, handed her some money from the petty cash tin and reminded her to give her father's apologies for missing the event. She went down the hill towards The Park, thinking that at least it was a pleasant day for a walk.

As she walked, Eleanor thought about The Park and its social hierarchy. Until her mother's death four years ago, she had been part of that world and she had been very glad to escape from it. The Park was physically and socially separate from the rest of the town. Most of Buxton's residents lived either in the oldest part of the town, perched high above the river Wye at the top of an escarpment and protected on three sides by steep cliffs, or in the lower part of the town which, since the more peaceful eighteenth century, had spread along the unprotected eastern bank of the river at the foot of the escarpment. People had been coming to the warm springs at Buxton for over three thousand years, either to worship at them or to bathe in them according to their religion. These visitors, in need of food and lodgings, had provided the impetus for a permanent settlement and the town had evolved slowly, following its own convenience without much concern for the overall plan. Farms, inns, lodging-houses, pubs, and shops had been built where and when they were needed, linked by track-ways which later became streets.

By contrast, The Park was of more recent origin and

planned specifically for those with a large income. The Duke of Devonshire owned the land and the original design for The Park was by Sir Joseph Paxton, of Crystal Palace fame, who had been employed by the Duke at nearby Chatsworth. In the opinion of its residents, these aristocratic origins gave The Park a certain caché which testified to their own unimpeachable taste and status and separated the area from the rest of the town. Large houses, each in a park-like garden setting, were set around a central circular road. In the late nineteenth century, The Park had attracted wealthy merchants, manufacturers, and professional men from the surrounding industrial areas who wanted to escape from the ugly, polluted cities they had created. The houses were large, architect designed, stone buildings of three or four floors, plus basement and attic. They were occupied by families cared for by servants, and surrounded by large gardens tended by gardeners. There was no commerce of any kind in The Park other than preparatory schools for the sons, who would go on to famous public schools in the south and then to Oxford or Cambridge, and schools for the daughters, who would be moulded into ladies and go on to matrimony and motherhood.

The wives of the local worthies ruled The Park. They formed a tightly controlled hierarchy of financially confident, socially insecure matrons, most of whom had acquired their wealth and social position within the last one or two generations. By tacit consent, they generously overlooked any imperfections in each other's ancestry, although oblique hints were sometimes thrown out if it was necessary to quash an arrangement or plan thought to be lacking in taste.

Lady Carleton-West was firmly ensconced at the top of this social hierarchy. She was the wife of Sir Marmaduke Carleton-West, a baronet of very little ability and even less charisma. His two achievements in life were inheriting a title from his grandfather, and marrying a woman who intended to make full use of that title. Lady Carleton-West also intended to make full use of the wealth which Sir Marmaduke's grandfather had accumulated as a result of diverting the resources of his cutlery factory to the manufacture of weapons for Her Majesty's Government during the Crimean War. For this sacrifice he had been doubly rewarded: he had made a fortune, to which had then been added a baronetcy.

Thirty-five years ago, Lady Carleton-West had moved the family from Sheffield to Buxton. She had purchased Top Trees, the largest house in The Park, had it lavishly furnished, engaged a butler and staff, and set about making it the focal point of polite society in the town and herself the arbiter of "good taste." Sir Marmaduke's only role was to sign cheques, which he did willingly on condition that he was free to hunt, shoot on the moors, fish in the river Wye, and visit his club when the weather was too poor for any of those activities.

Mrs Mary Giffard, on the other hand, had arrived in Buxton only about four years ago but she regarded herself as Lady Carleton-West's equal. She was full of energy, ambition, and plans. She chose a house called High Beeches, far too large for one person but commensurate with the social position she intended to occupy in the town. High Beeches had been renovated, completely redecorated, and renamed Manar. Several of the houses in the Park had a lawn tennis court but Mrs Giffard went a step further. Her tennis court had the latest type of clay surface and she had added a pavilion from which her guests could watch the players in comfort. She had also tried to match Lady Carleton-West in the matter of staff but, much to her regret, had been unable to engage a butler. There was a shortage of men owing to the War and she had had to be content with a parlour-maid to open the front door to her guests. Her staff also included a housekeeper, a ladies' maid, a cook, a kitchen maid, and a gardener. Two years ago she had also acquired a very expensive motor-car and a chauffeur. All of this grandeur and the expense involved was variously commented on, admired, or censured, by the other residents of The Park and left many people wondering at the size and source of her income.

Mrs Giffard was the first to volunteer for any of Lady Carleton-West's projects, offered the use of her house and garden for charity at every possible opportunity, and was forever pressing Lady Carleton-West to rely on her for "any little thing, no matter how small, if it would be of the least use" which annoyed the other ladies of The Park immensely. They considered that, despite their more modest financial resources, their long years of residence naturally gave them precedence over the newly arrived Mrs Giffard-pronounced-Jiffard. The words "pushy" and "full of herself" had even been muttered rebelliously on occasion.

Mrs Giffard was self-confident and domineering and might easily have been completely cold-shouldered but she was also very clever. On arrival in the town, she had sought introductions to influential people. She was assiduous with her morning calls and also left cards for any suitably distinguished, preferably titled, people visiting Buxton for the season. She kept up with all the local news and gossip and made discreet enquiries as to the financial status of her new neighbours. She soon discovered that the income and the entertainment budgets of some of The Park's residents had been seriously curtailed because of the War. Their depleted funds now made it difficult for them to give dinner parties and keep up appearances. Mrs Giffard was quick to realise that invitations to Manar would create a significant increase in the number of social engagements which these residents of The Park could enjoy without any expense to themselves. As soon as visiting etiquette permitted, she began issuing invitations to dinner parties, tea parties, afternoon bridge parties, theatre parties, after-theatre supper parties, and tennis parties. Every social occasion at Manar was a lavish affair at which the best food and drink were served. Thus the residents of The Park willingly accepted her invitations, ate and drank their fill, and withheld judgment. Such was the price of her acceptance and both she and the Park's residents were more than willing to pay it.

Chapter Two

Eleanor had strolled to Top Trees at a leisurely pace, postponing her arrival as long as she decently could but finally she had reached the freshly raked carriage drive. Two motor-cars were parked along one side of the drive. A black one, which she did not recognise, and a large dark green Bentley, which she knew had been recently acquired by her friend, Philip Danebridge. Eleanor had met Philip and his family six years ago when she was engaged to his cousin Alistair, and after Alistair's death in France, Eleanor and Philip had become firm friends, united by loss. Eleanor was amused to see the Bentley because Philip and his parents lived at Wood End, only about two hundred yards away from Top Trees. Eleanor would have been even more amused had she seen Philip that morning pacing around the garden wondering whether or not, given the mildness of the weather, it would be bad form to drive the short distance to Top Trees instead of walking. Quite a few people in Buxton now had motor-cars but he didn't want to be accused of showing off; nevertheless, pride in his new acquisition had won. Nearly everyone else had decided to walk.

By the time Eleanor arrived at Top Trees, Lady Carleton-West had abandoned the small drawing room and was presiding in the marquee.

'Good afternoon, Ash,' said Eleanor. 'The weather has been very kind to us today.'

'Good afternoon, Miss Harriman. Yes, we certainly have been favoured.'

Eleanor had been to Top Trees often enough to be greeted

by the butler by name. Before the War, the family at Top Trees had been served by a footman as well, but he had gone to serve his country instead of Lady Carleton-West and now lay buried in a Belgian field. Today, Ash handed Eleanor on to a female servant, saying: 'Miss Addison will take you through to the garden, Miss Harriman, if you will just follow her. You will find Lady Carleton-West in the marquee.'

Miss Addison was a thin woman probably in her mid-thirties and of a sombre appearance. Her face was not used to smiling and she wore spectacles which made her look very severe. Her dark hair was smoothed back and twisted firmly into a knot at the nape of her neck. She wore a very plain black dress, black stockings, and black shoes. The only bright touch was a black necklace made of jet which reflected the light. The necklace was beautiful and it seemed out of place against the plainness of her uniform. Eleanor did not recognise her as one of the servants at Top Trees and concluded that she must be new. She followed the servant through the conservatory and into the garden where a large marquee had been set up in the centre of the lawn.

'Miss Harriman, how lovely to see you,' squeaked Miss Pymble, the vicar's elderly cousin.

'So good of you to come,' twittered Miss Felicity Pymble, five minutes her junior and almost identical twin.

'Good afternoon, Miss Pymble, Miss Felicity,' said Eleanor, smiling at each in turn, and allowing herself to be steered into the marquee between them, a bony but steely hand gripping each of her arms. Eleanor was very fond of these two ladies. They still dressed in the fashion of their youth and retained the manners, morals, and good habits which had been instilled into them in a country rectory by a nanny and then reinforced by a governess. When they were thirty-five and still living at home, their father died and they were obliged to leave the rectory. Their cousin invited them to accompany him when he came to Buxton to take up his position as vicar. That was nearly thirty years ago and since then the Misses Pymble had lived at Waverton House on Bath Road and provided accommodation for visitors. They had taught most of the parish in Sunday School, supplied food or medicine to all the families in need, raised funds for the town's charities, and helped to run almost every Church fête or charity event. They had also welcomed every new curate with a good, hearty dinner and given him free accommodation until he got himself settled in.

'You've just missed the official opening,' said Miss Pymble.

'What a shame,' said Eleanor, trying to express regret.

'Unfortunately the Mayor is indisposed but the Deputy Mayor gave a lovely speech,' said Miss Felicity.

'Yes, I'm sure he did,' said Eleanor. The Deputy Mayor was well-meaning in his attempts to encourage civic pride but his speeches on such occasions were notoriously long-winded and pompous. Eleanor looked around the marquee and added: 'Goodness, the ladies have been busy. They must have been working very hard.'

'Oh, yes. This has taken weeks of preparation. Start at this end, Miss Harriman. You are sure to find something useful here,' said Miss Pymble.

'Do excuse us while we go and welcome these other newcomers,' said Miss Felicity.

'Of course,' said Eleanor. She smiled as she watched the two ladies advance in a pincer movement and capture another new arrival.

The marquee had been skilfully decorated with red, white, and blue bunting and large floral arrangements in the same colours. Trestle tables, each covered with either a red, white or blue cloth, were loaded with items created by the ladies for the sale. The marquee was full of people milling about, greeting each other, or exclaiming over various items of work. Although one or two of the ladies were still in black mourning, most wore brightly coloured afternoon frocks on which a great deal of money had been spent. The dresses were of the very latest style, but a style which, unfortunately for many of the ladies, aimed to create a fluid, sylph-like effect. On some, who should have followed Lady Carleton-West's advice, the draped fabric and floating panels simply refused to drape or float and, instead, clung unmoving against ample, firmly-corseted hips.

Eleanor tried to melt into the crowd, which was not an easy task, given that she was dressed soberly for work in a navy blue serge skirt and jacket, high buttoned blouse, and sensible shoes. She was conscious of the fact that People probably thought that she should have changed into an afternoon frock but Eleanor had never been particularly interested in her appearance and was not overly concerned by the opinion of People. Her preference for independence was much tutted over by the ladies of The Park who considered Eleanor's decision to become a solicitor and to work full-time as the most wilful and extraordinary behaviour. The ladies of The Park could not understand why someone whose mother was a member of the aristocracy and whose father was wealthy enough to support her, should choose to behave in this peculiar way and be allowed to ruin her marriage prospects.

Eleanor stared without enthusiasm at the arrangement of 'useful' items from which she was expected to choose her purchases: drawn thread-work table cloths, embroidered hand-towels, tapestry scissors holders and spectacle cases, draught excluders, pincushions, needle cases, handkerchief sachets, aprons and pot-holders. A whole array of household items for which Eleanor had no need; however, the honour of the firm was at stake so she dutifully considered the selection, listening to the conversation going on around her as she did so. The organisers and their supporters were greeting each other and commenting on the quality and variety of work.

'Isn't this simply too marvellous?'

'Lady Carleton-West and her team have done us proud.'

'As usual.'

'Oh, look, here's Daisy's tapestry. She spent months on that.'

'Darling, it's lovely to see you. Where have you been hiding? I haven't seen you for an absolute age. Come and look at this decoupage of Winifred's. Isn't it too clever?'

'Here's Muriel's water colour of Chee Tor. I do wish I had her talent.'

'Oh, I simply must have some of these embroidered egg-cosies. They are so cheerful.'

'That papier-mâché tray is absolutely stunning. I think I shall buy that.'

Rising above the general buzz, Eleanor identified the voice of Lady Carleton-West:

'Mrs Frampton, may I introduce Major Giffard and Mrs Giffard. They are staying at Oxford House. Mrs Frampton is one of our most tireless workers, Major.'

Eleanor turned to look at these newcomers but she could see only their backs. Her interest was aroused because Oxford House belonged to her younger sister, Cicely, who provided furnished apartments to visitors during the season.

Lady Carleton-West continued: 'The Major is staying here for the benefit of his health and, happily, is not in need of the Convalescent Fund himself. The Major and his wife have very generously come along to lend their support but the Major he tells me that there are a great many people of his acquaintance, including people from his former regiment, who are very much in need of assistance. Isn't it gratifying to know that our humble efforts are being appreciated?'

As Mrs Frampton was telling the newcomers how delighted she was to welcome them to the town and hoping that they would enjoy their stay, Mrs Giffard was talking to a young man in a brown suit. She detached herself from him and stood beside Mrs Frampton. Lady Carleton-West turned again to the Major and his wife, saying: 'And may I present another one of our able helpers? Mrs….' Then she stopped, looked confused, and said: 'Oh!… What a co-incidence! Mrs Giffard, may I introduce Major and Mrs Giffard.'

'How strange' said Mrs Frampton. 'You even pronounce your names the same way. Are you related by any chance?'

The Major bowed slightly towards the older Mrs Giffard, saying: 'I am sorry to say that, if we are, we can only be distantly so. I have no relatives in England as far as I am aware.'

'The Major and Mrs Giffard are visiting from Edinburgh,' interrupted Lady Carleton-West.

'I have lived in Scotland for most of my life,' said Major Giffard, 'although I was born in India. Calcutta actually. I left there many years ago as a child. Until now, I have not met anyone with the same name as mine. What a pleasure to find that there is, after all, someone else who shares my surname even though we may not be connected.'

Eleanor thought from the startled look on Mrs Giffard's face that she feared that there might well be a connection between them, and an unwelcome one at that. Mrs Giffard seemed to have been thrown off-balance and looked completely ill at ease. 'In fact,' thought Eleanor, 'she actually looks ill.'

Mrs Giffard did not respond to the Major. To ease the awkwardness of the moment, the Major's wife said: 'Of course, your name is Giffard by marriage, as is mine, so you may not know many of your husband's connections.'

The comment seemed to have been kindly meant but instead of staying to discuss the possibility of mutual relatives, Mrs Giffard fumbled an apology and said that unfortunately she had to rush away. This early departure had clearly not been planned and was certainly not approved of by Lady Carleton-West.

'How extraordinary! What can have caused her to rush off like that?' said Lady Carleton-West.

'Perhaps it was the mention of her husband,' said Mrs Frampton. 'She is a widow remember.'

'Oh dear,' said the Major's wife, 'I didn't think. I hope I haven't distressed her.'

Lady Carleton-West reassured the Major's wife as she steered her two guests away to the tables of work. Eleanor too began to turn away but the man in the brown suit pushed past her roughly and, without apologising, hurried after Lady Carleton-West and her party. A voice behind Eleanor said: 'Are you hurt, Miss?' and when Eleanor turned around she saw that Miss Addison, the servant who had shown her to the marquee, was standing behind her, accompanied by a maid carrying a tray. It was the maid who had spoken. Miss Addison's attention was fixed on the departing group. Eleanor assured the maid that she was uninjured and Miss Addison, recalled to duty, said: 'May I offer you a cup of tea, Miss?' She handed Eleanor a cup and saucer from the tray and moved on to the next guest.

Eleanor wondered about the significance of the scene she had just witnessed. The man in the brown suit and Miss Addison had certainly found it interesting. Eleanor sipped her tea and was contemplating how soon she could decently follow the example of the elder Mrs Giffard and leave the Sale of Work when Philip Danebridge approached her with a cheery: 'What ho, Eleanor!' Can I please talk to someone normal?'

'Good afternoon, Philip. I knew you were here somewhere. I saw your motor-car outside. What do you mean, normal? To whom have you been talking?'

'Aaagh!' he said, banging the side of his head with his hand. 'I've been having my ear bent by Mr Wentworth-Streate. I was stuck in the corner and just couldn't get away.

He's got a new addition to his rare plant collection. Wanted to tell me all the intimate details of its origins and life cycle. It's some rare thing from the Amazon. Poisonous probably, like the rest of his collection.'

'May I offer you tea, sir?'

Miss Addison was standing beside Philip and he turned and thanked her as he took the tea.

'I don't think all his plants are poisonous,' said Eleanor. 'Apparently his collection is very well thought of in horticultural circles.'

'So he has been telling me…at great length.' Philip sipped his tea. 'Apparently, some writer chap came recently and had a poke about in it. He produced a piece in the journal of some learned society for the preservation or promotion of something or other. I narrowly missed having the whole thing read out to me on the spot by Wentworth-Streate. Fortunately Mrs Apthorp turned up and rescued me. She wanted to buttonhole him about some fête or other at the hospital.' He took another mouthful of tea. 'Are you staying here long? May I offer you a lift back to the office?'

'Thank you, Philip. I shall be delighted to accept your offer of escape.'

'Jolly good. That justifies me bringing the motor. I knew I should need it.'

'Just let me do my duty and buy some things from the stalls. I'll get a few useful items but I want something frivolous to take back for Mrs Clayton.'

'Right. I'll help you.'

Some thirty minutes later, Eleanor and Philip managed to leave, with an assortment of items from the sale. As they walked down the carriage drive towards Philip's motor-car, Eleanor said: 'Did you discover who owns that other motor-car?'

'It's a Crossley,' he said, opening the car door for Eleanor.

'Yes, but did you find out who owns it?'

'I did.'

There was a provoking silence while he started the car and put on his driving gloves.

'Well, come on. Tell all,' said Eleanor.

'Rupert Brantlingham, lives in Manchester, drove down this morning. Bit of a chancer, I'd say. That's not his motor. He's a salesman for a firm in Manchester and it belongs to his employer. His cousin is one of Lady C's helpers. She told him about the Sale of Work and he asked her to get him in and introduce him to people. Apparently he thinks there is a market for his motor-cars here and he persuaded his employer to let him have one for the day on the grounds that there might be a sale, or at the very least some publicity, in it.'

'Which one was he?'

'The one in the brown suit,' said Philip in a tone which condemned both the suit and its wearer.

'Oh, yes. He bumped into me without apologising. I noticed him talking to Mrs Giffard.'

'Pronounced Jiffard,' said Eleanor and Philip in unison, laughing as they drove away.

CHAPTER THREE

The following morning, Edwin Talbot, the younger half of Harriman & Talbot, arrived at the office on Hall Bank. After hanging up his hat and coat and checking the appointment book with James, he took a file into Eleanor's office. He exchanged a greeting with Napoleon and said to Eleanor, with an innocent smile: 'Good morning, Eleanor. How was the Sale of Work? I am sorry I had a valid excuse for missing it.'

Eleanor pulled a face: 'I'm sure you are.'

Edwin Talbot was in his late forties and a happily married family man. He was self-confident, generous, and a very capable lawyer. Eleanor's brother, Edgar Harriman, had been articled to him with the expectation that Edgar would one day join the firm as a junior partner. However, at the beginning of the War, Edgar, never keen on a career in law, had chosen to enlist and had been killed in France, aged twenty. Edwin Talbot had welcomed Mr Harriman's suggestion that Eleanor should take Edgar's place. Eleanor had been a willing and capable pupil and Edwin had quickly realised that she was more interested in the work of a solicitor and better suited to the role than her brother would ever have been. He had never mentioned that to anyone except his wife but he had encouraged Eleanor and was very pleased with her progress. An easy, bantering friendship had developed between them.

'Did you lash out with the petty cash?' asked Edwin.

'I did my bit. The honour of the firm has been preserved. I brought back some odds and ends for the kitchen and an apron and a tea cosy that I thought Mrs Clayton might like for herself. She doesn't have much to spare for new things. I also got a scarf for her and one each for her two boys.'

'So who was there? All the usuals?'

'Absolutely,' said Eleanor, 'all in their appointed place, or should that be anointed place. All doing Lady Carleton-West's bidding and being worried by her sheep-dog, Mrs Giffard-pronounced-Jiffard. Just as you would expect.'

'It was good of you to go, Eleanor. I know you find those events very tedious and your father does appreciate it.'

'Well, there was some compensation, though.'

Eleanor described the encounter between the three Giffards.

'Mrs Giffard's behaviour was so uncharacteristic,' said Eleanor. 'She is usually so self-possessed and confident but yesterday she was literally lost for words.'

'It does sound very odd,' said Edwin. 'If the Giffards are staying at Oxford House, perhaps your sister will be able to shed some light on the subject. Now, enough chatting. I need you to do some drafting for me. Chillingham and Baynard's Bank is ready to proceed against Mr Wilde for that unpaid loan so we need to draft the claim. Can you do that for me? Then I can get it filed first thing Monday. Here's the file. If you have any questions, come and see me. Oh, and can you keep Napoleon up here? Mrs Hird is coming in for her new Will at eleven o'clock.'

Edwin left for his own office and Napoleon stationed himself at the window, dividing his attention between the people who were walking down Hall Bank towards the Old Hall and the Crescent and those who were strolling about on The Slopes. Eleanor settled down at her desk, pulled the file towards her, and started to draft the claim which was going to disrupt the life of the Wilde family. There had been a lot of work drafting claims and bankruptcy notices lately and Eleanor was only too aware that whilst it was good for their business, it was not good for the town. She sighed. One other misery to blame on the War.

As it was Saturday, the office of Harriman & Talbot closed at one o'clock. By then, Eleanor had drafted the claim, had it checked by Edwin, copied by James, and left ready for filing on Monday morning. Accompanied by Napoleon, Eleanor went off to play tennis. The season had just begun and she wanted to be in top form when the Lawn Tennis Club began its campaign to win the trophy at this year's Peak District tournament.

At two thirty that afternoon, the ladies of The Park were assembled at Top Trees for a committee meeting. A new kitchen and dining room had been planned for the Devonshire Hospital and Princess Mary was coming the following year to lay the foundation stone. Various civic events were being organised by the town to mark the occasion and the ladies of The Park were meeting to discuss the part they intended to play in these events.

'Well, ladies, shall we begin?' said Lady Carleton-West. 'I shall take the chair as usual, shall I?' The ladies knew from experience that this was a statement of intention not a question.

'Mrs Giffard isn't here yet,' said Mrs Frampton, warily.

'She is usually very punctual,' volunteered Mrs Wentworth-Streate, timidly.

'Shall we start without her, ladies?' said Lady Carleton-West. Another statement disguised as a question.

'I could telephone to Manar and ask if she is on her way,' said Miss Pymble tentatively.

'That won't be necessary' said Lady Carleton-West, firmly.

'It is most unusual,' said Miss Felicity.

'And she is our secretary,' said Mrs Apthorp.

'Someone else can take the minutes,' said Lady Carleton-West. 'Mrs Frampton, I would be very grateful if you would oblige.'

'Certainly. But I believe Mrs Giffard has the correspondence, and the response to our invitation to the Princess to attend the Ladies Auxiliary afternoon tea.' Mrs Frampton added, deferentially, 'That was to be the principal reason for today's meeting.'

'Then we shall assume that Her Royal Highness will accept our invitation and move on to the next item on the agenda which is the arrangements for the decorations. We can manage without Mrs Giffard for that, I think,' said Lady Carleton-West, icily.

It was clear that Her Royal Highness was to have no further say in the matter and would be expected to do exactly as Lady Carleton-West decreed. Mrs Giffard's failure to attend had been noted and would no doubt be dealt with in due course.

Chapter Four

For almost thirty years, the Harrimans had lived at The Park in a large house called Hare Wood but, like many other families in Buxton, their lives had been disrupted and altered by the War. Several years before the War, the two eldest daughters, Amelia and Alice, had married and moved away from Buxton, although they returned to Hare Wood with their children each year for the summer holidays and Christmas. Then Cicely, the youngest daughter, had married and only Eleanor and Edgar, the only son, were left at Hare Wood. Then Edgar had been killed in France and, the following year, Cicely's husband, Wilfred, had been killed. Cicely and her young son, Richard, moved back to Hare Wood and then Mrs Harriman had died.

After Mrs Harriman's funeral, Mr Harriman and his four daughters agreed that the memory of happier times at Hare Wood was in danger of being blotted out by ghosts and they decided to sell Hare Wood. It was agreed that Cicely would move to Oxford House, a property on Broad Walk which Mr Harriman had purchased many years ago as an investment, so that she could offer accommodation to visitors and support herself and her son, and Mr Harriman and Eleanor would move to Hall Bank and occupy the two floors above their office at Hall Bank.

Mr Harriman decided to employ a housekeeper for Hall Bank and had been lucky enough to find Mrs Clayton. Her husband had been killed at Gallipoli in 1915 and she and her two young boys had moved in with her brother and his family. Mrs Clayton came to Hall Bank during the day, organised the household, cooked meals as required for Mr Harriman and Eleanor, and supervised the maid who came in to do the cleaning and the rough work. In the evenings she went home to be with her two boys. The original Georgian kitchen in the basement was turned into storage for the client's file boxes and office equipment and a modern kitchen was installed for Mrs Clayton in the freed-up space on the first floor. The new arrangement suited everyone perfectly. They worked as a team and provided mutual support as they each tried to pick up the pieces of lives fragmented by the War.

Mr Harriman was aware that moving from The Park and "going to live above the shop" was regarded by some of his acquaintances as a "come down" and by others as dangerously eccentric. Many people shook their heads and put his odd behaviour down to the loss of his wife who, they were sure, had been "a steadying influence" on him. However, Mr Harriman was more concerned about the effect this move would have on Eleanor's social prospects than his own. Eleanor had assured him that she did not mind in the least what People thought and that her real friends would not care a bit. As she continued to get more invitations from The Park than she wanted, Mr Harriman had ceased to worry.

On the Sunday after the Sale of Work, Eleanor, accompanied by Napoleon, walked from Hall Bank along Broad Walk to Oxford House to visit her sister, Cicely, and nephew, Richard, who was nearly six years old. Oxford House was one of several large houses built on Broad Walk fifty years ago to accommodate visitors to the spa. It was a substantial, three storied stone building with large, bay windows facing west towards the Pavilion Gardens and an uninterrupted view of Corbar Hill. It was ideally placed for visitors wanting to enjoy all the facilities that the town had to offer during the season between May and October. Eleanor and Napoleon usually visited Oxford House on

Sunday afternoons and, when the weather was fine, they accompanied Cicely and Richard to the Pavilion Gardens to listen to the band and feed the ducks. On this Sunday afternoon, they strolled in the Gardens and then, whilst Richard and Napoleon played with a ball, Eleanor and Cicely sat down to chat. Cicely had not been at the Sale of Work, although she had supplied cakes for the stall and loaned her maid, Susan, for the afternoon to help serve the teas. Eleanor had been too busy to call in at Oxford House since then so there was quite a bit of catching up to do.

Cicely said: 'Tell me about the Sale of Work. I heard a bit about it from Susan.'

Eleanor described the afternoon at Top Trees including the curious encounter between Major and Mrs Giffard and Mrs Giffard-pronounced-Jiffard. Eleanor was an excellent raconteur and her animated description of the event amused Cicely and made her laugh.

'Of course, now that I offer accommodation for a living that puts me in trade as far as the ladies in The Park are concerned and you, as a solicitor, are quite beyond the pale. I wonder that we are still welcome.'

'I'm sure that even when we lived at Hare Wood we were only ever included because Mummy was an Honourable. Otherwise, father's being a local solicitor would certainly have counted against us,' said Eleanor.

'I suppose,' said Cicely, putting on a very posh accent, 'when there are tradesmen lurking in one's recent past, it is absolutely essential to leave all that firmly behind. One has to be so very careful with whom one associates. One does not want to be judged by the company one keeps.'

'I hoped we would be putting The Park firmly behind us when father sold Hare Wood,' sighed Eleanor. 'I really hoped the invitations would cease. Still, if I hadn't been invited to the Sale of Work I would have missed the encounter between the Giffards.'

'What a co-incidence. About the names, I mean. And both pronounced Jiffard. And also a co-incidence that the Giffards are staying with me.'

'Yes, Lady C said they were.'

'They arrived last Tuesday,' said Cicely. 'They live in Edinburgh and they're on their way to London. They came here to break their journey and allow the Major to rest. Apparently, he has been having treatment and has to go to London for one more consultation which he is hoping will be his last.'

'How long are they staying?'

'They will be leaving on Thursday but they have booked to come back for a whole month next July which will be marvellous for my takings. They are such lovely people, too. Definitely my nicest guests so far, although, I have been lucky, I will admit.'

'Yes, I did wonder how you would cope providing accommodation. You are such a private person and you now have to deal with all-comers, some more demanding than others I should imagine, but you seem to be managing extremely well,' said Eleanor.

'Really, it has not been too difficult so far. And I am really pleased that the Giffards are coming back. They are so appreciative of everything and so kind to Richard. He's in awe of the Major, especially since he discovered that he's got a DSO, the same as Wilfred.'

The mention of Cicely's husband brought the conversation to a temporary halt and they sat watching Richard and Napoleon playing. Leaving Napoleon in possession of the ball, Richard came up to Eleanor and asked: 'Aunt Lella, are you coming home to tea with me?' The name, Eleanor, was difficult for a child's tongue to master and, at first, Richard could manage only Lella and the name had stuck.

'Richard, I would really like to come but I have to go to

a meeting.'

'What meeting?'

'The Girl Guides' committee meeting. They want me to help them write a letter to Buckingham Palace and ask for someone to come and meet the Guides.'

'I know the Palace,' said Richard proudly. 'We see it when we go to catch the train.'

'No, that's the Palace Hotel. It's next to the station. Buckingham Palace is in London. It's where the King lives.'

'Is Kingham Palace a hotel? Does the King live in a hotel?'

'No, he lives in Buckingham Palace. You ask too many questions.'

'No, I don't,' said Richard.

There was a pause and it was obvious that he was thinking things through. Then he asked: 'Aunt Lella, why do you have to write a letter? Why do you want the King to come here?'

'Because the Deputy Mayor and the townspeople want to make this town more important so that people will want to come and stay again like they did before the War. They think that if we have lots of royal visitors it will encourage other people to come too.'

'Why won't they come anyway? It's nice here.'

'Yes, it's very nice here but people can't come because they don't have as much money as they used to have and also they are very tired because of the War.'

'Oh,' said Richard. He thought for a bit and then said confidently: 'But the King won't come. Not if he lives in London. He'll be too busy.'

'You're right,' said Eleanor. 'Perhaps he will send someone else.' She smiled at Cicely. 'I'm glad we've resolved that. Now, I must go or I shall be late for the meeting. They want Princess Mary to meet the Guides when she comes next year to lay the foundation stone at the hospital. Come on

Leon.'

'Aunt Lella, can Napoleon come home with me for tea, if you're not?' asked Richard.

'Yes, if you promise to look after him and if Mummy agrees.'

Richard and Napoleon both looked at Cicely. Unable to resist the steady gaze of two pairs of brown eyes, Cicely said: 'Come on then. We'll walk Aunt Lella back to the gate and then we'll go home.' They all headed across the Gardens towards the Broad Walk entrance and, as they passed the boating lake, Eleanor noticed Rupert Brantlingham surrounded by a group of young men. 'Trying to sell motor-cars, I suppose.' thought Eleanor.

On the following day, Monday, Eleanor and Napoleon had finished their lunch-time walk and were sitting in the sunshine on Broad Walk. Eleanor was reading the newspaper and Napoleon was watching the passing parade. The Broad Walk formed the eastern boundary of the Pavilion Gardens. Keeping to the higher ground, it followed the contour of one of the natural terraces formed by the river Wye. Originally a practical footpath from the Crescent to the Cold Bath on Macclesfield Road, it had now become a fashionable promenade. Along one side of Broad Walk, facing the Pavilion Gardens, was a row of elegant, stone built houses with large bay windows designed to catch the sun. The houses were separated by wide, sweeping carriage drives and exuded an air of openness, languor, and luxury. They provided accommodation for the wealthier visitors and the perfect backdrop for the daily promenade of people engaged in an unhurried stroll, taking the air, greeting friends, and nodding to acquaintances. Sauntering along the Broad Walk was a tonic strong enough to banish all thought of the bustling, crowded, dirty industrial cities from which most of the visitors came.

Eleanor looked up briefly from her newspaper and noticed Major and Mrs Giffard strolling along in one direction and another group approaching them from the opposite direction. Two women were walking arm in arm accompanied by a dapper gentleman sporting a panama and a cane. One of the women detached herself from this party and, rushing forward, accosted the Giffards with:

'Good afternoon, Major and Mrs Giffard. We met at Lady Carleton-West's. At the Sale of Work.'

The Giffards stopped and looked slightly confused.

'Mrs Apthorp,' said the lady, helpfully, extending her hand to Mrs Giffard. 'My husband is one of the surgeons at the Devonshire Hospital. May I introduce my cousin, Mrs Rathbourne? And, her husband, Colonel Rathbourne?'

The introductions completed, Mrs Apthorp continued: 'My cousin and Colonel Rathbourne arrived early this morning from Rutland. Wasn't it a pity they were not able to get here for the Sale of Work?'

The Colonel showed no visible sign of regret. The ladies began a conversation about the amount of money raised at the Sale and the Colonel and the Major oriented themselves by exchanging information about regiments.

Eleanor was glad that, in her eagerness to greet the Giffards, Mrs Apthorp had not noticed her. She kept her head down and her eyes on her newspaper; she was not in the mood for conversation today. Napoleon, on the other hand, watched the group with undisguised interest. The Colonel had a very loud voice and Eleanor heard him say, telegraph style: 'Giffard, eh? Knew a chap called Giffard. Out in India. Civil service, I think. Calcutta. Any connection of yours?' Eleanor could not hear the Major's reply but it apparently was in the negative because the Colonel then said: 'Umph! Probably just as well. Something not quite right about the fellow. Disappeared or something. Can't quite recall.'

Mrs Apthorp, sensing gossip, abandoned her conversation about the Sale of Work and tuned in to this conversation instead. She said, in her usual unbroken stream of thoughts: 'I wonder if perhaps the gentleman you mention was any relation to Mrs Giffard at Manar? I believe that she was in the Far East for many years. It is a rather unusual name and the same pronunciation too. I must ask her when I see her next. I didn't see her yesterday at Church, although she is always there, and I was expecting to see her this afternoon at our regular Monday bridge party. It was to be at Manar today, which is her house, of course, but she sent a note first thing this morning cancelling. It was most inconvenient because I had to telephone to everyone else in time to put them off.'

No-one had anything to add to this, so she invited Major and Mrs Giffard to change direction and the whole party headed along Broad Walk back towards the Crescent. Mrs Apthorp was notorious for being one of the busiest gossips of The Park. She engaged everyone she met in conversation, squeezed every possible drop of information from them, and then used it as she saw fit. Eleanor had no doubt that speculation about Mrs Giffard and the possible reasons for her absence were already circulating around The Park.

Eleanor folded her newspaper and stood up, saying: 'Come on Leon. Time's up. Back to work.'

As she did so she noticed Rupert Brantlingham sitting on the next seat along and wondered what he had made of the conversation, which he must surely have overheard.

News generally travelled fast in the town. Mrs Apthorp made sure that it spread throughout The Park during the course of the day and the people who were employed as live-out servants in The Park took it back with them at the end of the working day across the Pavilion Gardens to the main part of town. In addition, almost every household in Buxton was connected in some way or another to the network of delivery men and boys employed by the town's tradespeople, who carried gossip with them just as efficiently as goods. By Tuesday morning, the news that something unusual had happened at Manar had reached Oxford House. Cicely had heard it when Susan arrived early that morning. Susan had heard the news from her brother who was the baker's delivery boy. The baker had let him off work early the evening before because his last delivery of the day, which was to Manar, had been unexpectedly cancelled. In fact, two orders at the baker's had been cancelled that day by Mrs Giffard's housekeeper. When Susan arrived at Oxford House, it was her opinion that: 'Summat's def'nitly 'oop. Them cakes an' things was for a bridge party, an' the cook ordered the bread special to make sandwiches for the theatre supper. An' that's tonight. An' it's been cancelled, an' all.'

At the offices of Harriman & Talbot, news generally arrived via Mrs Clayton. She placed orders with the local tradespeople who supplied Hall Bank and took delivery of the gossip at the same time as she accepted the ordered goods. Thus, at eleven o'clock on Tuesday morning, when she brought Eleanor a cup of tea, Mrs Clayton was able to inform her, with confidence, that Mrs Giffard had left town.

After the Hall Bank office had closed for the day, Cicely and Richard arrived to have tea with Mr Harriman and Eleanor. While Mrs Clayton put out a selection of cakes and biscuits and made the tea, Richard played a game of marbles with Mr Harriman and extracted a promise from him to read his new story-book to him as soon as he had finished his tea.

Mr Harriman was dining at his club that evening and Eleanor had arranged to have dinner with a friend so Mrs Clayton was able to leave early. Once the tea table had been loaded to her satisfaction, she said goodnight, went downstairs, and had just reached the outer door when the doorbell rang. She opened the door, ushered Philip Danebridge in, and then departed.

'Hello, all,' said Philip. 'I'm just on my way home from the station and thought I would call in. I've been in Manchester today.'

'Philip, this is not on your way home from the station at all and I suspect, therefore, that you have news to impart. Important news, probably. Come on, out with it,' said Eleanor.

'It's not fair. Richard, your aunt Lella reads me like a book. I can't keep anything from her,' complained Philip. 'Is she like that with you?'

Richard had just taken a mouthful of cake and didn't respond.

'We were just having tea. Won't you join us?' said Cicely, setting out another cup, saucer, and plate.

'Thank you,' said Philip. 'That's just what I need. I didn't manage to have lunch today I was too busy.'

'So, what is the big news? What were you doing in Manchester?' asked Eleanor.

'My negotiations with, or should I say badgering of, Messrs Willis, Wise and Campbell have finally paid off. Those worthy gentlemen who, and I quote from the brochure, pride themselves on being in a position to supply superior antique furniture and quality decorative items, unquote, have agreed to open a showroom here in Buxton and condescended to appoint one as manager.'

'Oh, Philip. That is wonderful news,' said Eleanor.

'I'm very pleased for you, Philip. Willis, Wise and Campbell is a very reputable firm. You will do well with them,' said Mr Harriman. 'And they are lucky to have you.'

'It's what you have always been interested in,' said Eleanor. 'You have such a good eye for quality. It just comes naturally to you. I know you will do exceedingly well. Have some tea and some of Mrs Clayton's cake to celebrate. I'm afraid we don't have champagne.'

'Congratulations, Philip,' said Cicely. 'Well done. I'm sure you will be a great success. Where will the showroom be?'

'That's still being decided,' said Philip, 'possibly on Cavendish Circus.'

'I know how much this means to you. You have wanted to get involved with that sort of work for such a long time,' said Eleanor. 'On Saturday, we shall all go to the Hydro to celebrate properly.'

After tea, when the excitement of Philip's news had died down, Mr Harriman and Richard were engrossed in the new book and the conversation naturally progressed to the news of the town. Eleanor, Cicely and Philip began discussing Mrs Giffard and the town's opinion as to events at Manar.

'It's the timing that I find interesting,' said Eleanor. 'Mrs Giffard was plainly taken by surprise when she was introduced to the other two Giffards at the Sale of Work. She literally went white and I really did think she was about to faint. And then she rushed off saying she had another engagement and that was clearly not true. Mrs Giffard obviously was not aware that the other Giffards were in town otherwise she would have been prepared for the meeting and not so shocked. And, on Sunday morning, although she is a pillar of St John's, she did not attend Church.'

'Yes,' said Philip. 'My mother noticed her absence on Sunday and apparently the Rector was also surprised. He knew nothing about it.'

'And then,' said Eleanor, 'the next day she cancelled all her engagements, without giving any reasons.'

'Miss Pymble told me that she also missed the committee meeting on Saturday afternoon at Top Trees to discuss the arrangements for the visit of Princess Mary,' said Cicely.

'Now, that is serious,' joked Philip. 'She has been giving her opinion for months about the plans for that event and her role in it.'

'And to quote Miss Pymble again, when Miss Felicity went to enquire at Manar she was told by the parlour-maid that Mrs Giffard was indisposed,' said Cicely.

'So, that's three days when no-one has seen her, two days when engagements have been cancelled, and now,' said Eleanor, 'according to Mrs Clayton who, as you well know, is extremely reliable in the news department, Mrs Giffard has gone to visit a cousin in Shrewsbury.'

'Does she have a cousin there?' asked Philip.

'I don't know. I've never heard her mention one, or any relatives at all for that matter, but really I know very little about her,' said Cicely.

'Cicely, how long had Major and Mrs Giffard been staying with you before the Sale of Work?' asked Eleanor.

'Three days,' said Cicely. 'They arrived last Tuesday.'

'Then, how is it that Mrs Giffard hadn't met them or at least heard of them before the Sale of Work?' said Eleanor.

'Yes,' said Philip. 'Visitors are always considered fair game when it comes to breaking the monotony of the social round, especially if the visitors have any kind of rank or distinction and the Major certainly has that.'

'And the co-incidence of their names would have been bound to crop up in conversation before the Sale of Work,' said Eleanor. 'Mrs Giffard would certainly have been forewarned by the time she got to Top Trees. Especially if Mrs Apthorp had been doing her job properly. But Mrs Giffard was definitely not prepared.'

Cicely said: 'I can explain that. The Giffards…'

'Also pronounced Jiffard,' interrupted Philip.

Cicely frowned at him. 'The Giffards didn't get here until the late train and Major Giffard was not well when he arrived. He needed rest and they spent almost all of the next day in their rooms. And then on Thursday, he didn't leave the house all day and neither did Mrs Giffard, as far as I know, apart from a stroll along the Broad Walk just before supper.'

'How did the Giffards know about the Sale of Work, then?' asked Eleanor.

'Well,' said Cicely, 'on the Thursday evening, the Pymbles called to collect the things I had made for the Sale. The Giffards were just coming in from their walk as the Pymbles were about to leave. The Giffards just said "good evening" and "lovely weather" that sort of thing. I didn't introduce them. Then the Pymbles left. They had been so intent on talking about the Sale of Work they left without realising that they had not asked about the Giffards. You know how difficult it is to get a word in when they are in full flight. So, when the Pymbles got to the Sale of Work, they would certainly have recognised the Giffards but they would have had no idea what their name was.'

'So the co-incidence of their name would not have arisen until Lady Carleton-West introduced them to Mrs Giffard,' said Eleanor, 'but why were the Giffards there? At the Sale of Work, I mean. Who invited them?'

'Well, I did. Indirectly. By the Friday morning, the Major was feeling so much better and I told him and Mrs Giffard about it and suggested that they might like to go. I thought that, as it was to raise funds for returned servicemen, he would be interested in it.'

'So, there was no opportunity for Mrs Giffard-pronounced-Jiffard to know of the existence of the other Giffards until she was introduced to them at the Sale of Work?' asked Philip.

'That's right,' said Cicely.

'And has the Major said anything about it. Does he think

they are related?' asked Eleanor.

'No, he hasn't mentioned it and I didn't think it appropriate to ask. I still don't see why it's important though.'

'Neither do I.' said Eleanor. 'Perhaps when Mrs Giffard deigns to return from visiting her cousin in Shrewsbury we shall find out.'

CHAPTER FIVE

Eleanor was fully occupied with legal matters the next day so she paid no attention to the social life of the town. She and Edwin had travelled on the train to Manchester to attend a hearing in court and it was just before closing time when they arrived back at the office. James said:

'Major Giffard, the gentleman staying at Oxford House, telephoned this afternoon, Miss Eleanor. I have made an appointment for him for ten o'clock tomorrow. He asked specifically for you.'

'Oh! Did he say what it was about?' asked Eleanor.

'Only that it was a matter about which he needed advice. When I pressed him in order to make sure that he saw the right person, he said it concerns an inheritance. I told him that you would be able to help him.'

'Ah. Thank you James.'

The following morning, the Major arrived punctually at ten o'clock and James escorted him up to Eleanor's office. After the formalities had been gone through the Major said, solemnly:

'Your firm has been very highly recommended to me, Miss Harriman. I am staying at Oxford House and when I asked Mrs Sherringham to recommend a solicitor she named your firm and you in particular. Then I discovered that you are her sister.' The Major smiled. 'So, it is not a totally unbiased testimonial, but I decided to come to see you anyway.'

'Ah, yes.' Eleanor laughed. 'I should warn you, Major Giffard, that my sister is my most ardent supporter and family recommendations are not always very objective. However, I promise to do my very best to come up to your and my sister's expectations.'

'I am sure you will. Naturally I am surprised to find a lady in the role of solicitor but times are changing, are they not?'

'My father was blessed with four daughters before, finally, my brother was born. My father intended to take him into partnership and he was articled to Mr Talbot when the War began but he went to France and was killed. At Loos. There were no other sons to take over then so I am doing what I can to fill the gap.'

'I see,' said the Major, nodding. He chose not to comment further, because there was so little to be said in the circumstances. There was a brief silence between them which conveyed his sympathy and then he said: 'Miss Harriman, I decided to consult a solicitor because I received this yesterday.'

He handed to Eleanor a small, white envelope. Eleanor took the envelope and noted that it was addressed to Major E. A. Giffard, DSO. Then she removed a square card from inside the envelope.

'As you can see, it is an anonymous letter. It arrived yesterday at Oxford House in the afternoon post.'

Eleanor examined the card. It was white, made of good quality paper, and had a deckle edge. The envelope was made of the same heavy quality paper and was post-marked Buxton. A message was written on the card in black ink:

> *Sir,*
> *I advise you to enquire into your father's Will. All may not be as it should be. I can say no more.*
> *A well-wisher*

'The letter has been very carefully written,' said Eleanor, 'and there seems to have been no attempt to disguise the handwriting. As the writer has not resorted to letters cut from a magazine and pasted on to paper, we can probably assume that the need for anonymity is not due to an intention to blackmail you or threaten you in some way. Possibly the writer is just as described: someone who wishes you well, who wants to help you but, for some reason, is unable to do so publicly.'

The Major nodded.

'The envelope is of good quality and the card is the sort used for responding to formal invitations to social engagements, so unlikely to be found in every household in Buxton,' said Eleanor, 'which suggests that the author is someone who is in the habit of using these cards or else has access to someone else's stock of them.'

'Quite,' agreed the Major.

'So the letter could come from someone within your circle of acquaintance.'

'Yes,' said Major Giffard, 'except that the letter is postmarked Buxton so the author must be here and, apart from the people I met at the Sale of Work, I know no-one in this town.'

'Hmm,' said Eleanor, looking at the envelope. 'The way that the envelope is addressed suggests that the author is someone who knows you or at least knows something about you because it uses both your initials. I assume they are correct.'

'Yes,' agreed the Major.

'The author also knows how to address you correctly in terms of your rank, which might argue against a servant, although not necessarily so, but it does suggest someone to whom proper regard for rank is important. Possibly someone of rank himself? More persuasive of the author being of some rank is the confidence with which the letter is written.

I also sense from that opening "Sir" that the author is a man not a woman.'

'Hmmm,' said the Major. 'Excellent deduction. Just like Sherlock Holmes. I am impressed.'

'Thank you, Major, but impressive or not, it is pure guess work and probably totally wrong.' Eleanor laughed. 'Quite honestly Major, I am not sure how I can help you. Anonymous letters really are police business, although I do not think that the police would take an interest in this letter because it does not threaten you or appear to put you in any danger.'

'No, you misunderstand me, Miss Harriman. I am not asking you to trace the author of the letter, although I admit that I am curious as to his identity. No, I intend to take the writer's advice. What I should like you to do is to enquire into my father's Will. I want to know if he made one and, if so, whether his instructions were carried out properly. Would you be able to do that?'

'Oh, I see. Yes, I can certainly do that.' Eleanor reached for her pen. 'I shall need some details, though: your father's full name, last address, date of death....' The Major raised his hand and interrupted Eleanor.

'You will think me a complete fool but I don't have that sort of information. That is why I need your help. I know very little about my father and, until now, I have not been at all curious about him or my family. Since I have been here in Buxton, the family name has been the subject of comment and that, taken together with this letter, has caused me to wonder if there is something about my family that I ought to know.'

'You mean the co-incidence of you and Mrs Giffard at Manar having the same name and pronouncing it in the same way? I overheard your conversation with her at the Sale of Work recently.'

'Yes,' said the Major, 'my surname is relatively

uncommon and, until now, I have not met anyone of that name.'

Eleanor put down her pen. 'Perhaps if you tell me what you do know about your father I shall be able to see a way forward. Rest assured that anything you say to me will be treated by this firm as confidential.'

'Thank you. As I think you know, I am on my way to London to see a specialist. The medicos have been gradually patching me up and when they are done I hope to be able to return to my former profession of schoolmaster. I expect to take up the position of deputy headmaster at a boarding school in Edinburgh in September and, naturally, I am hoping eventually to progress to headmaster. It is a very well regarded school and the boys are drawn from the best families. That means the staff must be of unimpeachable character. This anonymous letter has caused me concern and I need to be sure that there is nothing regarding my family which would interfere with my position in the school. I have discussed it with my wife and we have agreed that, although our financial resources are limited at the moment, we should make some enquiries just in case. I should explain that my only income is my Army pension and a few pounds a month from a small annuity. Do you think that you can help me?'

'Certainly, Major,' said Eleanor. 'I understand that you and your wife need peace of mind.' Eleanor recalled the conversation she had overheard on Broad Walk and wondered if the man in Calcutta that Colonel Rathbourne had mentioned was at all relevant. 'I suggest that we make some preliminary enquiries which will not be costly and then decide how to proceed from there.'

The Major continued: 'Thank you, Miss Harriman. At the back of my mind there has always been a vague thought that there was something unusual about my family, something which I did not understand. Now, I am wondering if perhaps there is a skeleton in the cupboard and I am beginning to be afraid of the unknown.'

'And this anonymous letter.' Eleanor flicked the card with her finger. 'Does it suggest to you any clues, any avenue of investigation we might take?'

'No, the letter is puzzling because I know nothing about a Will or an inheritance. In fact, I know nothing at all about my father.'

'I see. So, when did your father die?'

'I don't know. This must sound very stupid on my part, uncaring even, but I have no idea whether he is alive or dead. I know almost nothing about my family.'

'All right. Tell me as much as you can. Perhaps a line of enquiry will suggest itself.'

'I know that my parents were English and that they were in India and living in Calcutta when I was born. My father was in the Civil Service. When I was five years old, I was sent to Scotland to a preparatory school near Edinburgh.'

'That is very young to be sent so far away from one's family,' said Eleanor.

'Yes, but many of the sons of the civil servants and the soldiers serving in India were sent to that school so from that point of view, my childhood wasn't particularly remarkable. At first, I received letters regularly from my mother, for about a year I think, and then suddenly they stopped. Then the headmaster informed me that my mother had died but I was given no details.'

'So you were six then?'

'Yes.'

'And did you hear nothing from your father?'

'No, I had only ever received letters from my mother. After she died, I received nothing at all. The school was strict about letter writing and we all had to write to our parents at least once a month. So, after my mother died, I wrote to my father but I never received a reply. Then, several months after my mother died, the headmaster told me that my great aunt, Adeline Frencham, had been appointed my guardian. I was not told why and I had no idea who this great aunt was. I had never even heard of her and she lived in Kent which is rather a long way from Edinburgh. During the summer holidays the year I finished at the preparatory school, Aunt Frencham invited me to stay with her. The invitation was kindly meant but it was not a success. Aunt Frencham was not used to having children about, especially boys. She had never married and she had three female servants who looked after her. I quickly got the impression that, in her house, the male of the species was regarded as unnecessary clutter.'

Eleanor laughed. 'I have had to deal with great aunts and I know what they are like. I can imagine how difficult it must have been for you as a young boy.'

'Yes,' said the Major. 'She really had no idea what to do with me. I was sent outside to play with the gardener's boy for most of the time. It was very generous of Aunt Frencham to accept the role of guardian because she had absolutely no obligation to do so. I saw her once more, briefly in London when I was about to go up to Cambridge and she died about six months after that. Aunt Frencham's solicitor contacted me to tell me that she had left me an annuity in her Will. I had always assumed that my father had paid my school fees and was paying my Cambridge fees and living allowance but the solicitor told me that Aunt Frencham had paid for everything. She had never let on and, naturally, when I heard what she had done for me, I felt guilty that I had not made more of an effort to see her. I wished I had been able to express my gratitude. Apparently, she had had no contact with my father and the solicitor knew nothing about him. He explained that Aunt Frencham had been appointed my guardian because there was no-one else. My mother was an only child so there were no brothers or sisters who could look after me. My grandmother, who was Aunt Frencham's sister, and my grandfather had been killed in a railway accident before I was born. Apparently, my mother's only other relatives were some cousins who had a coffee plantation in Kenya.'

'When you were at school, did you not think it strange that members of your family didn't contact you?'

'No, you see, most of the boys from India had little contact with their parents. During the holidays it was not possible to go back home. Those who had relatives in Scotland or England went to stay with them and those who had no-one just remained in school. We filled the gaps for each other. The headmaster's wife was very good to us and included us in the activities she arranged for her own children.'

'And your great aunt didn't give you any information at all about your father?'

'When I tried to ask her about him she was evasive. So was the headmaster's wife. They must have known something but, as a child, you soon sense when adults consider your questions inappropriate and you cease to ask.'

'Your birth certificate will give us the name and occupation of your father and his address at the time you were born, which is a useful starting point.'

'I know this is going to sound very odd but I have none of those personal papers. I've never really needed any. Aunt Frencham's solicitor always made all the necessary arrangements for me, even when I went up to Cambridge. Aunt Frencham had appointed him her trustee and, after she died, he continued to take care of everything until I turned twenty-five.'

'What about the Army, did they not ask you for your birth certificate as proof of your age?'

'When I joined up, if you looked fit enough to fight they were willing to believe anything you told them. I realise now, telling you all this, that it must seem as though I've rather just left everything to other people all my life and never made any decisions for myself. I suppose that's true, in a way. Until now, I have never tried to find out anything about my parents.'

'Major, please don't answer this if you don't want to, but I assume that you and Mrs Giffard are married?'

'Good Lord, yes. Why do you ask?'

'Well, did you not need your birth certificate then?'

'Oh, I see what you mean. Well no, we got married in France. After I had been wounded, I ended up at No 9 Red Cross Hospital at Longueness. Isabel, that's my wife, and her sister were VADs there. Isabel's brother was at my college at Cambridge and I was in hospital long enough to get to know Isabel. When we heard that the Army was planning to ship me back here, we decided to get married straightaway. The padre did the honours and one of the local French worthies did the civil bit and the paper work. It was all done at my bedside and, to be honest the shape I was in, I don't think they were too anxious about the formalities because they thought I wouldn't pull through. But it is all legal and above board. I checked later. After a couple of months, Isabel managed to wangle herself a transfer back to London to the hospital where I had been sent.'

'I see,' said Eleanor. 'Well, I can arrange for searches of the official records. We should be able to obtain an extract of your birth certificate as a first step, and then we can trace your father from there. What is your date of birth, please?' Eleanor picked up her pen again.

'The eighteenth of December 1888.'

'I shall also order a search of the Civil Service records at The India Office. Do you have any idea what year your mother and father went to India?'

'No, but I think they were married in India so they must have been there before 1888. And they were still there in June 1894 when I went to school.'

'And your father's full name?'

'Edward. I was named after him. I know that much. I am Edward Alfred. I am not sure of my mother's name. The servants always referred to her as the Memsahib, of course, and my father called her Missy, but I think that must have been a pet name. It can't have been her real name, can it?'

'It does seem unlikely,' said Eleanor, making notes. 'And she would have died in about 1895, if it happened shortly after you went to school. She must have been quite young.'

'Yes, although my parents did not seem young to me. Children don't have much of a perception of age, do they? Everyone seems old to a child of five or six. I don't honestly think I have much of a recollection of them at all and I have no photographs of them. I am sorry to be so vague but, growing up in India, one saw very little of one's parents. I had an ayah who looked after me but I spent a great deal of time alone.'

'I am sure that it will be possible to discover something about your father. Although most of the important events took place in India, many of the records we need will be in London but it may take a little time before we have any useful information. I wonder if your great aunt's solicitor has any documents still, although I suppose if he had known anything about your father's Will he would have told you, surely.'

'I'm certain he would have. He was a very decent old chap but he's gone now. Died just before the War. Miss Harriman, I have to go to London tomorrow and I expect to be there for about two weeks and then I shall travel straight back to Edinburgh. Can I ask you to find out what you can and write to me in London?'

'Certainly but I don't expect to have learnt very much in two weeks and finding your father's Will may take longer than that.'

'Of course.' The Major smiled. 'I have been in ignorance

for so long that a few more weeks will make no difference.'

'Major Giffard, I appreciate your coming to see me and having confidence in me but, if you are going back to Edinburgh, would it not be more convenient for you if you were to instruct a solicitor there? You could do that when you get back home and I am sure he would have London agents to carry out searches, just as we do.'

'Possibly, but I am rather curious to know more about that anonymous letter. It must have come from someone here in Buxton, so there might be more chance of something coming to light if you carry out the enquiries here than if I ask an Edinburgh solicitor to do the work.'

'I understand, Major,' said Eleanor, smiling. 'You have discovered by now that everyone in this town takes an interest in their neighbour's affairs and what you are really hoping is that I will hear some gossip which will provide a clue as to the anonymous writer's identity. Rest assured, I shall do my very best to solve this puzzle and put your mind at rest.'

'Thank you, Miss Harriman. I am certain you will. Your sister was right to have confidence in you.'

Eleanor accompanied the Major downstairs and, after he had left, she said to James:

'The Major needs our help, James. Will you write to our London agents please, and get them to make some enquiries at Somerset House and The India Office. I will give you a list of the information we need.'

'Certainly, Miss Eleanor. I shall see that it gets into the next collection.'

Once the letter had been sent, there was nothing further Eleanor could do for the Major until she received a reply from the London agents so she turned her attention to the work needed for the firm's other clients.

♣♣♣

That evening, Mr Harriman returned from an appointment just as James was closing the office. Eleanor and Edwin were in the sitting room enjoying a pre-dinner glass of sherry and Mr Harriman joined them there. The three lawyers often had an informal meeting after the office had closed because it allowed them to discuss any difficult legal issues that had arisen during the day. The law on a particular point can sometimes be uncertain and a vital part of a lawyer's work involves examining a legal question from all sides and playing devil's advocate. Also, by discussing the facts of a case, one lawyer might notice something that the other had overlooked, or might see the relevance of a fact that the other had regarded as insignificant. Eleanor enjoyed these sessions because they gave her the opportunity to seek advice and to learn her craft from the two more experienced lawyers. Eleanor told her father and Edwin about the Major's visit and the anonymous letter.

'So,' said Eleanor, 'I am wondering who could possibly have sent the letter. Is it a visitor who, by co-incidence, is here at the same time as the Major, or is it a resident who has discovered that the Major is visiting?'

'Perhaps the writer has been in possession of this knowledge for some time but, until now, has not had the means to pass it on,' said Mr Harriman, 'and has simply taken an opportunity which has unexpectedly presented itself.'

'Either way,' said Edwin, 'it is obviously someone who knows more about the Major's family than he does. It is curious that he knows so little about them. I suppose he is telling the truth and not holding anything back.'

'He remembers very little about his parents,' said Eleanor, 'and he seems not to have asked any questions about them, or perhaps he asked but received no answers.'

'Remember that he was only five when he was sent away to school. Not that much different from young Richard. How much would Richard remember about us if he were sent away tomorrow to a school in a different country and never saw any of us again?' asked Mr Harriman.

'Well,' said Eleanor, 'it seems that the writer of the letter is someone who wants to help the Major and not someone who means to harm him.'

'Given the Major's history, I think the writer is most likely to be someone who has a connection with India,' said Mr Harriman. 'Who is there in town in that category?'

'There's Colonel Rathbourne, who was visiting Mrs Apthorp but he seemed to know nothing other than that a person named Giffard disappeared in India,' said Eleanor.

'And, of course, there's Mrs Giffard-pronounced-Jiffard,' said Edwin.

'No, the letter cannot have come from her because she was away from Buxton when it was posted. Although, I think she knows something about Major Giffard because I am sure she is avoiding him. Perhaps I should try to find out if Mrs Giffard is related to the Major in some way. Do you think I should get our London agents to search for information about her?'

'Well, my dear,' said Mr Harriman, 'you may be right about Mrs Giffard. Her behaviour does seem out of character and I admit that Giffard is not a very common name but even supposing that there is a connection, with so little information to go on it would have to be a wide ranging search. We know absolutely nothing about Mrs Giffard and we can't really spend the Major's money ordering searches of every Giffard listed in the records at Somerset House. Even if they are a rare breed, it would still be a costly exercise.'

Edwin said: 'Let's think this through a bit. Mrs Giffard is a widow so presumably there was once a Mr Giffard. He is the one who would have been related to the Major not Mrs Giffard so finding out who her husband was would be more relevant than finding out about her. There must be a death certificate for him. Do we know where he died?'

'No,' said Eleanor. 'All we know is that he died before Mrs Giffard came to Buxton, and before that Mrs Giffard lived somewhere in the Far East.'

'Which leaves a lot of territory to cover,' said Mr Harriman.

'Then I shall see what local gossip can do,' said Eleanor. 'I shall consult Cicely. She hears a lot of things. Landladies always do.'

'I shall not tell Cicely what you just said,' said Mr Harriman, laughing. 'I don't think for one minute she regards herself as a landlady.'

Edwin said: 'I might be able to help with the gossip. I shall be in London on Monday. That matter in the Chancery Division that we have Sir Giles Benson briefed in. It was listed for the following week but his clerk rang James today to say that it has been brought forward because the previous case has settled. I shall be staying at my club so I can ask around if you like. There's always some ex-Indian army officer or civil servant willing to talk about the old days and retail colonial gossip in return for a drop or two of decent whisky. If there really was a Giffard who disappeared, or a scandal of some kind, someone is bound to remember something about it. Now, I must get on home. I'll see you both tomorrow.'

On Friday morning, Major and Mrs Giffard left for London as planned and, in their absence, The Park forgot about them. They remained part of Buxton only in the form of a file on Eleanor's desk.

On Saturday evening, Mr Harriman, Eleanor and Cicely joined Philip and his parents for dinner at the Buxton Hydropathic Hotel to celebrate the beginning of Philip's new career. The older generation went home after dinner but Cicely, Eleanor and Philip stayed on for the Cinderella dance. They met various people whom they knew so there was no shortage of partners for the two sisters. Gliding happily around the ball-room floor, Eleanor forgot all about the Giffards and concentrated on enjoying herself.

Chapter Six

Sunday was a perfect summer day. Eleanor and Napoleon, Cicely and Richard went for their usual stroll in the Pavilion Gardens and, taking advantage of the sunshine, Eleanor and Cicely organised deckchairs and joined the crowd sitting around the band-stand listening to the band. Richard and Napoleon sat on the grass and alternated between teasing each other and wrestling.

'Mrs Giffard-pronounced-Jiffard is back,' said Cicely, when the band had stopped briefly to rearrange its music. 'I saw the Misses Pymble when I went to collect Richard from Sunday school this morning. Evidently they saw Mrs Giffard in the Devonshire Arcade yesterday afternoon. They were rushing with one of their charity parcels to catch the last post collection and didn't have time to cross over the road to speak to her. By the time they had finished at the Post Office she had gone. They were frightfully disappointed to have missed her. You know how much they like to be up to date with everything that is going on in town.'

'Yes,' said Eleanor, laughing, 'I don't think people appreciate just how valiant the Pymbles are with their information gathering. They would have made excellent spies during the War. They look harmless enough but they are as sharp as tacks. What would this town be without them?'

'Well, whatever it was that caused Mrs Giffard to cancel her engagements and leave town so suddenly it has obviously been dealt with. It is most unusual to just cancel things like that though, isn't it? Particularly for Mrs Giffard. There is something happening practically every day at

Manar. She never lets up, especially during the season.'

Eleanor said: 'When did the Major and his wife leave for London?'

'Friday morning.'

'Hmmm, they left on Friday and on Saturday Mrs Giffard reappeared at Manar. I think that the timing of those two events is not a co-incidence. It is impossible to keep anything secret in this town so Mrs Giffard would have known fairly quickly that the Major and Mrs Giffard had left for London and that it was safe for her to return. Which train did the Giffards catch?'

'Oh, the early train. Old Tom came at seven to take them to the station.'

'Well, there you are then. Old Tom lives with his daughter and son-in-law, who would have known that he had an early start that morning and probably also knew who it was that he was taking to the station. And, of course, Old Tom helps his son-in-law deliver the milk to The Park so the news of the Major's departure could have got directly to Manar, probably before breakfast and even before the Major and his wife had got as far as Derby. This coming and going is not random.'

'You may be right about Mrs Giffard avoiding the Major and his wife, but what reason could she possibly have?'

'I have no idea but I am very curious to know what it is.'

The band started up again. Eleanor and Cicely relaxed in their deckchairs and Richard and Napoleon lay on their sides on the grass watching the crowd sideways. When the band stopped for the next break, Eleanor decided that the afternoon would not be complete without ice-cream and, taking orders for flavours, went in search of the ice-cream vendor.

Eleanor returned and handed out the ice-creams. She said to Cicely: 'That motor-car salesman from Manchester was in the queue ahead of me, buying ices for a group of girls he had in tow. He seems to spend a bit of time here. He must find it worth his while.'

'I heard that he had sold a motor-car to the Hampsons and I also heard that he'd been visiting at the Apthorps. He seems to have squeezed his way in to The Park.'

'All on the introduction of his cousin, I believe. That girl in the pink hat is one of the maids from Top Trees. Perhaps he met her at the Sale of Work.'

Cicely looked across at the group sauntering past and added: 'And the one in the blue dress is one of the maids from Manar.'

'He is in demand.'

'Here comes Rufus Wentworth-Streate,' said Cicely. 'Doesn't he look smart?'

A tall, young man dressed in a well-tailored linen suit and Panama hat, was walking confidently along the promenade, swinging a cane. He lifted his hat politely as he reached Brantlingham and his group of girls. Eleanor and Cicely watched as Brantlingham skilfully detached himself from the girls and strolled off with Rufus Wentworth-Streate towards the park gate, both of them talking animatedly. The abandoned girls consoled themselves by finishing their ice-creams and listening to the band.

'I do wonder what is going to happen to girls like those, growing up with such a shortage of men,' said Cicely. 'The Pymble sisters were telling me the other day about their ideas for the Girls' Friendly Society and the new activities they are planning. They want to give the girls something to be interested in and somewhere to go.'

'So many of these young girls are without hope of a family life now,' said Eleanor. 'In a way, I think the Pymble sisters themselves are the best inspiration they could possibly have. Those two really are remarkable. So energetic and full of fun. They're not at all the usual spinster types.'

'When they were growing up it must have been very

difficult to avoid becoming the unwanted spinster sister or aunt, the one who is always made use of by the rest of the family but they seem to have escaped and made a life for themselves instead,' said Cicely.

'Perhaps,' said Eleanor, 'it makes a difference their being twins. There have always been two of them so they are never alone, as typical spinsters are. They provide support and encouragement for each other. In many ways, though, they are still regarded as typical spinsters and treated accordingly. It does not matter how one sees oneself, a spinster is labelled as a type and People expect one to behave according to type. There are so many rigid rules about the way you dress, the way you live, how much you earn, what you can and can't do, what you are allowed to talk about, and what topics you are supposed to know nothing about. So many limitations. The world has changed for married women but single women might as well still be living in the last century.'

'Is that how you regard yourself, Lella?' asked Cicely in surprise. 'A spinster?'

'No, but that is how I am regarded by others. For father's sake, I have to accept invitations from the ladies at The Park but I do hate going to their parties. Because I'm not married, I'm not supposed to know anything about worldly topics. I feel as though they are making allowances for me all the time because I am not married. I can only admit this to you, Cicely, because I know you won't think I'm boasting, but I know that intellectually I am their superior. I am far better educated and know more about the world than most of them ever will. The most ironic thing is that while they are talking down to me I am talking down to them.'

'What do you mean?'

'When I am at work with father and Edwin I have normal conversations about any topic that is relevant to our work but in the company of the ladies at The Park I have to steer clear of any serious topic of conversation. They leave that sort of thing to their husbands. Not only that, I have to limit my vocabulary to avoid using words which they probably wouldn't understand. They would just think I'm showing off but for me, during the day, that vocabulary and level of mental activity is normal. Father and Edwin treat me as an equal even though I don't yet have their level of experience. The ladies at The Park patronise me. They give the impression that they are doing me a favour, giving me pleasure which, as a spinster, I would otherwise be deprived of.'

'Many of them have lost sons or husbands so they no doubt feel sympathy with you because of Alistair,' said Cicely mildly. 'I am sure they are trying to do their best.'

'I know they are and it is mean of me to criticise them but their rigid way of thinking does really make me furious sometimes. The world they believe in, the world we were brought up for has gone. The War has destroyed that. Things we were taught to regard as important are no longer valued and, in many ways, are no longer even relevant. The rules have changed. We have to change but the ladies at The Park don't see that. They assume that because I am a spinster, I must be unhappy and frustrated and that I am just waiting for someone eligible to come along so that I can leave my job and get married.'

Cicely didn't respond immediately. She paused to reflect on what she was going to say and then she said: 'Lella, I know that, even though you were not married to Alistair, his death was just as painful for you as Wilfred's death was for me and, because of his death, your life is very different from the one you planned, but I don't think of you as an unhappy or frustrated spinster.'

'You are right. It was painful losing Alistair and it was painful for all of us losing Edgar but if Edgar had survived he would have joined father and Edwin in the firm instead of me. To be brutally honest, the War has given me an opportunity that I would never have had otherwise. It makes me feel guilty sometimes.'

'You shouldn't feel guilty. When I hear you wrangling with father and Edwin over some legal point, I do wonder whether you ever would have been satisfied with the role of wife and mother, even with Alistair. You are very clever, Eleanor, and you are naturally suited to the work you do. I am sure Edgar would be very proud of you. In fact, I am not sure that he wouldn't be relieved. I doubt that he would have been truly happy as a solicitor, not the way you are. He would have done a good job but it would only ever have been a job not a passion, not the way it is with you. I think that might be why he enlisted. He wanted to do something he cared about. He once confided in me and said that he was very interested in architecture and would have preferred that to law.'

'Why did he never say so? I'm sure father would have listened to him.'

'I suppose because, from the day he was born, there was an assumption that he would join the family firm, just as father did. That is what mother wanted. She was very keen on there always being a Harriman actually in the firm and not just on the nameplate.'

'Well, there still is and there will be for a while because you are right, Cicely, I am not very interested in marriage right now. But who's going to carry on after me? Richard perhaps? Or what about Amelia and Alice. Are any of their boys likely to be interested? Of course, they are not Harrimans, so even if they did join the firm, it wouldn't be the same.'

'There are quite a few families in town in the same position. The "& Son" is no longer a reality and they are left with an heir in name only.'

'All the old certainties are gone, aren't they?' said Eleanor.

'Yes,' said Cicely very quietly. 'I got a letter from

Wilfred's mother yesterday. She has invited Richard and me to stay at Wyvern Hall in August. It will be the fifth anniversary of Wilfred's death and they are going to unveil a memorial plaque in their church. The one where Richard was christened.'

'And where, no doubt, Wilfred expected to be buried.'

'Yes. It's a lovely old church and with so many generations of his family christened, married and buried there, a plaque does seem appropriate. It is very thoughtful of them to invite me and, of course, I shall go but it won't change anything.'

'What do you mean?' asked Eleanor.

'Well, I suppose the anniversary of his death is a date which is more significant for them than other days, but not for me. The feeling of loss is the same for me every day of the year and no greater on the anniversary than on any other day. There is not one day when I don't remember something about him or about the things we did together. I still cry for him. I keep going for Richard's sake, of course, and in that way I know I am luckier than many. At least I have had the joy of a husband and a family life, if only for a short while, and because of Richard I have something of Wilfred that is with me every day and will live on.'

They sat in silence for a while. Then, Cicely said: 'Do you think one day there will be someone else again for you, Eleanor?'

Eleanor shrugged. 'It's unlikely don't you think? The way things are now.'

At one o'clock on Monday, Eleanor informed Napoleon that they needed to walk to Manar instead of taking their usual lunchtime route in the Pavilion Gardens. She had decided that, while she was waiting for the London agents to send information about the Major's father, she would try to find out something more about Mrs Giffard. The two of them headed down Hall Bank and along St John's Road towards The Park. When they had reached the corner of the low stone wall at the boundary of Manar they turned along a narrow lane which ran parallel with the wall. The house was a good distance from the lane and between it and the lane there was an extensive lawn interspersed with large specimen trees and box hedging. The lane led around to the tennis court at the back and the only part of the house visible was the side roof and two attic windows. Through the trees, Eleanor could see part of the carriage drive but there was no-one about apart from the gardener who was wheeling a barrow load of hedge clippings towards a compost heap. There was a gate in the side wall leading out on to the lane. While the gardener's back was turned, Eleanor let Napoleon off his lead and threw his ball into the garden. Napoleon, unable to resist, leapt the boundary wall and raced in pursuit of the ball. Eleanor let herself into the garden through the gate, calling to Napoleon to come back. The gardener turned to see what the noise was about. By the time he had walked back towards her, Eleanor had attached Napoleon to his lead again and hidden the ball in her pocket. Napoleon sat meekly by her side, gazing up innocently at the gardener. Eleanor apologised profusely for the disturbance and then said: 'This is Mrs Giffard's house, isn't it?'

'Pronounced Jiffard,' said the gardener automatically. 'Aye.'

'It must be about four years since she came here.'

'Aye.'

There was a pause.

'Where did she live before she came here?' Eleanor asked casually.

'Somewhere foreign,' said the gardener, decisively. He resumed clipping the hedge.

'I heard that she moved here from the Far East? Or was it India?'

'Summat like that.'

Eleanor stroked Napoleon, leaving another pause so as not to look too eager for information.

'Mrs Giffard is a widow, I believe.'

The gardener did not reply.

'Have you ever heard anything about Mr Giffard?'

The gardener shook his head and continued clipping.

'How long ago did he die, I wonder?'

The gardener shrugged.

'Have you worked here long?'

'Aye.'

'Before Mrs Giffard came?'

'Aye.'

'How long have you been gardener here?'

'Fifteen year come Michaelmas.'

Eleanor conceded that this line of enquiry was not going to lead anywhere. She was about to leave when she heard a car engine and, looking towards the carriage drive, saw a car pull up. A man got out and walked towards the house.

'That's Mr Brantlingham, isn't it?

'Him with the motor?' said the gardener.

'That's right.'

'Aye. Makes a right mess of that drive every time. An' extra work for me 'avin' to rake it again.'

'Has he been here before, then?' asked Eleanor in surprise.

'Aye. A nuisance, that's what he is.'

'Yes, I'm sure he is,' Eleanor sympathised.

Bidding the gardener "good afternoon" Eleanor guided Napoleon through the gate and they turned back the way they had come so as not to walk in front of Manar and be seen. Eleanor wondered what Brantlingham was doing at Manar. Mrs Giffard already had the latest model Silver Ghost and a chauffeur to drive it. Surely she could not be intending to replace it with a Crossley and it seemed unlikely that she needed two cars. And, if she did want a new car, why would she go to Brantlingham and not to Mr Sanders as everyone else in town did?

On her way back from Manar, Eleanor re-thought her strategy for getting information about Mrs Giffard and, at five o'clock that afternoon, she and Napoleon headed to Bath Road and rang the bell of Waverton House. The Misses Pymble were always glad of visitors. Eleanor was welcomed enthusiastically and Napoleon was an old friend. He consented to be made a fuss of, looked around for the cats he knew inhabited the house and, in their absence, settled down obediently beside Eleanor's chair.

After tea and home-made cake had been offered and served, and all the fresh gossip had been exchanged, Eleanor said: 'Miss Pymble, Miss Felicity, I've come to ask for your help.'

'Of course, dear,' said Miss Pymble, attentively. 'What can we do for you?'

'I am not at liberty to tell you why, but I need to know something about Mrs Giffard at Manar.'

'Oh, I thought you were going to ask us to take in a stray cat or something,' said Miss Pymble.

'Or a stray curate,' giggled Miss Felicity.

Miss Pymble frowned at her sister. Napoleon had raised his head at the word "cat" and was looking expectantly towards the door.

'No, Napoleon,' said Miss Felicity, 'the cats are upstairs so it's no use looking for them.'

The Pymble sisters were notorious for leading a conversation down a side-track so Eleanor pressed firmly onward.

'Do you know anything about her? Who she is? Where she lived before she came here?'

'Let me see,' said Miss Pymble. 'I believe she was living somewhere in the Far East and when her husband died she decided to return to England. Her husband left her very well-off and there are no children, so she only has herself to please.'

'Do you know when her husband died?'

'Well,' said Miss Pymble, 'I had just assumed that it was shortly before she returned to England and that she was only recently widowed. But now that you ask, I'm not really sure what gave me that impression.'

'I think she said something about her husband one day when we were at a working bee at the church,' said Miss Felicity, 'but I can't recall exactly what. Was it perhaps that her husband had something to do with tea? That's in the Far East, isn't it?' She paused. 'Where is the Far East, exactly? China? Or maybe Singapore?'

'Is it important, Miss Harriman?' asked Miss Pymble, ignoring her sister's questions.

'Yes, rather,' said Eleanor.

'Well then,' said Miss Pymble, 'I think that a little snooping is justified. Mrs Giffard's young kitchen maid comes to the Girls' Friendly Society meetings so I know her well. I will see if she knows anything. We meet on Wednesday evenings. Will that be soon enough?' Before Eleanor could reply, Napoleon raised his head and gave a low growl. 'Oh, that will be the butcher's boy. Will you excuse me, Miss Harriman?'

'Of course,' said Eleanor, as Miss Pymble disappeared.

'And we must be going, Miss Felicity. Come on, Leon. Thank you for the tea and the delicious cake,' said Eleanor as Felicity Pymble accompanied them to the front door.

♣♣♣

Chapter Seven

The following morning, Eleanor had gone to Court for the Mentions List because Edwin was in London for the appeal. When she returned to the office, James said: 'Mrs Wentworth-Streate rang three quarters of an hour ago, Miss Eleanor. Could someone go to Garroch Brae as soon as possible? Mrs Wentworth-Streate wouldn't say what it was about but apparently it concerns a Mr Brantlingham. Mr Harriman is out and I said you would go as soon as you returned from Court. I didn't specify when that would be, so you have time to have a cup of tea first, if you would like one.'

'Thank you, James. Efficient as ever and yes, I am longing for a cup of tea.'

'Mrs Clayton has just been down with mine so it will still be fresh.'

Eleanor dumped a bundle of files on James' desk and went upstairs to the kitchen to see Mrs Clayton. She was greeted at the top of the stairs by Napoleon who had been supervising the cutting of cake in the kitchen.

'Here you are, dear, a nice cup of tea, fresh made,' said Mrs Clayton, 'and a piece of cake to keep you going while you're at Garroch Brae. I heard James take the telephone call. You'll need it if that Mr Brantlingham's involved.'

'Do you know him, Mrs Clayton?'

'A nasty piece of work. All smarmy if he thinks he's impressing you and getting his own way but quite nasty behind your back. He was up at our Alf's yesterday trying to persuade him to buy a motor. Fortunately for Alf, I was in the back room finishing the cleaning so I heard him going on.'

Alf, Mrs Clayton's brother, was one of the local funeral directors. Alf prided himself on being a "go-ahead" business man anxious to move with the times, and he was very enthusiastic about the latest developments in the funeral industry in the United States of America.

'That Brantlingham chap, he kept telling Alf how impressed people would be if he turned up at people's houses in a motor-car and how useful it would be for him to have a motor for collections. He even told Alf he could get a motorised funeral coach built for him. They're the coming thing according to him. Very popular in America. I'm glad I was there. I could see Alf was weakening. I said to him not to be so silly. What do we want with that nonsense? I know what those Americans are like. I've seen them at the Picture House.'

Mrs Clayton was much addicted to the matinee at the local cinema and had formed her opinion of Americans accordingly.

'So you don't like the idea, Mrs Clayton?' said Eleanor, who was always entertained by Mrs Clayton's strict notions of what was proper and what was not.

'I do not,' she said firmly. 'Who wants to be carted off to the cemetery in a van? And how are the men supposed to walk respectfully beside a motor? As I said to Alf, it's just not decent. There's nothing more dignified than a proper horse-drawn funeral coach. It's what people expect. That's what's right for folks in Buxton and the sooner that Brantlingham person goes back to Manchester where he belongs, the happier I'll be.'

'I thought Mr Brantlingham had only come for the Sale of Work but I've definitely seen him in Buxton several times since then.'

'So have I. And I've heard that he's been getting chummy

with the maids at The Park. Pumping them for information about the size of people's incomes. I expect he's trying to find someone to buy his motors. And he was certainly here on Saturday. That's when he was pestering Alf.'

'And I saw him in the gardens on Sunday. Well, thanks for the tea, Mrs Clayton,' said Eleanor, setting down her cup and saucer. 'And the delicious cake. I'd better go and see what Mrs Wentworth-Streate wants. No, Leon, you stay here. He's not to have any more cake, Mrs Clayton, even if he tells you otherwise.'

Napoleon's brown eyes looked at Eleanor in reproach.

At Garroch Brae, Eleanor was shown into the morning room where Mrs Wentworth-Streate was sitting on a sofa and looking anxious. She got up and went forward to greet Eleanor: 'Miss Harriman, thank you so much for coming. I do hope you can help me. Please, do sit down. Can I offer you tea or coffee?'

'No thank you Mrs Wentworth-Streate, I have had morning tea. I understand you want to talk about something which concerns Mr Rufus.'

'Yes. That horrid Mr Brantlingham has persuaded my son to buy a motor-car. It happened yesterday apparently, but I only found out about it this morning. He got Rufus to sign a contract. My son had to tell me about it because there was something about a guarantee but I don't understand these things. Naturally, I leave financial matters entirely to my husband but he knows nothing about this, of course, for the moment at least. I simply haven't had the courage to tell him. I know he will be very cross. Is there anything that can be done? I am hoping that you can advise me so that I won't have to tell Mr Wentworth-Streate about it.'

'Please tell me about the contract,' said Eleanor.

'That man Brantlingham is simply evil. He invited Rufus out saying that he wanted to see Tideswell and needed Rufus to show him the way. Then, after they had only gone a little way, he invited Rufus to drive the motor-car. My son was in the Ambulance Corps during the War but he's not registered to drive as a civilian, of course. Then Mr Brantlingham asked Rufus to give him lunch at the Union Club and while they were there he persuaded Rufus to buy the motor-car. He is a dreadful man, Miss Harriman.'

'May I see the contract, please, Mrs Wentworth-Streate,' said Eleanor calmly.

'Of course. How silly of me,' she said, going over to her desk and getting the document out of a drawer. She handed it to Eleanor. 'I didn't want to leave the papers lying around where any of the servants or my husband might see them.'

'I'll just take a minute or two to read this document if you don't mind,' said Eleanor.

She had been taught never to let an anxious client rush her into an opinion, so she took the time to read the contract carefully and made sure that she had understood it. After a few minutes, she looked up and said: 'And this is your son's signature?'

'Oh yes. The foolish boy! He signed that document and gave Mr Brantlingham a cheque. What does it mean, Miss Harriman? What has he agreed to?'

'Mrs Wentworth-Streate, the terms of this document are very clear. Your son has entered into a contract with the company which employs Mr Brantlingham and he has agreed to purchase a motor-car which will be manufactured and delivered to him in two months' time.'

'Oh, no!' said Mrs Wentworth-Streate, putting a tiny lace handkerchief up to her nose. 'The silly boy! Can nothing be done to stop this?' Then she said, trying to control her voice: 'Rufus cannot afford such a purchase, Miss Harriman, and neither can my husband. Not at the moment, at least. It is out of the question.' She paused and was obviously considering how much she should say. 'Miss Harriman, can I trust you not to let this information about our finances go any further?'

'Oh, course, Mrs Wentworth-Streate. Whatever you tell me is entirely between the two of us.'

'At present, we are all suffering the effects of the terrible financial situation our nation is in, are we not? And the motor-car, I'm afraid that a debt such as that, coming just now, would be too much. It could very well ruin my husband. That is why I have been afraid to tell him. Oh, this is too dreadful. We have a position to keep up in this town.'

Eleanor could see that Mrs Wentworth-Streate was fighting to keep control of her emotions and that only her rigid training was preventing her from breaking down completely. Eleanor was silent for a moment. She had been taught to listen very carefully and to pay attention to even the smallest of details when interviewing clients. She did a quick mental calculation and then she said: 'Mrs Wentworth-Streate, you said that Mr Rufus knows how to drive but that he is not registered. Does that mean he's not old enough to be registered to drive as a civilian?'

'That's right. He will be twenty-one next month. I think he was hoping that we would give him the motor-car as a birthday present and that he wouldn't have to pay for it himself.'

'He looks older than twenty-one.'

'Yes, he does. That is why he was able to enlist. He was only seventeen and he went without our permission. He has always been a difficult boy to control. But I don't understand. What is the significance of his age?'

'Well,' said Eleanor, 'it is very significant and Mr Brantlingham should have considered that before he set his sights on your son. Mr Rufus is very lucky that you acted as quickly as you did. You see, in law, he is still classed as a minor, that is, a person under the age of twenty-one, and if a minor enters into a contract it cannot be enforced against him if it is not for the supply of "necessaries" and I do not think that, in your son's case, a motor-car could be regarded as a necessity.'

'I don't think I really understand, Miss Harriman. What does it all mean?'

'It means,' said Eleanor 'that you may not need to worry any further. I would like you to telephone your bank manager immediately and ask him to stop the cheque that your son gave to Mr Brantlingham. I suppose it was for the deposit. It will not have been cleared yet. Then Mr Rufus must go to Mr Brantlingham straightaway and inform him that he does not intend to proceed with the contract. I shall draft a statement for him to sign and hand to Mr Brantlingham and then you can tear up that contract.'

'Is it really that simple? How easy you make it sound.'

'Yes, it is that simple. However, your son may be reluctant to act as he clearly wants the motor-car and there is also the risk that Mr Brantlingham will try to intimidate him.'

'Yes, I see what you mean. You are probably right.'

'So, I would suggest that you tell Mr Wentworth-Streate everything, straightaway, and ask him to go with your son to see Mr Brantlingham.'

'Yes, I think that would be best.'

'So, unless there is anything else I can tell you, I shall leave you to make your telephone call to the bank manager. I shall go back to the office and draft the document to give to Mr Brantlingham.'

'Miss Harriman, you've been wonderful,' said Mrs Wentworth-Streate as she rose from the sofa and rang for the maid. 'I cannot thank you enough. It is such a relief to have this sorted out. I shall tell Mr Wentworth-Streate immediately what has happened. And thank you so much for coming to see me. It would have been very inconvenient for me to come to your office. I mean, if I had been seen. Naturally I would not like any of this affair to become the subject of gossip and I know I can rely on your discretion.'

'Absolutely.'

'Please ask your clerk to send your account to Mr Wentworth-Streate.'

'Thank you, Mrs Wentworth-Streate. And please let me know if Mr Brantlingham makes any difficulty about this or if I can be of any further assistance.'

'Miss Harriman, your father was very sensible to have confidence in you. Giving you a legal training was an unusual thing to do. We all thought so at the time, but you have proved him right. Now, I must make that telephone call. Jane will show you out and thank you again.'

Eleanor made a mental note to avoid Mr Brantlingham in future in case he discovered that it was she who had allowed young Wentworth-Streate to wriggle out of his contract. Although, thought Eleanor, after this set-back he might decide to go elsewhere to sell his motor-cars. Unless, of course, selling motor-cars was not his only purpose for visiting the town.

When she arrived back at Hall Bank, Eleanor went in search of Mrs Clayton. Accepting a cup of tea from her, Eleanor said: 'Mrs Clayton I know I can depend on you not to say anything about this matter at Garroch Brae. It is to be kept confidential so I know that you will not mention to anyone that I visited there today.'

'Never fear, Miss Harriman,' said Mrs Clayton, cheerfully. 'You can rely on me. Silent as the tomb. I just hope that Mr Brantlingham gets his come-uppance.'

'I can tell you, Mrs Clayton, without breaching any confidences that by this afternoon Mr Brantlingham will not be a happy man.'

'That is excellent news,' said Mrs Clayton. 'I am very glad to hear it.'

Eleanor drafted the document for James to copy and have delivered to Garroch Brae. Later that day, Mr Brantlingham returned to Manchester, furious and temporarily vanquished, but undeterred.

When the next post arrived later that day, James brought a letter to Eleanor's office. It was from the London agents and Eleanor unfolded it with anticipation. There were several sheets of paper which was a promising sign. Clearly the agents had something to report. The letter stated that they had searched the records at The India Office and were able to provide an extract of the registration of the birth of the Major and the marriage of his parents. Edward Alfred Giffard was born in Calcutta on 18 December 1888. His father was listed as Edward George Granby Giffard, civil servant, and his mother as Mary Rosa Ferrers. They were married on 16 June 1887 at Simla.

The London agents had also located, at The India Office, the record of employment for Edward George Granby Giffard which showed that he was born on 14 March 1853 at Marlow on Thames and had been employed by the Indian Civil Service in the revenue office in Calcutta from 8 March 1873 to 28 February 1896. This file also contained a record of his civil service examinations and his employment history. The agents had not thought it necessary to copy this information because it was very detailed and possibly not relevant. However, they did note that the last entry on the employment record was dated 31 March 1896. It stated: *Salary unpaid. No forwarding address. File to remain open.* The agents could find no record at The India Office of the death of Edward George Granby Giffard and had concluded that either he was still alive or had died somewhere other than India. They then reasoned that, if Mr Giffard was still alive, he would have been eligible for a Civil Service pension. They had found a pension file in the name of Edward George Granby Giffard but no claim had been made for a pension.

The London agents had not searched the records of Somerset House to see if there was a record of death for Mr Giffard because, as they pointed out, such a search would have had to cover more than twenty years. They were concerned about the cost and said they would await further instructions from Harriman & Talbot. They were still searching for information concerning Mary Rosa Giffard and would report again shortly.

Just before the office was due to close for the day, Eleanor took the Giffard file to her father's office and left him to read the report from the London agents, saying: 'I would very much like your opinion about this conundrum. May we talk about this report when you have read it?'

'Certainly,' said Mr Harriman and, when he had finished reading the report, he took it back into Eleanor's office and sat down. Napoleon rested his chin on Mr Harriman's knee and closed his eyes contentedly as Mr Harriman stroked him. Mr Harriman said: 'The records at The India Office clearly belong to the Major's father but, I agree, they are puzzling. If Mr Giffard is still alive, he would have become eligible for his pension about six or seven years ago but it appears that no claim has been made.'

'Does that mean he is dead?' said Eleanor.

'Well, if a civil servant dies, his widow *is* entitled to claim his pension. Now, we know that the potential widow, the Major's mother, died in 1895 so if Mr Giffard is dead and there is no widow, the file should have been closed. Of course, he may have remarried but, if so, why has that widow not made a claim?'

'So, either Mr Giffard is still alive or he has died and no-one has notified the Civil Service office.'

'But,' said Mr Harriman, 'if he is still alive, why has he not claimed his pension? We're going around in circles.'

'His employment file is still open as well and the last month's salary was never paid to him. Does that mean he disappeared?' said Eleanor. 'I wonder if he is the man Colonel Rathbourne recollected? The man called Giffard who disappeared from Calcutta? If a person just disappears it does suggest that he has something to hide or has been involved in a scandal of some kind and can't face continuing with his old life. Perhaps the Major's father disappeared to protect himself or to avoid being arrested for some crime and that's why he can't reappear and collect his salary or his pension. Is that too fanciful an explanation?'

'It's a theory, certainly, but we still have no evidence that there is any connection between the missing Giffard that Colonel Rathbourne remembers and the Major's father,' said Mr Harriman.

'But surely it must be more than mere co-incidence that someone called Giffard is known to have disappeared in Calcutta and someone called Giffard who worked in Calcutta has failed to collect a month's salary or a pension, to which he is entitled.'

'Possibly,' said Mr Harriman. He paused for thought. 'The other unexplained thing is that the anonymous letter gives the impression that the Major's father is dead. How does the writer know that when the official records suggest otherwise?'

'Yes. What knowledge does the writer of the anonymous letter have that we do not have?'

'The only reliable evidence of Mr Giffard's death would be either a death certificate or a grant of probate of his Will,' said Mr Harriman, 'and, as our London agents have pointed out, finding a death certificate would be a very lengthy exercise. It requires a search of twenty odd years' worth of records and that would be far too costly for the Major. We know his resources are limited.'

'Then I can't see how we can help him because unless we find his father's Will we cannot do what the writer of the anonymous letter suggests we do. We have come to a full stop.' Eleanor drummed her fingers on the desk top while she considered the problem. 'We cannot just leave it there.'

'No, we cannot. There must be a way around the problem,' said Mr Harriman.

'What if we assume that the Major's father *is* dead and, that he died in India. There would be a record of the grant of probate at The India Office. He has an unusual surname and one of his Christian names is Granby. There can't be many people called that so if the agents did find a record in that name we could be certain that it was the right person. What if we also assume that the death occurred relatively recently? Otherwise why would the writer of the letter be contacting the Major now and not years ago? Based on those two assumptions, we could ask our London agents to work backwards through the records. That way they would possibly have to cover less ground.'

'Yes, possibly that could be the solution.' Mr Harriman was a cautious man, and he added: 'Perhaps you should ask them to limit the search, initially at least. To the last ten years, say.'

'I'll do that. I shall draft the letter before I finish for today and then James can send it off first thing tomorrow.'

'I'll leave you to it then,' said Mr Harriman.

Eleanor stayed at her desk and drafted the letter to the London agents. She left it on James' desk for him to send the next morning.

♣♣♣

CHAPTER EIGHT

Edwin Talbot had returned from London very late the previous evening and Eleanor had to wait until he arrived at the office the next morning to find out the result of his enquiries. He came into her office. 'Well, Eleanor,' he announced. 'I have managed to find a Mr Giffard for you but I am not sure whether he is your Mr Giffard.'

'Oh, well done. Do tell.'

'I caught up with an old Oxford friend at the Club and he introduced me to a family friend: Sir James Knowle. He was out in India for many years and he remembered that there was a civil servant named Giffard in Calcutta and there was a scandal of some sort. He couldn't recall what exactly because it was twenty or so years ago but he thought that there was an Army officer involved. A woman had died suddenly and there was a rumour that she had killed herself but when I pressed him for details he said he couldn't be sure whether it was Giffard's wife or the Army officer's wife who had died.'

'I see,' said Eleanor. 'Well, Mrs Giffard is alive and well at Manar, so that Mr Giffard can't have been her husband. In which case, he might well be the Major's father because we know that the Major's father was a civil servant and that his wife died in about 1895. The timing is possibly right. Did Sir James know what happened to Mr Giffard after his wife died?'

'No, but he did give me the name of someone he thought might remember the incident. A Colonel Westerbrook. He lives in Derby now but his regiment was in India and Sir

James thought that the Army officer concerned was one of his officers.'

'Oh, that sounds very promising. Do you think we could telephone this Colonel and see if he does know anything?' asked Eleanor, eagerly.

'I am not sure that telephoning is appropriate for a conversation of that kind. For one thing, one never knows who is at the exchange and likely to overhear personal information about the Major. And for another thing, I understand that the Colonel is in his late seventies so he probably doesn't trust the telephone at all. Older people don't. So I think that he is unlikely to feel comfortable using it to speak to a complete stranger about a scandal if, in fact, that is what we are dealing with.'

'Yes, you are right. I understand. Anyway, he's probably deaf as a post; they always are.'

'Even more reason why arranging a personal interview would be preferable to having a telephone conversation,' said Edwin, laughing.

'So, I shall write to the Colonel and arrange to visit him.'

'Hmm,' said Edwin.

'What?' said Eleanor. 'I know that look.'

'Retired Army Colonels, especially those who have been in India, can be very prickly. He might not agree to see anyone so don't get your hopes up too much.'

'All right. I won't. But thanks for your help Edwin. I really do appreciate it.'

'Glad to be of service. When you are free, can you bring in those files of mine you were minding for me?'

'Of course. I'll bring them in now. They're all up to date.'

Edwin went back to his own office followed by Eleanor. She gave him the files and discussed what had been done and then went back to her desk to think about the prickly Colonel and how best to word the letter requesting an interview. There would only be one chance at this so she didn't want to risk his just refusing outright. And then, even assuming that he was prepared to see someone, would he be willing to answer questions about some chap's past misdoings, especially if it was someone from his own regiment? Eleanor tried to picture the Colonel. The only image that she managed to conjure up was based on memories of numerous military gentlemen she had seen taking the waters at Buxton during the season. Red faced, bad tempered, and bossy for the most part, and not very comfortable in the company of women. Eleanor realised that, even if this description did not fit the Colonel completely, he was probably unlikely to agree to a meeting with a young woman, and even more unlikely to speak frankly to a female of any age about a scandal in the regiment. 'But,' thought Eleanor, 'he just might be prepared to speak to an older man, someone closer to his own age.'

Eleanor accepted that, for the sake of the client, she sometimes had to put aside her personal feelings and conform to the limits society placed on women, frustrating though that was. Those limits had ensured that, from time immemorial, women who wanted to achieve their goals were forced to persuade men to take the action they were barred from taking themselves. Eleanor paused a moment to reflect, not for the first time, on how unjust it was, in those circumstances, to blame women for being manipulative. After a few minutes spent considering the lot of womankind, she sighed and moved on to thinking about how to persuade her father to visit the Colonel. The difficulty was that the Colonel might not know very much at all and the meeting could prove to be a fruitless exercise. Mr Harriman would certainly not approve of the expense involved in a speculative trip to Derby. Eleanor decided that the first step was to draft the letter and then she would deal with her father.

When she had finished the draft, Eleanor took it downstairs to James. The firm of Harriman & Talbot had been connected to the telegraph and then to the telephone for many years, but it had not yet felt the need to employ a typist. All of the correspondence was still sent out in James' immaculate copperplate.

'James, this is the Giffard matter. I have drafted this letter to a Colonel Westerbrook in Derby asking if he will see Father but don't write it up yet. I haven't spoken to Father about it and I am not even sure that he will agree to go because of the expense but I was wondering what day I could suggest for the meeting.'

'Well, I think I just might be able to help you there, Miss Eleanor,' said James, entering into the conspiracy. 'Mr Harriman has a meeting in Derby next week. Perhaps he will be able to find time to see the Colonel that day. Let me just check the diary....Yes, Thursday at eleven. He should be finished by twelve thirty, one o'clock at the very latest. Shall we suggest two o'clock for the Colonel?'

'That's marvellous. Thank you James. I shall put that in the draft and then work on Father.'

Just before the office closed for lunch, Eleanor said to Napoleon: 'Right, now to tackle Father and the interview with Colonel Westerbrook.' They went into her father's office. He was tidying up his desk and locking away files ready to leave for his Wednesday afternoon round of golf. Once a week, the professional gentlemen of the town met on the golf course to keep themselves up to date with the town's affairs. Eleanor explained about Colonel Westerbrook, and said: 'He might know something useful. I think we have enough information to put some specific questions to him rather than just making a general enquiry. Something might jog his memory. This Mr Giffard who disappeared in

India may well be the Major's father. It must be more than co-incidence. Surely it is unlikely that two Mr Giffards would have disappeared in the same place and at about the same time?'

'I understand that you want to help the Major, Eleanor, but we are still speculating, and that, as you know, can be expensive. The time involved in going to Derby might incur significant unnecessary cost for the Major. The money would be better spent on enquiries which we know will produce results.'

'Well,' said Eleanor, adopting as neutral a tone as she could manage, 'it might be possible to see the Colonel and keep expense to a minimum. You are due to go to Derby on Thursday next week, you know. Could you, perhaps, see the Colonel while you are there?'

'Eleanor, why do I get the impression that I am being manoeuvred into something?'

Eleanor smiled sweetly at him and said nothing. Her father sighed. 'Very well. If the Colonel agrees to a meeting I shall see him. But don't get your hopes up. There may be a perfectly simple explanation for this so-called co-incidence of yours.'

'Such as?'

'Your Mr Giffard may have a brother who has done something reprehensible.'

He put on his hat, went downstairs and told James that he was going to his Club for lunch and then to golf – purely for the sake of the firm and not for his own pleasure, of course.

At three o'clock that afternoon, James said: 'Mr Danebridge on the telephone for you, Miss Eleanor.'

'Lella, I need your help.'

'Hello, Philip, what do you want?' she asked, without

enthusiasm.

'Mrs Giffard is back and has organised a tennis party at Manar for this Saturday afternoon. There's to be a tournament so there's quite a crowd going. My parents were invited and they accepted on my behalf as well. There's a shortage of men as usual, so Mother volunteered me to help make up the numbers. She's only just owned up and it's too late for me to pull out now. My lungs won't last more than one set and you play well enough for two people, so be a pal. Come and be my partner in the mixed doubles, will you? And save me from disgrace.'

'This Saturday?' Eleanor was getting ready to frame an excuse not to go.

'Yes, and don't try to pretend that you've got another engagement because I know you haven't. I asked James before he put me through and he says you're free.'

'Very well, Philip, I shall come. But only to help you out, mind. I'm certainly not doing it to accommodate Mrs Giffard. I will deal with James separately.'

'Thanks awfully, Lella. I'll call for you at three o'clock.'

As she put the ear-piece of the telephone back on its cradle, it occurred to Eleanor that a visit to Manar might provide the opportunity to find out more about Mrs Giffard. Saturday might prove to be more enjoyable than she had first thought, so she stopped being cross with Philip.

When Eleanor came in from walking Napoleon the next morning, James was already at his desk. He said: 'The second report from the London agents has arrived, Miss Eleanor. I've put it on your desk.'

'Thank you, James. What have we got on today?'

'Dr Norton is coming at twelve for Mr Harriman. A codicil to his will. There are two completions this afternoon.

The files are ready for you but will you do a final check to make sure all the documents are in order. Mr Harriman has instructions for the purchase of a property in Marlborough Road which needs some preliminary advice. I have put that file on your desk too. Mr Hampson will be in at eleven to see Mr Talbot regarding a dispute over some land at Wormhill and Mr Talbot says will you sit in and take notes.'

'Right. I'll just read this Giffard report quickly and then get on with the other things.'

Eleanor settled down at her desk, Napoleon at her feet, and opened the report from London hoping that it was going to be useful. As instructed, the agents had searched the death register for the year 1895 and for the three years on either side of that date. They had found no record of a death in the name of Mary Rosa Giffard. In fact, for the whole of that seven year period, there was only one entry in the name of Giffard. Although the name was not an exact match and the place of death was different, the death had occurred in 1895. They had made a note of the entry in case it was relevant. The date of death was 9 September 1895, which certainly did match the Major's story, but the place of death was Darjeeling, not Calcutta. The name of the deceased was Mary Giffard not Mary Rosa Giffard. Then Eleanor's eyebrows shot up. The cause of death was described as "poison by the administration of an excess dose of morphine."

Eleanor stared at the paper and thought about the significance of this information. It was possible that this was a suicide. If this was the Major's mother, it would explain why the details of her death had been kept from him, a small school boy. But this record must surely belong to some other Giffard unrelated to the Major, because the name was not an exact match and the place of death was not right. And yet, thought Eleanor, the agents had found no other deaths recorded in the name of Giffard. This must be the Major's mother, otherwise it meant that either she had not been in

India when she died or she had not died in 1895, as he had been told. And if she had not died in 1895, had she, like his father, also disappeared? It was baffling. The report had raised more questions than it had answered. It seemed that the more information they had the more complicated the puzzle became. Eleanor quickly drafted another letter to the London agents asking them to search the newspaper archives for September 1895 to see if they could find a report of the death of this Mary Giffard in Darjeeling. She gave the draft to James for him to send and, for the rest of the day, had her head down dealing with other files and drafting documents.

Just before the office was due to close for the day, James announced that Miss Pymble had called to see her. Eleanor asked him to show her up. She had almost forgotten that she had asked Miss Pymble for information about Mrs Giffard at Manar. Miss Pymble was in a high state of excitement. She said she had come to report.

'Last evening after the Girls' Friendly Society meeting, I spoke to Ellen, the kitchen maid at Manar, as we agreed I should. She told me that Mrs Giffard sometimes receives letters with a foreign stamp. They are "official looking letters" according to Ellen. When the envelopes are thrown out, Hannah, the parlour-maid, retrieves them from the waste paper basket and gives them to Ellen. She takes them home to her younger brother because he collects stamps. I asked Ellen which country the letters came from but she isn't interested in stamps, so she didn't know.'

Miss Pymble paused for breath and Eleanor said: 'Well, that has been very helpful, all the same, Miss Pymble. Thank you very much.'

'Oh, but Miss Harriman, that is not all,' said Miss Pymble, proudly. 'You see, I decided to use my initiative and that is what has delayed me in providing my report. I know that I have gone outside the strict line of enquiry you authorised and I hope I haven't done the wrong thing but I did feel it was important to complete the task you gave me. And I think when you hear what I have to say you will understand. This afternoon I found Ellen's brother, and interviewed him, and I found out about the origin of the stamps. He's Mr Dawson's delivery boy, you know, so I had to wait for him to return from his rounds and I've come straight from there to see you.' Miss Pymble took a deep breath. 'I am able to inform you that the letters come from Ceylon.'

'Oh, well done, Miss Pymble! That's excellent.'

'Ceylon is where the tea comes from, isn't it, so my sister may be correct in thinking that Mrs Giffard's husband was somehow involved in tea.'

'Yes, I think you may be right. Did Ellen say how often these letters come, by any chance?'

'No, Miss Harriman, but her brother showed me the stamps he had. He's very proud of them because not many of his friends have foreign stamps. He said he had four from last year and one so far this year and was hoping for three more. That would suggest a letter every quarter would it not? Especially if it was something official.'

'Yes, it certainly would. Miss Pymble, thank you again. You have been a tremendous help.'

Miss Pymble, still beaming, was shown out courteously by James.

After Miss Pymble had gone, Eleanor re-read the report from the London agents in case there was anything she had missed. Edwin had taught her to draw a chronology when preparing a case for hearing because if the facts were assembled in that way it was easier to detect patterns or to spot missing pieces of evidence. Eleanor now made a list of all the events, known and rumoured, and put them into date order. She studied her list and considered the information which she had so far. A record of the Major's parents' marriage. A record of the Major's birth. Two missing parents who may or may not be alive. An entry for the death of someone who may or may not be the Major's mother. She sighed at the unsatisfactory nature of the list.

Edwin came into her office bringing a file which he put on her desk. Seeing the frown on her face, he sat down and asked: 'What's that you're puzzling over?' Eleanor gave Edwin the list and explained about the absence of a record of death for the Major's mother. As Edwin scanned the list, Eleanor said: 'We don't yet have certain evidence that the Major's mother is dead. When he was six or seven years old, he was told that she had died but he was given no details. He has no tangible evidence that she is dead other than that he stopped receiving letters from her. He wasn't at her funeral and he doesn't know anyone who was. What if his mother didn't die then? What if she had done something which the family considered so disgraceful they felt justified in simply pretending that she was dead? Does that sound too far-fetched?'

'Something such as?'

'Well, run off with another man, for example. In 1895, a woman who left her husband and ran off with someone else would have been shunned by her family, shown the door probably and never mentioned again. To all intents and purposes, she would have been dead as far as the family was concerned.'

'It's possible, I suppose.' said Edwin. 'And there have been instances of women wrongly certified as insane and incarcerated for life in an asylum as a punishment for having had a clandestine affair. Or for having an unorthodox opinion about life, for that matter. So sending a woman away and pretending she is dead is not that different from locking her up. But where does this theory lead you?'

'Well, suppose the Major's mother is still alive. Perhaps Mrs Giffard is avoiding the Major because she knows the truth,' said Eleanor.

'You mean she is some sort of relative of his and,

therefore, knows the family secret?'

'It is possible. She is supposed to have lived in the Far East before she came to Buxton. And I have just discovered that she regularly receives letters from Ceylon. Is Ceylon classed as "the Far East" or is that not far enough east?'

'I would consider China or Japan, or Singapore even, as the Far East,' said Edwin, 'but not Ceylon. It's right next to India.'

'There must be some connection with Mrs Giffard. At the Sale of Work when the Major was introduced to her she looked startled, no shocked. And it really was too severe a reaction to be caused by a mere co-incidence of surname. Suppose she knows that the Major's mother is still alive and knows that he has been lied to. Perhaps she knows the reason for the lie and can't bear to face him. It would explain why she left town and avoided meeting the Giffards again.'

'Well, yes, if there is some deep, dark family secret it would be dashed awkward for her having to meet him socially and pretend that she knew nothing. But if there was such an event, it would have been, what? Twenty-five years ago? Would it matter so very much after all this time? And how would Mrs Giffard have known that the Major was connected to this supposed family scandal?' asked Edwin.

'When Lady Carleton-West introduced the Major to Mrs Giffard, he mentioned that he had been at school in Scotland. If Mrs Giffard had known his mother at that time that piece of information would have meant something to her. It would have dispelled any doubt in her mind as to who he was.'

'Well,' said Edwin. 'It's a theory but I am afraid I am inclined to pour cold water on it. There isn't much else to go on at the moment though is there?'

'No,' said Eleanor. 'So, I shall hang on to my theory until we find something better but I do confess that it is all idle speculation and, as father says, speculation costs money. I can't afford to spend any more time on this file and, besides, it is time for Napoleon's walk.'

'I too have finished for today, so I shall bid you goodnight. I'll see you tomorrow, Eleanor.'

'Goodnight, Edwin. Come on, Leon. Time for a walk. How am I going to face Mrs Giffard at her tennis party with thoughts about dark family secrets going around in my head? Perhaps it will rain and I shall be saved the embarrassment.'

Edwin laughed as he went downstairs and headed for home.

Chapter Nine

It did not rain on Saturday for the tennis party. It was a perfect summer day and when Eleanor and Philip arrived at Manar, there were already about thirty guests, milling around on the side lines or scattered about the lawn. Reverend Pymble was occupying the umpire's chair and Mrs Giffard was moving about from group to group, handing round the list of players and organising partners. The four players at the top of the list were warming up ready for the first match of the tournament. Mrs Giffard welcomed Eleanor and Philip and then said: 'Now, I have you both down in the third match and, Miss Harriman, would you mind awfully filling in for us in the fifth as well. We are so dreadfully short of men, as usual, and I know you are a very strong player. Would you be very kind and partner Miss Andrews, otherwise she will not be able to play.' Eleanor graciously agreed and accepted several repeated expressions of gratitude from Mrs Giffard. This, she thought, was her punishment for last night's theories.

The tennis court had been laid out towards the rear boundary of Manar and was protected on three sides by tall bushes. The fourth side was bordered by a wide strip of lawn scattered with deck-chairs for the players and spectators. Running parallel with the edge of this lower lawn was a shallow grassy bank punctuated at regular intervals with sets of stone steps which lead to a larger upper lawn. In the centre of the upper lawn was a large wooden pavilion, positioned to give a good view of the court. The pavilion was protected and separated from the rest of the upper lawn by a clipped box hedge about four feet high. Deck-chairs were also scattered about on the upper lawn on either side of the pavilion. Most of the guests were still down on the lower lawn, greeting new arrivals or working out when and with whom they were to play.

Eleanor and Philip decided to sit on the upper lawn to watch the first two matches. A group of five ladies, headed by Mrs Apthorp, was crossing the upper lawn ahead of them intending to take possession of the pavilion. Eleanor and Philip, by tacit agreement, avoided the pavilion and took two deckchairs which they positioned on the other side of the hedge which separated the pavilion from the lawn. They settled down to watch the first match.

On the court, a fierce competition got underway. One of the women was a very strong player, returning the ball from the male player at the other end without difficulty. Eleanor recognised her. Violet Sanderson was a young widow whose husband had been killed in 1917. Before the War, she had certainly not been such a confident player. In fact, Eleanor could not recall her playing very much at all.

'Violet's playing well.' The disembodied voice of Mrs Apthorp came from the pavilion.

'She's been taking lessons,' said her daughter, Helena.

'She seems to have recovered from the loss of Sir Samuel,' said Mrs Apthorp.

Mrs Frampton said with a sigh: 'Oh, how well I remember that day when he and the rest of the boys left for the Front. We went to the station to wave them off and there was Violet all alone on the platform watching the train pull out. We thought her so brave. Smiling proudly, with no hysterics, not even the sign of a tear. Not like some of the girls. And such a sacrifice, too, letting him go like that, a married man with four children.'

'Hardly a sacrifice. She was glad to be rid of him,' said Mrs Frampton's daughter.

'Oh, Daphne! Really! How could you say such a wicked thing when Violet was being so wonderfully patriotic?' said Mrs Frampton.

'Because he was no great loss,' said Daphne, 'so it was easier for her to be patriotic than it was for some.'

'Whatever do you mean?' asked Mrs Frampton, shocked by her daughter's forthrightness.

Eleanor and Philip exchanged glances. As the ladies were speaking so frankly, they must be unaware that they could be overheard. Philip raised an enquiring eyebrow which conveyed the question: "Should we leave, or stay and eavesdrop?" Eleanor smiled and settled more deeply into her deckchair.

'Violet was desperate for marriage at any cost,' said Daphne. 'She wasn't really concerned who the bridegroom was. She just wanted to get away from her mother.'

'Daphne, really! You forget yourself!' said her mother.

'It's true,' said Daphne, rebelliously.

'It is true,' said Helena. 'Daphne is right. Violet hated being at home. Her mother wouldn't let her do anything or go anywhere. She said Violet could do as she pleased when she was married but until then she would do as she was told. So Violet wanted to be married and have a life of her own.'

'And becoming Lady Sanderson was just an extra prize as far as Violet was concerned,' said Daphne.

Mrs Apthorp gave a long drawn out 'Well' as she considered the proposition and then continued. 'It is true that Violet's mother was determined to get a title for her daughter if at all possible. And Samuel being a Sir was very much in his favour despite the age difference. And it is also true that even his family would have to admit that he was not very bright.'

'I do think that's a bit harsh,' said Mrs Frampton.

'But it didn't take Violet very long to realise how fearfully dull marriage was,' said Daphne.

'And,' added Helena, 'four children in nearly as many years does rather take the shine off.'

'Well really!' admonished Mrs Frampton.

'Anyway,' said Daphne, 'we needn't feel sorry for her now. She's got everything she ever wanted.'

'Yes,' said Winifred, Helena's friend, as she joined in the conversation. 'Mother told me that Violet's father-in-law has given her a very generous allowance because, after all, she has provided an heir and two extra sons. And they've given her a nanny as well.'

'So she is a free woman *and* she has plenty of time and money for tennis coaching,' said Daphne. 'It's no wonder that her game has improved so much.'

'Girls, girls! It's very naughty of you to say such things,' said Mrs Frampton. 'I suppose you think you are being clever and very modern. But really! I don't know what the world is coming to.'

To avoid a lecture, Daphne said: 'Look, Violet's finished now and she's won. Who's up next?'

There was a pause while they looked at the list of players pinned up in the pavilion.

'Oh, I say,' said Helena. 'Philip Danebridge is down to play in round three. Isn't he still suffering with his lungs?'

Daphne said: 'Yes, but look. His partner is Eleanor Harriman, so she'll back him up. She's an excellent player.'

'What do you make of those two?' said Mrs Apthorp, addressing Mrs Frampton.

Eleanor and Philip looked at each other and grinned. They were both curious to hear the reply to this question.

'Eleanor does not seem at all interested in marriage,' said Helena.

'Mother says it's because she's got a job,' said Winifred.

Mrs Frampton interrupted: 'I was extremely shocked when I heard that Mr Harriman was going to allow Eleanor to work in his office. I wouldn't dream of letting Daphne do anything like that.'

'I shouldn't want to,' said Daphne, sulkily.

'Mother says working at any job distracts a woman from her real purpose in life and doing a man's job is out of the question,' continued Winifred, 'especially now that so many returned servicemen are looking for work.'

'Well, it's because the son was killed, isn't it?' said Mrs Apthorp. 'Eleanor took his place.'

'Yes, I understand that, but that still does not make it suitable,' said Mrs Frampton, firmly. 'Certainly not for someone of her social position. Her mother was very well connected and I don't think she would have approved. I know lots of girls had to take on jobs during the War but it's not as if working as a solicitor was helping the War effort. She could have joined the VAD if she had wanted to work. That would have been much more use.'

'But she did do war work. Have your forgotten? She was driving ambulances before she started working for Mr Harriman,' said Daphne.

'Perhaps she'll marry Philip Danebridge,' said Winifred. 'Then she'll have to stop working.'

Philip winked at Eleanor. Eleanor put her hand over her mouth to stop herself from laughing.

'They do go about together quite a lot,' said Helena.

'I don't think he's the marrying kind,' said Daphne.

'Well, if she wants him she will have to get on with it because he is very eligible, despite his condition,' said Mrs Apthorp. 'I know Mrs Ellery has been thinking of him for her daughter.'

Philip looked indignantly at Eleanor. 'Talking about me as if I were a few yards of cloth to be made into a suit,' he said, in a low voice.

Eleanor stifled a giggle. She was highly amused by the look of horror on Philip's face. She and Philip were under no illusions as to where they stood with each other. They were very close friends but they both knew that marriage was out of the question. Consequently, they were very comfortable and at ease with one another and this conversation caused only amusement and not embarrassment, or in Philip's case wrath.

'We'd better get ready,' said Eleanor, as she stood up. They abandoned their deck chairs and walked down to the lower lawn. Eleanor was very tempted to turn and wave to the ladies in the pavilion but she resisted. Had she done so she would have enjoyed the look of consternation on their faces when they realised that the subjects of their conversation had probably overheard everything that had just been said.

Having finished his match, Philip went to relax in a deck chair in the shade of a large beech tree. From there, he watched Eleanor salvage the shots missed by her partner, Miss Andrews, and win the match for them. Eleanor came to join him and collapsed into a deck chair beside him.

'Right,' said Eleanor. 'We've done our bit for Mrs Giffard and her tournament. I think we can rest on our laurels now.'

'I'm not sure there will be any laurels for the two of us,' said Philip. 'You played really well, though. That backhand of yours is deadly, but I deserve the wooden spoon after my performance.'

'Nonsense, you managed to keep up.'

'Thanks awfully for coming, Lella. I would have had a miserable time otherwise and Mother is happy because we all turned out. She's always anxious to please Mrs Giffard although I can't think why. She's far too bossy and it's clear she wants Manar to replace Top Trees as the centre of society in this town, which is a bit disloyal, don't you think?'

'Well, the tennis court is jolly good. I've not played on it before. It's absolutely the latest type of hard surface and much better than the one at Top Trees so that counts in Mrs Giffard's favour.'

They lazed in their deckchairs watching the other players and eventually two maids came out of the house and headed past Eleanor and Philip to the tennis pavilion. They were carrying trays with jugs of lemonade and plates of sandwiches. The maids were followed by a tall, thin woman dressed in black who was obviously the housekeeper come to supervise the maids. Eleanor thought she recognised her but could not place her.

'That's not Mrs Giffard's usual housekeeper,' said Eleanor, 'but I'm sure I have seen her before.'

'At the Sale of Work probably. She was on loan to Top Trees because they needed extra staff.'

'Ah, yes, that's it. Miss Addison. What's happened to Mrs Brompton, I wonder?' said Eleanor, idly and not expecting an answer.

'She's gone off to look after her sister. Miss Addison is her temporary replacement. From the agency. She's been here about three weeks, I think.'

'How do you know these things, Philip? Do you spend all day gossiping about the servants?'

'No, I overheard my mother telephoning to the vicar. He's praying for Mrs Brompton's sister. He's wasting his time, though. If God has decided your time's up, that's it. You're finished.'

'I know. No amount of praying is going to make the least difference. I tried that with Edgar, and with Alistair, and with my mother.'

'Oh, Lella. What has reduced us to this? We've become so cynical.'

'I know. We're too young to be this cynical. It's not normal.'

'It's the damn War! Sorry, language. In the trenches, I

used to think when it was all over, things would go back to the way they were. After all, that was what we were fighting for, wasn't it? To preserve our way of life. But things haven't gone back as they were, have they?'

'No, far from it. And they never can. Not now.'

'I'm left with a ropey pair of lungs, your sister is left without a husband, and you're minus a brother and a fiancé.'

'And a mother. I know that my mother was already ill when Edgar left to go to France but she was recovering. I'm sure she was. But when he was killed she just seemed to give up.'

'I think you are probably right. I know Aunt Muriel hasn't been the same since Alistair was killed. She doesn't talk about him but I know she is thinking about him all the time. It's eating away at her, little by little. She puts on a brave face but when she isn't aware that someone is watching her, she lets down her guard. I'm sure you think about Alistair all the time too. And Edgar. And Wilfred.'

'Yes, but one just has to keep going, there is no alternative no matter how pointless it all seems,' said Eleanor. 'I suppose that as time passes it will become less painful and it will be easier to see some purpose to one's life, but one does get awfully tired of just "keeping on" without any reason to do so.'

'I know what you mean. So many of our friends have gone. It's an odd feeling. It's as though they have gone somewhere and somehow one has been left behind.'

'Yes. That is exactly the way I feel.'

They sat in silence for a while staring at the tennis court without really seeing it. Then, as the final two players shook hands at the net, Philip said:

'Buck up, old girl. That was the last match. It's nearly time for the prize giving and we have to put on a smile as we accept the loser's trophy. I'll get us some lemonade, shall I?

♣♣♣

On Tuesday morning, shortly after the office had opened, Eleanor went downstairs to say good morning to James. He greeted her with: 'Good morning, Miss Eleanor. The Misses Pymble have called but they didn't want to disturb you so they just left this advertisement for you. There's to be a Thé Chantant at the Crescent Hotel and they were hoping someone from the office would attend. The proceeds are to go to St Dunstan's. For the blind soldiers and sailors.'

'Thank you, James. What are they offering us?' said Eleanor, looking at the paper James handed her. 'Thé Chantant. Four o'clock to six o'clock. Table d'Hôte, Tea and Entertainment, two shillings,' she read. 'Giving it a fancy French name doesn't make it any more appealing as far as I am concerned.' She continued to read. 'Tea, sandwiches, cakes and scones will be served. Entertainment to be provided by Miss Elsie Saunders, mezzo-soprano, and Mr William Owen, The Welsh Tenor, in capital letters, no less. Oh, Lord! They are sure to be singing those sentimental songs about dead babies and lost chords and Maud who never will come into the garden when she's called.'

'And there is Mr Arthur Tomlin, the humorous entertainer at the Piano,' added James, wryly. 'Miss Pymble assured me that his monologues are most entertaining and quite in good taste.'

'Perhaps you would like to go then, James?'

James simply smiled and raised one eyebrow at her little jest.

'Do you think it is the sort of thing Mrs Clayton would enjoy?' asked Eleanor. 'I'm sure she doesn't get out very much. Perhaps she would like to take her sister-in-law.'

'I think she probably would enjoy it,' said James.

'Can you find out for me? We'll have to make a donation anyway so we might as well buy some tickets instead. If she does want to go, can you organise some tickets for her and tell her we can manage without her for once. Father and I can dine out.'

'Very good, Miss Eleanor. I shall let you know what she decides.'

Eleanor was about to go back upstairs when James added, raising an eyebrow archly: 'You will be interested to know that a letter arrived in the early post from Colonel Westerbrook confirming that he would see Mr Harriman on Thursday as requested. I've put the letter on Mr Harriman's desk.'

On Thursday, when Mr Harriman arrived back from Derby, Edwin Talbot had left for the day, James had locked up the office, and Eleanor and Napoleon were in the Gardens. Feeling that he could do with some fresh air and exercise, Mr Harriman decided to postpone dinner and go in search of his daughter and her dog. He found them at the croquet lawn. Napoleon was solemnly watching the croquet game in progress and Eleanor was standing chatting to one of the players. Eleanor greeted her father and she took his arm as they walked slowly along the path that circled the boating lake. Napoleon dawdled along happily beside them. They were out of earshot of other people in the Gardens and Mr Harriman described his meeting with Colonel Westerbrook.

'The Colonel was in Bengal with the King's Shropshire Light Infantry. We had to have a long chat about the old days first, of course, but eventually I managed to get him round to 1895. His battalion was stationed in Calcutta that year and when I mentioned the name Giffard and asked if he had known anyone of that name he said he assumed that I was referring to Mr Giffard and his wife who was poisoned. He said that he did not know them personally but he knew who they were.'

'Ah,' said Eleanor. 'So, the Mary Giffard who died in

Darjeeling. Was she the wife of the Mr Giffard who disappeared?'

'Yes. Apparently, there was some doubt at first as to whether the woman had taken her own life or had been poisoned by someone else. Eventually the wife of one of the Colonel's officers was accused of murder and the Colonel had to deal with the consequences. The officer's wife was tried and sent to a mental asylum and the scandal was too much for the regiment. The officer had to resign. After the trial, Mr Giffard packed up and left Calcutta.'

'So if the Mary Giffard who died in Darjeeling is the Major's mother, I may have to tell him that his mother was murdered? I wonder how he would take that. It is one thing to know that one's mother has died without knowing what she died of, or even that she committed suicide but it is quite another to find that she was murdered.'

'If this is his mother,' said Mr Harriman, 'one can understand why nobody told him the truth at the time. I wonder how much his headmaster knew about the incident.'

'I have already asked the agents to see if there was a newspaper report regarding the death of Mary Giffard in Darjeeling so that should arrive soon. We should be able to take things further when we get that. The Colonel has certainly given us a better idea of what we are looking for. There may even be an official report at the India Office.'

They walked in silence for a while, each trying to picture the incident in India and imagining the sequence of events which would have taken place. Then Eleanor said: 'But why would Mr Giffard disappear after his wife died if he wasn't the one accused of killing her? Why did he feel he had to leave Calcutta?'

'Grief, perhaps. When your mother died I found it difficult to stay here at first. I could easily have run away from the memories.'

'Oh, I know that feeling. What stopped you?'

'Well, you of course, and Cicely and Richard.'

'Then why didn't Mr Giffard go to England to be with his son?'

'Pass.'

'Even if Mr Giffard did feel he needed to get away at first, that feeling wouldn't have lasted forever. He would have recovered in time and he would still have been able to find his son.'

'Pass.'

'Did the Colonel have any idea where Mr Giffard had gone?'

'No, but his opinion was that if the fellow had had any sense he would have gone further east. You suggested that we should widen the searches and I was cautious because of the cost but now that I have heard the Colonel's story I agree with you. It seems that the two cases are linked and we should try to find out more about this Mary Rosa Giffard. I must congratulate you, Eleanor. Your judgment has proven right on two counts. You were sure that Colonel Westerbrook's information would be of use, and it is. And then secondly, you very cleverly persuaded me to go and see Colonel Westerbrook instead of going yourself. The Colonel is as crusty as you had imagined. He was more than willing to talk about India but I had great difficulty getting him around to the scandal involving someone in his regiment. I am certain that he would not have spoken to you about it. In fact, I doubt if he would have agreed to let you into his house. He is one of those narrow minded types who believe that women were put on this earth for only one reason.'

'To provide support and comfort to a man?'

'Yes, and certainly not to do what he regards as a man's job. I am sure that if you had turned up saying that you are a solicitor, you would have aroused all of his prejudices.'

'Well, I am very grateful that you agreed to go. The information he gave you is certainly useful. Now we just have to establish whether our Mr Giffard is alive or dead. We should receive something more from the agents by tomorrow.'

'In the meantime, I need my dinner so, speaking of a woman's proper role, let us go and see what Mrs Clayton has got for us tonight. Come on Napoleon. Dinner time!'

Chapter Ten

The following morning, a letter arrived from the London agents responding to the request for information about the poisoning death of Mary Giffard. They had located newspaper reports published at the time. The letter also stated that their enquiries regarding the Will of the late Edward Giffard were almost complete and a report would follow shortly. They enclosed transcripts of three relevant newspaper articles and a note of two further items.

The first transcript was of a newspaper item headed Report of Death, 10 September 1895.

> DARJEELING, Tuesday. Mrs Giffard, the wife of Mr Edward Giffard, a civil servant in the revenue office at Calcutta, was found dead at home yesterday afternoon. It is believed that the lady died from poisoning and that suicide is suspected. Mrs Giffard was found by a neighbour, Mrs Florence Bryant, who alerted staff at the Giffard household and arranged for a doctor to be called.

The second transcript was headed Report of Inquest, Darjeeling, 3 October 1895.

> DARJEELING, Thursday. The inquest into the death of the late Mrs Edward Giffard was held today at Darjeeling before Sir Linton Cartwright, CMG.
>
> The pathologist, Dr. Robinson, MD, FRCP, gave his opinion that the cause of death was the ingestion of a lethal dose of morphine.

Evidence as to Mrs Giffard's state of health was then given by her treating doctor, Dr Fraser, MD, who said that he had been treating Mrs Giffard for the past ten months for headaches and difficulty sleeping. He said that the onset of these symptoms appeared to have coincided with her young son leaving India to go to school in Scotland. Dr Fraser had prescribed laudanum which, he confirmed, contained morphine. Asked if the prescribed dose was sufficient to cause death, Dr Fraser replied in the negative. It had been prescribed merely as a sleeping draught. However, he did agree that, if the deceased had mistakenly taken an additional dose, that could have been fatal.

Mr Giffard, the widower, gave evidence that he had last seen his wife alive at about 2.30p.m. when she retired to her sitting room after luncheon. He had an urgent matter that had to be attended to that afternoon, so he had returned to his office and did not leave it until about 4.00 p.m. when he was alerted by his clerk to the fact that his wife had been found dead. Mr Giffard gave evidence that his wife had not been well lately and was suffering from nerves. However, he believed that when he last saw her at luncheon she appeared to be quite well.

The last witness was Mrs Florence Bryant, the wife of Captain Geoffrey Bryant who holds a commission as an officer of the King's Shropshire Light Infantry. Mrs Bryant explained that she was a neighbour of the Giffards and had gone to visit the deceased on the afternoon of 9 September. She could not be sure of the time but thought it was just after about three thirty. She had not rung the door-bell because she knew that the indoor servants would be in their quarters resting at that time in the afternoon. Instead, she went around to the courtyard to the French doors which open on to the verandah. On looking through the French doors, she saw that someone was lying on the floor of the sitting room. She went into the sitting room and found that it was Mrs Giffard. Mrs Bryant then went across the courtyard and called for help from the servants. Mrs Bryant confirmed that she had observed an empty glass on the table next to where the deceased was lying when she found her. The glass was later tested and found to have contained morphine.

The coroner's verdict was that the deceased had died on 9 September 1895, between 2.30 p.m. and about 3.45 p.m., as a result of ingesting poison, namely morphine, and that there was insufficient evidence to determine whether the poison was self-administered or administered by person or persons unknown.

The third transcript was an item published in *The Times of India* and headed Report of Trial at Calcutta, 24 February 1896.

CALCUTTA, Monday, From Our Court Reporter.

TRIAL OF FLORENCE LILIAN BRYANT charged with the murder of Mrs Mary Giffard at Darjeeling on 9 September 1895. The hearing commenced on Monday before His Honour Mr Justice Castles and a jury of twelve men.

In opening the case, Mr Miles, Q.C., for the prosecution informed His Honour that there may be an issue as to the fitness of the accused to plead due to her current state of mind.

In the absence of the jury, the judge heard submissions from counsel and from Dr Mathers, the accused's treating doctor. He testified that he had been treating the accused for neurasthenia, a nervous condition which had developed as a result of the death of her infant son some twelve months previously and that, since her arrest, the accused had suffered a complete nervous collapse. In his opinion, she was not fit to give evidence. The judge then heard the evidence of Dr Roger Hampton, MD, FRCP, a specialist in treating hysteria. His Honour then ruled that the trial should proceed.

Throughout the hearing, the accused sat in the dock staring straight ahead of her and did not seem able to hear or comprehend what was unfolding in front of her. She had, clasped in her hands, a necklace made of jet beads and during the hearing she fingered these beads incessantly passing them between her fingers in the manner of a rosary. The writer understands that the necklace was a gift from her husband on the birth of their daughter.

Medical evidence was heard regarding the circumstances of the death of the victim and reports were admitted into evidence regarding the tests which had established that the cause of death was a lethal dose of morphine. Superintendent Morgan, the police officer who had been in charge of the investigation, gave evidence that the deceased had been found by the accused some time shortly after 3.30 p.m. on the afternoon of 9 September last year. The accused had apparently alerted the staff at the Giffard house, who called a doctor. A glass, left on the table next to the deceased, had been tested and found to contain morphine.

Evidence as to the deceased's state of health was given by her treating doctor, Dr Fraser, MD. He said that he had been treating Mrs Giffard for the past ten months or so for headaches and difficulty sleeping and that he had prescribed laudanum, which contains morphine.

The first lay witness to be called was Mr Kahar, one of the Giffard's indoor servants, who testified that, on the afternoon of 9 September 1895, he had been in the courtyard. He was unable to say what time that was. He said that he had looked across the courtyard and through the French doors into the sitting room where he had seen the accused and the deceased. Until that moment he was not aware that the accused was in the house. The doorbell had not been rung and he had not opened the door to anyone. He recognised the accused because she was a regular visitor to the house and she was wearing a shawl of a distinctive pattern which he had seen her wearing on previous visits. He saw the accused put something into a glass and offer the glass to the Memsahib. When asked by the defence counsel why he had not come forward to give evidence at the inquest he said that he was away visiting his family for the Diwali festival at the time and knew nothing about the inquest.

Miss Hepworth was then called. She stated that, in September 1895, she was employed as governess to the accused's daughter, Lilian Bryant. She had been in that post for eight months and had left on the day after the accused was arrested. Miss Hepworth gave evidence that the two families, the Bryants and the Giffards, were neighbours in Darjeeling having rented bungalows in the same street for the summer months. They were on very familiar terms. She said that she and Mrs Bryant were frequent visitors at the Giffard's house and entering the house informally via the courtyard was not unusual.

Miss Hepworth said that the accused had left the Bryant's house at about 3.30 p.m. to visit the Giffard's house intending to return a book she had borrowed and to ask Mrs Giffard if she had any gold thread which she, Miss Hepworth, needed because she was making a fancy dress costume for the accused's daughter to wear at a forthcoming children's party.

Miss Hepworth said that the accused had a supply of laudanum which she regularly took to help her sleep.

Asked if she knew why the accused had difficulty sleeping, Miss Hepworth said that the accused had believed that her husband, Captain Bryant, was engaged in an illicit liaison with the deceased.

That concluded the prosecution's case and there was no evidence called for the defence. The judge summed up and the jury retired to consider its verdict.

The London agents reported that a brief newspaper article dated a week later stated that the accused had been found guilty and, instead of being sentenced to death or a prison term, had been committed to a mental asylum.

The final note from the London agents was a death notice from *The Times of India*.

BRYANT, Florence Lilian, late of Calcutta, wife of Captain Geoffrey Bryant (retired), died 30 April 1896.

When Eleanor had finished reading these reports, she thought what a sad sequence of events they portrayed. She had a very clear mental picture of the accused sitting in the Court totally impassive and powerless. She considered the facts as reported. Florence Bryant seemed to have had both the means and the opportunity to commit murder and the evidence of the governess certainly gave her a motive. That evidence appeared to have sealed Florence Bryant's fate.

Eleanor was very good at isolating facts and analysing them. She read through the account of the trial again, slowly, absorbing each detail carefully before moving on to the next. She was not sure whether it was the report of the trial or the trial itself but she was left with the feeling that something was unsatisfactory. Either way, she felt certain that there was more to the story than had been revealed in these summaries. Without a full transcript of the evidence, it was difficult to judge but it seemed to Eleanor that Florence Bryant had been convicted on the flimsiest of evidence.

Eleanor said to herself: 'Why is it that I feel more concern, compassion even, for Florence Bryant than for Mary Giffard? Florence was the killer. I should feel more for Mary. After all, she was the victim. It's back to front. Somewhere in all of this, something is wrong.'

Eleanor took out her list of events and added all of the new facts to her chronology. When she had finished she had a niggling feeling at the back of her mind that there was some relevant fact or some important detail which she had missed. She knew that if she concentrated on other things, the facts of this case would fall into place in her mind and when she next looked at the file, things would be clearer. She put the Major's file away and opened another file. Nevertheless, she sighed as she did so, and wondered how Major Giffard was going to react to all of this. She hoped that it would all turn out to be a mistake and nothing to do with him at all.

True to their word, the London agents had completed their search for the Will of Edward Giffard and their report arrived with the first post on Tuesday. By working backwards through the records as Eleanor had suggested, they had found an application dated 18 June 1914 made in the Indian High Court for a grant of probate in relation to the Last Will and Testament of Edward George Granby Giffard. The Will was dated 2 July 1888. The agents had transcribed the Will and the documents accompanying it and they had drawn attention to the fact that probate had been granted by the Indian High Court on 25 November 1914 and then the grant had been re-sealed in the High Court in Colombo on 28 February 1915. Eleanor read the documents, then slowly analysed the facts, and arrived at a conclusion. She now understood the reason for the strange behaviour of Mrs Giffard and her shock on being introduced to Major Giffard at the Sale of Work. She went over the facts again and, when she was certain she had missed nothing, she went in to see her father. Eleanor said: 'The Major's father is dead.'

'I see,' said Mr Harriman.

'He died in 1913. His Will was witnessed by a solicitor in Calcutta in 1888 and, judging by the date, it was made in anticipation of the Major being born. It is a very simple Will. It provides for a life interest to his widow and, on her death, everything goes to any surviving children of the marriage. Mary Giffard died in 1895 so she doesn't get her life interest and, as far as we know there were no children other than the Major. On the death of his father, Major Giffard was entitled to all of his father's estate.'

'And yet Major Giffard has not received his inheritance,' said Mr Harriman.

'No,' said Eleanor, 'which means that the writer of the anonymous letter was absolutely correct. His message to the Major was: *All is not as it should be*. And it certainly is not.'

'So probate was granted in India because that is where the Will was made,' said Mr Harriman. 'Who is the executor?'

'When probate was granted, the Calcutta solicitor, the one who drew up the Will, was replaced by a solicitor in Colombo on the grounds that Mr Giffard had no assets in India. All of his property is in Ceylon.'

'So the unpaid salary and the pension are not mentioned as assets?' asked Mr Harriman.

'No. I suppose it is possible that the Colombo solicitors knew nothing about them. But this is the disturbing thing. Mr Giffard died nearly seven years ago but the executor has not yet filed final accounts. That is because Mr Giffard left a widow who is still alive and she is receiving the benefit of the life interest granted by the Will.'

'A widow? A second Mrs Giffard? But that can't be right,'

said Mr Harriman.

'Well, the interim accounts show quarterly payments being made to the widow, named as Mary Giffard. And, this is an even more disturbing thing. Look at this. The address on the last line.'

Eleanor handed a piece of paper to her father. He read the last line and then looked up. Eleanor and her father regarded each other in silence, then Mr Harriman frowned and said: 'Hmmm.' Mr Harriman looked at the piece of paper again and, still frowning, drummed his fingers lightly on the top of his desk while he contemplated the facts. Then he said: 'This needs careful analysis, Eleanor. I think we may be treading on very unfirm ground here.'

'Quite,' said Eleanor. 'We need to be absolutely sure of our facts before I report to Major Giffard and provide him with advice.'

'There are several possible explanations, of course,' said Mr Harriman. 'Let's examine each of the facts in turn and decide which we are certain about and which we are unsure of.'

'I'll make notes as we go, facts in one column, speculation in the other,' said Eleanor.

First fact: We can be certain that we have the correct Will. The name is very distinctive and it matches exactly the name on the Major's birth certificate.

Fact Two: The Will was made in 1888 when the Major's mother, Mary Rosa Giffard, was still alive.

Fact Three: Mary Rosa Giffard is the person referred to as my wife, Mary Giffard to whom a life interest is granted although her second name Rosa has been left out.'

'I think,' said Mr Harriman, 'that is a safe assumption.'

Eleanor resumed her list.

'Fact Four: We know that a Mary Giffard died in Darjeeling in 1895 and again, the second name, Rosa, was not used but with the other information we have it is safe to assume that the Mary Giffard who died in Darjeeling was Mary Rosa Giffard, the Major's mother.'

'Yes,' said Mr Harriman. 'Given the details in the report of the inquest and the trial of Florence Bryant, there can be no doubt of that.'

' So, Fact Five: The Major's father gave a life interest in his estate to the Major's mother but she died eighteen years before the Major's father so the gift of the life interest cannot take effect. Therefore, the whole estate should have passed to the Major on the death of his father in 1913.

Fact Six: If the Major's father had remarried after 1895, his 1888 Will would have been automatically revoked by that second marriage.

Fact Seven: The Colombo solicitors applied for a grant of probate using the 1888 Will so they must have known, or assumed, that it was still valid.'

'Fact Eight,' said Eleanor. 'If there is a second Mrs Giffard, she would only be entitled to a life interest in the estate if there was a second Will. But there isn't a second Will.'

Eleanor stopped writing and grinned at her father. 'This is like one of those WitchFinder General tests, isn't it? When you are accused of being a witch and you are thrown into the pond.'

'What?' said Mr Harriman. 'If you float you're guilty, and if you sink you're innocent but either way you die.'

'Yes,' said Eleanor, 'that's the one. If you are not married to Edward Giffard, the 1888 Will is valid but you get nothing because you are not the wife referred to in that Will. Everything goes to the son. And, if you *are* married to Edward Giffard as his second wife, the 1888 Will is no longer valid because it has been automatically revoked by your marriage. You still get nothing. So, is this widow floating or sinking?'

'From where I am sitting, she is floating and in very troubled and rather murky waters,' said Mr Harriman. He continued: 'Fact or speculation? The Colombo solicitors were not told and did not realise that the Mary Giffard referred to in the 1888 Will had died in 1895. They must also not have realised that the widow who was alive in 1913 was not the person referred to in the 1888 Will. They have been making payments to the wrong person.'

'That is what I thought. So, where do we go from here?' asked Eleanor.

'Let's look at the grant of probate,' suggested Mr Harriman.

Eleanor said: 'According to the probate application Edward Giffard died on 12 December 1913 at Kandy, Ceylon. The list of assets attached to the grant shows only property in Ceylon and nothing in India. The main asset which provides the income for the life interest is a tea plantation named Singhapitiya Gardens, purchased in 1897.'

'So it seems that when Mr Giffard disappeared from Calcutta he went to Ceylon and became a tea planter.'

'Yes. Since the beginning of 1914, quarterly payments have been made to the widow out of the income from the plantation,' said Eleanor.

'Well,' said Mr Harriman. 'There are only two explanations here. Either the Major's mother did not die in 1895 and she is the person currently receiving the quarterly payments as per the 1888 Will, or….'

'The person currently benefiting from the life interest is the second wife of Edward Giffard who is posing as the first Mary Giffard referred to in the 1888 Will,' said Eleanor.

'Hmm,' said Mr Harriman.

'And,' continued Eleanor, 'as the tea plantation named Singhapitiya Gardens is at a place called Manar, I think we both know who that imposter is. It would certainly explain why Mrs Giffard has been avoiding the Major and his wife. And I know from Miss Pymble's sleuthing that Mrs Giffard receives a letter from Ceylon every quarter.'

Eleanor stared for a moment or two at the paper she had been making notes on and then she looked at her father and said: 'What do we do now? Is the evidence strong enough? Or, have we jumped to an unfounded conclusion?'

'No, I don't think we have jumped to the wrong conclusion. We have a lot of facts and only a small amount of speculation. One thing is certain. We have an obligation, at this point, to report the facts that we do have to the Major and ask him for further instructions.'

'The cost of obtaining proof that he is the rightful heir could be quite high, couldn't it?'

'Yes, I'm afraid so. It has to be his decision as to what action we take next. He could contest the grant of probate and that would have to be done in India, of course. And then there would have to be proceedings in Colombo. But before he can make a decision, we need to find out the remaining value of the estate. Let us begin by sending him a letter setting out the facts and explaining his options. And, in the meantime, we shall keep our suspicions about Mrs Giffard to ourselves. Although, we shall bring Edwin up to date, of course.'

'Absolutely,' said Eleanor, 'I shall draft the letter to the Major straightaway and wait for his response before doing anything further.'

'There is one unanswered question, though,' said Mr Harriman, 'the anonymous letter writer must know about the Will. Who is the writer and how did he come by the information?'

While the office was closed during lunch, Mr Harriman discussed the Giffard matter with Edwin. When Eleanor came back into the office after having taken Napoleon for his lunch-time walk, she joined in the discussion. 'You do agree, don't you,' said Eleanor, addressing Edwin, 'that the evidence points to Mrs Giffard being somehow involved in fraud or, at the very least, deception.'

'It is certainly difficult to think of an explanation which does not involve dishonesty of some kind,' agreed Edwin, cautiously. 'And, if there had been no deception and she is indeed the rightful beneficiary, it would mean that she is the Major's mother.' He laughed. 'It would certainly explain her shock at meeting him at the Sale of Work.'

'Goodness, yes,' said Eleanor, laughing. 'I hadn't thought of that. What a delicious complication that would be, but she isn't the Major's mother because she is not old enough. The Major is thirty-two and Mrs Giffard could only be in her late forties at the most, which makes her only about fifteen years older than he is.'

Mr Harriman said: 'It is clear that Mrs Giffard of Manar is not the Mary Giffard referred to in the 1888 Will. And if she is indeed receiving quarterly payments of a life interest, either she told the Colombo solicitor that she was that Mary Giffard, or she remained silent and allowed him to assume that she was.'

'So who is she and what claim can she have had on the Major's father?' asked Edwin.

'She must be someone he met in Ceylon. His first wife was dead by then, so he would have been free to marry again,' said Mr Harriman. 'That would at least make her his legitimate widow even if it bars her from the inheritance.'

'But if she had produced her marriage certificate, the Colombo solicitors would have told her that the 1888 Will had no effect and they would not have applied for probate,' said Eleanor.

'Well,' said Edwin, 'if she was married to Giffard and he didn't make a second Will, she would have received only what the law allows to a widow, which is not a great deal and certainly not enough to maintain a place like Manar.

Judging by the way Mrs Giffard lives, there is a very substantial amount of money involved and that would provide a big incentive to fraud.'

'Yes,' said Mr Harriman, 'we know from experience that a very wealthy person who makes a Will in terms that displease his or her relatives provides a large incentive for litigation or deceit. The law reports are littered with cases of unhappy beneficiaries, some of whom resort to murder as well as fraud.'

Eleanor said: 'The only possible way she could have made a claim on the estate was to pretend to be the first Mary Giffard. And the Will made it easy for her because it doesn't say "to my wife Mary Rosa Giffard" it just says "to my wife Mary Giffard" and I know that the Christian name of Mrs Giffard is Mary, the same as the Major's mother, so if she told the Colombo solicitor that she was Mary Giffard she would not have been telling a lie. How was he to know that she was the wrong Mary Giffard?'

'I agree. It's a feasible explanation,' said Mr Harriman. 'We know that Mr Giffard left Calcutta not long after his wife's death. It seems that he went to Ceylon and established himself as a tea planter. So, once there he meets someone whose name is Mary. If he simply introduces her as "my wife, Mary Giffard" who's to know that she was not the original wife. He would have had to be careful to avoid people who might have known him or the first Mary Giffard in India, of course.'

Edwin said: 'It does depend on the Colombo solicitors not being too particular about evidence of identity.'

'Not necessarily,' said Eleanor. 'Maybe the second Mary Giffard just used the first Mary Giffard's documents. There are no photographs on identity documents and, until a few years ago, not even on passports. She could have just told the solicitor that she had stopped using the name Rosa because she didn't like it and was now just Mary. I think we have to accept that there has been deception of some kind.'

'Sadly, I think you are correct,' said Mr Harriman. 'I wonder if the deception was solely on the part of Mrs Giffard after Mr Giffard's death or was Mr Giffard also involved?'

'You mean,' said Eleanor, 'did Mr Giffard intend, after his death, that the second Mary Giffard would use his first wife's identity in order to claim the life interest? Or did Mrs Giffard decide to make the claim only after Mr Giffard had died?'

'But surely, if he had intended the second Mary Giffard to have a life interest,' added Edwin, 'he would have made a new Will in her favour.'

'Perhaps he didn't want to leave anything to the second Mary Giffard,' said Eleanor, 'but didn't have the courage to tell her. He might have expected the 1888 Will to be used so that the Major would inherit everything and that was his way of making amends for having abandoned him as a child. Maybe he felt guilty about what he had done.'

'It would be nice to think so, for the Major's sake, but I suppose we shall never know,' said Edwin.

'Well,' said Mr Harriman, 'Eleanor has done what Major Giffard asked her to do and the rest is up to him. We shall have to wait for his instructions before taking any further action.'

'And any action we do take will be expensive,' said Edwin. 'Perhaps we can confront Mrs Giffard and see if we can shame her into confessing and giving up the money.'

They looked at each other with expressions that showed how little hope they thought there was of that happening.

'Perhaps,' suggested Eleanor, 'we could telegraph to the solicitors in Ceylon and ask for more information?'

'That's not a bad idea,' said Edwin.

'I think we need the Major's instructions first before we take such a step but it is certainly a sensible plan and could save a lot of unnecessary expense later if he does choose to pursue the matter further.'

♣♣♣

In the afternoon post that day there was a letter for Mr Harriman from Colonel Westerbrook and Mr Harriman took the letter into Eleanor's office saying: 'Colonel Westerbrook seems to be taking an interest in the Giffard case. I have just received this.'

'He must have been charmed by my letter,' said Eleanor.

'Well, he writes to say that after I had been to see him…'

Eleanor interrupted him saying: 'Ah, then it was your visit that charmed him, not my letter.'

'…he was at a regimental dinner and met one of his old cronies, a Major-General Williamson. The Major-General was in Calcutta at the same time as Colonel Westerbrook. This is what the Colonel has to say:

Having been reminded of the Giffard incident because of your recent visit, I asked Major-General Williamson if he recollected it at all. He did recall the incident but knew very little about it. However, he believed that his wife had been friendly with some of the people involved. Mrs Williamson will be in Buxton next week and I am writing to let you know of her visit as I thought you may wish to call on her. I believe she will be staying at the Buxton Hydropathic Hotel.'

'Oh, what a piece of luck,' said Eleanor. 'Good old Colonel Westerbrook. That was kind of him to take the trouble to write. I take back anything I may have said or thought about his being old and crusty. I hope Mrs Williamson really does know something. But how odd that she should be coming to Buxton.'

'Yet another co-incidence in a case full of them?' asked Mr Harriman as he left the letter on Eleanor's desk and returned to his own office.

Chapter Eleven

On Saturday night, Eleanor and Cicely had tickets for a comic opera which was playing at the Buxton Opera House. Cicely, looking very glamorous, arrived at Hall Bank with Richard in time for the two sisters to have a glass of sherry with Mr Harriman before walking down to the theatre. In their childhood, Eleanor and Cicely had been allies against their two older sisters and had always shared everything. Now they shared the bond of bereavement. At first, when the inevitable telegrams came, they had been too numb to feel anything. Then they had gone through a stage of disbelief in which they tried to comprehend the loss of their loved ones. That had merged into a feeling of hopelessness. At the end of the War, they did not celebrate what the government and the newspapers described as "the Victory" and felt only a sense of relief. At last, the lists of casualties would stop and they would be released from the ever-present fear that today they would read yet another familiar name, another friend whose death was to be mourned.

A year ago, on the anniversary of Wilfred's death, the two sisters had made a pact. They had agreed that, for their own sakes as well as for Richard's, they had to face the reality of life without a partner. They vowed in future to find things about which they could be positive and to look for enjoyment in life again. It seemed ungrateful not to do so given the sacrifice of so many lives which had made it possible for them to continue to live. They had been gradually returning to the things they used to do before the

War and, this evening, they were going to the theatre for the first time in years, dressed in evening frocks and jewellery instead of the practical clothing suitable for War work. Cicely was dressed in an evening frock of midnight blue silk patterned very faintly with silver flowers and the fabric draped and flowed as it was intended to over her slender figure. The dress was set off with silver accessories and a silver necklace. Eleanor wore a rich burgundy gown in velvet and silk with pearl trimmings, and long red velvet gloves, which emphasised her tall, elegant figure. They admired each other's frocks and Cicely showed off a new pair of evening shoes. They were in the mood to be entertained.

As a special treat, Richard was allowed to stay at Hall Bank with Mr Harriman and Napoleon. Richard and Mr Harriman began an energetic game of Snap. This was one of their favourites and the pack of cards they played with was now slightly the worse for wear. It had been bought for Amelia, the eldest of the Harriman children, many years earlier when the game first became popular and had been handed down from one sibling to the next and then used to entertain the sisters' children when they visited. Now it was Richard's turn. Matching the cards was not easy because, unlike ordinary playing cards, these did not have the symbols of hearts, diamonds, clubs and spades grouped in patterns. This pack had the original Tenniel drawings. They were caricatures of people and the designs were not easy to distinguish apart. Because Mr Harriman believed in teaching children to earn their prizes, he only allowed Richard to win often enough to keep him interested in the game. As a result, Richard had developed a quickness of eye and hand which allowed him to win cards by his own effort. This evening, Richard was very pleased with his own performance and was making sure his audience knew it. Eleanor and Cicely finished their drinks and left him to it.

The entertainment at the Buxton Opera House was usually provided by professional companies but, from time to time, there was a performance by the Buxton Amateur Dramatic and Operatic Society, a very talented amateur company of near professional standard. The proceeds of their productions were donated to charity and, as the company received enormous support from the local community, the amounts raised were considerable. This evening they were performing a comic opera called *Dorothy* and it was their first full-scale production since the interruption caused by the War. The company's return to the stage was welcomed with eager anticipation. Tonight was opening night and the air was electric. Many of the audience had friends or relatives in the cast, and Buxton society had turned out in full force for the occasion. When Eleanor and Cicely arrived at the Opera House there was quite a crowd milling around outside under the lights. The two sisters stood to one side of the entrance, watching the scene and enjoying the sense of occasion and anticipation.

'Isn't it marvellous,' said Cicely. 'Everyone has made a real effort tonight. It's almost back to the way it was.'

The gentlemen were looking suave in their black and white evening dress and shiny patent leather shoes. The ladies were glamorous in evening frocks and jewellery, stoles languidly draped over one shoulder. As people arrived and greeted each other, groups formed, dissolved, and re-formed, leaving an impression of shimmering, moving colour. Occasionally a chauffeur-driven motor-car pulled up and the female occupants were handed out by their partners. Then, a very large, immaculately polished Rolls Royce drew up to the kerb. The chauffeur opened the door and stood to attention. The lady companion got out of the car and, with the right degree of deference and fuss, supervised Lady Carleton-West's descent to the pavement. Obviously Sir Marmaduke had another engagement that evening. Lady

Carleton-West paused to survey the scene with approval and make sure everyone had noticed her arrival. Then, the two ladies processed grandly across the forecourt of the Opera House and up the entrance steps, Lady Carleton-West graciously acknowledging acquaintances as she went.

'Buxton Royalty,' said Eleanor to Cicely. 'The management has forgotten to put out the red carpet.'

Cicely giggled: 'I know. But what would we do without them? You must admit they give a certain air of importance to the occasion.'

'They certainly do. I agree. And Lady Carleton-West is far less dangerous than some,' she added, darkly.

The bells started ringing for the beginning of the performance. The sisters had agreed to splash out on tickets for the Dress Circle so they joined the crowd which was edging its way slowly up the main staircase. The theatre, although small, was built in the grand style, with all the customary Belle Epoque features: ornate plasterwork lavishly trimmed in gold and decorated with an abundance of cherubs, masks, and lyres. The auditorium was the traditional three tiered horseshoe with private boxes at each side of the stage, a dress circle set back above the stalls and an upper gallery above the dress circle. The front panels of the dress circle and upper circle balconies swept in two continuous curves around the theatre from one side of the proscenium arch to the other. These two curves were also decorated with gilded plasterwork which caught the light and reflected it throughout the theatre. High above the auditorium there was a wonderful moulded and brightly coloured painted ceiling also edged in gold. The glamour and elegance of the audience added its own shimmer to the theatre and there was a sense of occasion which the audience embraced with anticipation.

Eleanor and Cicely had seats towards the centre of the dress circle and three rows back from the edge of the balcony. They settled themselves and took it in turns to look through the programme or to survey the rest of the audience. Because of the horseshoe shape of the theatre it was possible for those in the dress circle to see and to be seen. Eleanor watched with interest as people arrived, found their seats. Some nodded to acquaintances before taking their seats, others just paused, half turning so that people in the rest of the theatre had time to notice them in all their finery. Eleanor recognised many people she knew. She also noticed that Lady Carleton-West had now taken possession of one of the boxes and was talking animatedly with her group of followers and directing which seat each guest was to occupy.

Cicely said: 'There's Philip,' and she and Eleanor exchanged waves of greeting with him.

'We'll find him at the first interval,' said Eleanor and turned her attention to the programme.

Cicely asked: 'So, what is *Dorothy* about? Is it the usual nonsensical farce?'

'Absolutely,' said Eleanor. 'Where would the world of comic opera be without a rich young hero incognito, a young and silly heroine, and a story based on mistaken identity?'

'Tell me more,' said Cicely.

'When the curtain goes up we shall be in Kent in 1740 in a hop garden,' said Eleanor. 'The chorus members are dancing around a hop pole, involving themselves in the affairs of the local landlord (played by Mr Roberts, our bank manager and a character part, no doubt) and talking about the betrothal of his daughter, Phyllis (played by Miss Amelia Allardyce, she's Lady Carleton-West's niece, isn't she?). The local squire's daughter, Dorothy Bantam (played by Miss Daphne Frampton, remind me at interval to tell you about her conversation at the tennis party), and her cousin, Lydia (that's Miss Pym from the Devonshire Library), are in disguise, romping with the village girls and serving as barmaids. The reason for this disguise is undisclosed but no doubt these two well-bred young ladies are looking for a bit of fun away from their governess. Dorothy and Lydia are against matrimony in general but then along come two handsome and rich young gentlemen (played by Mr Allen from the Post Office and Dr Flint from the hospital), who set about having a dalliance with the two barmaids. Naturally, these young gentlemen are going to fall in love with what they assume are village maidens and then get themselves into hot water when, later on, they meet Dorothy and her cousin in their real setting as young ladies up at the wealthy squire's house. Dorothy is apparently betrothed to one of these young gentlemen, who is actually her cousin, although she has never seen him before, and that young gentleman is tempted to renounce the idea of marriage to Dorothy in favour of the village maiden. So, they have three acts in which to sort out the confusion created in the first scene.'

'Honestly, Eleanor,' said Cicely, laughing, 'you never stop being a lawyer, do you? You reduce everything to just a few bland propositions, and remove all the fun into the bargain. Next you will be analysing the facts to decide whether or not there has been a breach of promise.'

'Sorry,' said Eleanor. 'I am sure I have covered the essential parts. Here, you read the programme and see for yourself. Anyway, the performance will be enjoyable and I am very much looking forward to seeing our Mr Roberts in 1740s knee breeches.'

Cicely giggled at the thought and looked through the list of people who were in the chorus, most of whom they knew. Then, the house lights began going down, conversation started to tail off, the stragglers found their places, and the audience got ready to enjoy the performance. Applause broke out as the conductor appeared in the orchestra pit. He bowed to the audience, turned to the orchestra, raised his baton to begin the overture, and then froze, arms in the air.

The door at the rear of the box on the left hand side of the dress circle had opened and light flooded into the auditorium. A group of people, talking loudly to each other, entered the box and began discussing who was going to sit where. One voice soared above the rest. The audience was silent at first and then started tutting quietly.

Cicely nudged Eleanor and whispered: 'Mrs Giffard and party.'

'Obviously too important to get here on time like the rest of us,' responded Eleanor.

The audience looked towards the box, as did the conductor, his arms still poised in mid-air. Mrs Giffard appeared to interpret his pose as a sign that the performance had been delayed pending her arrival. She gave a gracious bow in the direction of the conductor, acknowledging his courtesy in waiting for her. She sank majestically down on her chair, rested one arm delicately on the edge of the box, and inclined her head towards the stage as a signal that the performance could begin. Eleanor was very tempted to applaud this consummate performance of self-aggrandisement but contented herself with whispering to Cicely:

'What a performance. You have to admire her, for sheer gall if nothing else.'

'Isn't she wonderfully irritating,' agreed Cicely.

Eleanor looked across to Lady Carleton-West's box and said: 'If ever there was a murderous look, that is it. The actors would do well to study that expression and store it for future reference.'

Finally, the performance began.

During the first interval, Eleanor and Cicely found Philip who was in the company of the local theatre critic. They were discussing Mrs Giffard's performance and Eleanor said: 'Do you remember that wonderful letter to the editor, Cicely? Father read it to us once. How did it go? Something about 'bad imitators of gentility.'

'Yes,' said Cicely, 'I remember. It was about not having any manners at a concert in the Octagon.'

'I know the letter you mean,' said the theatre critic. 'I have often wondered whether the author was a local resident or a visitor. A visitor, I suspect. If I remember correctly he accused the latecomers of being parvenus and of "spending too much time occupied with making money to permit of them devoting any of it to the acquisition of manners." Very Oscar Wilde. Of course, it was written thirty or so years ago and, although it might have applied to some people in the audience at the time, I have always thought it very unkind and unwarranted. However, after tonight's performance, I am not so sure. Perhaps he did have a point.'

That performance, however, proved to be Mrs Giffard's last.

Chapter Twelve

Eleanor had three friends who, like her, had origins in The Park but were not keen to be full members of its society. They were all single women establishing an independent role for themselves in the town through their careers and had no ambitions to define their status by presiding over a mansion in The Park and playing dictator to a husband. One was a doctor, one was a senior mistress at a girls' boarding school, and one was a trainee draftsman at a firm of architects. Even though they were all daughters of people of impeccable pedigree, The Park asked itself uneasily whether it was "quite nice" for these young women to be so independent. They discussed politics and had even been known to attend a meeting at which "social improvement" was discussed, which was dangerously close to communism as far as The Park was concerned. They were setting a precedent which The Park did not want its daughters to follow.

The four friends, oblivious to the trepidations of The Park, met once a month during the season to spend Sunday afternoon walking along the local footpaths and rights of way. Out of earshot of the town, they could have open conversations about topics that interested them and provide mutual support for the challenges which, as single women, they had to deal with every day in their professional lives. For their walk on this Sunday, the four women, escorted by Napoleon, had taken the train to Chapel-en-le-Frith. They intended to follow a circular route from there around the Combs reservoir and then, after stopping for refreshments at the Beehive Inn, take the path out of Combs village to the south to join the old Manchester Road and so make their way back to Buxton. Their progress was always leisurely with plenty of stops to admire the scenery and they did not expect to arrive back in Buxton until at least eight thirty in the evening.

At five o'clock on that Sunday afternoon, the walking party was seven miles from Buxton, enjoying the hospitality of the Beehive Inn. In Buxton, the sun was illuminating the great fan-shaped windows that Sir Joseph Paxton had designed for the two adjoining railway stations and inside these buildings there was a great deal of noisy activity. The waiting rooms and platforms were full of passengers either arriving or leaving. On the outward bound platforms, the day trippers were going home to their small terrace houses in the grimy industrial areas of Manchester and Sheffield. They were milling about, hurrying to get tickets, anxiously asking which platform they needed, making sure they had all their belongings, and had not left any of their souvenirs or their children behind. Those leaving after a longer stay were assembled in groups, some in wheelchairs or leaning on sticks, standing beside piles of luggage, or searching for porters to load their luggage on to the train.

On the inward bound platforms, there was an equal amount of frenzied activity. Those who were arriving to stay during the coming week or were lucky enough to be coming for the season, were descending from carriages, calling for porters, asking for directions to their various hotels or lodging houses, or looking for a station taxi. There was a great deal of noise: people talking animatedly or calling to each other, carriage doors being slammed, guard's whistles signalling departure, engines hissing steam, and great clanking noises as moving carriages collided with stationary buffers. In all of this commotion, no-one noticed Major and Mrs Giffard descend from the Derby train.

Several hours later, the walking party arrived back at Buxton and, as they neared the end of Long Hill, began to disperse as each walker headed for home. Eleanor and Napoleon walked up Hall Bank, tired and dusty but happy. Eleanor took a bath, had a light supper, fed Napoleon, and went to bed. By the time Mr Harriman came back from his Club, she and Napoleon were sound asleep. Cicely and Richard were the only people in Buxton who knew that Major and Mrs Giffard had returned to Oxford House that afternoon.

Monday was a very busy day at Harriman & Talbot. Edwin was at Court all day. Eleanor and Mr Harriman had spent the morning drafting documents and at twelve-fifteen had left the office and driven to Chinley. They had lunch there and then went on to visit one of their long-standing clients, John Wainwright, a gentleman who had retired after a lifetime as a mill owner in Manchester. Mr Wainwright wanted to create a trust to secure the future of the mill and its employees and, as he had been a client of Harriman & Talbot for many years, Mr Harriman had no difficulty in agreeing to visit him at his home. Eleanor went with him to take notes because it was good experience for her, and also because Mr Harriman was very proud of his daughter and wanted to introduce her to one of the firm's valued clients.

They drove to a large house of Arts & Crafts design about two miles north of Chinley which looked out over the valley in the direction of Kinder Scout. The parlour-maid showed them into Mr Wainwright's study where he greeted them warmly. After two hours of intense discussion and note taking, Mr Wainwright's affairs had been analysed, re-assessed, and re-structured to his and Mr Harriman's satisfaction. Mr Wainwright then invited Eleanor and Mr

Harriman to join him and Mrs Wainwright for tea. Mr Wainwright ushered them into an elegant sitting room which afforded a magnificent view of the valley and the hills beyond.

Mrs Wainwright came forward to greet them.'Mr Harriman, how nice to see you again. Do come in.'

'Mrs Wainwright, how are you?' said Mr Harriman. 'May I introduce my daughter, Eleanor?'

'Miss Harriman, how do you do? Won't you sit here? I expect after all that talking you are ready for some tea.'

'I think we have earned it, my dear,' said Mr Wainwright. 'We have talked long and hard and, despite numerous obstacles, we have reached a most satisfactory arrangement. Now, what have you got to offer us?'

'Cook has prepared a few things and she has made some of your favourite ginger biscuits,' said Mrs Wainwright.

An impressive array of finger sandwiches, cakes and biscuits was set out on a small side table and the parlour-maid wheeled a tea trolley forward. Mrs Wainwright began dispensing tea and the maid carried around the plates of food. When Mrs Wainwright's attention was free from her duties as hostess and the maid had left, Mrs Wainwright said to Eleanor: 'Your fame has preceded you, Miss Harriman. I have heard all about your triumph over that horrid motor-car salesman from Manchester.'

Eleanor wasn't sure how to respond to this as she had been asked to keep the matter confidential and she wondered how the news had got out. Mrs Wainwright saw her surprise.

'Don't worry, my dear. You won't be breaching any confidences. Mrs Wentworth-Streate is my cousin. She telephoned me and told me all about Rufus' little adventure. We actually know the person you were up against. In fact, Mr Wainwright had cause to report him to the authorities in Manchester in 1917.'

'Yes,' agreed Mr Wainwright. 'Brantlingham got himself

involved with some people who were supplying goods on the black market and he tried a spot of blackmail. He was lucky not to be sent to jail. I cannot understand how he got the job with the motor-car company. They seem a thoroughly respectable crowd.'

'He probably told untruths or persuaded someone to vouch for him,' said Mrs Wainwright.

'From what I know of him, he would have found it hard to get someone to give him a good reference,' said Mr Wainwright.

'Well, you have no idea how grateful my cousin is, Miss Harriman. Thanks to you, Rufus had a very lucky escape.'

'I am just pleased to have been able to find a solution for them,' said Eleanor. 'I think the person concerned has left Buxton but I shall keep in mind what you have told me about him in case he returns to look for another victim.'

The conversation continued happily during tea and eventually Mr Harriman and Eleanor said good-bye and drove back to the office. By the time that they arrived back at Hall Bank, the office was closed and both Edwin and James had left for the day. Mrs Clayton and Napoleon were upstairs in the kitchen preparing Eleanor's dinner. Mr Harriman was going to a meeting and then he was dining with a friend at his club. Napoleon came out of the kitchen to welcome Eleanor, followed by Mrs Clayton who greeted her with the news that Mrs Giffard-pronounced-Jiffard was dead.

Eleanor, stunned, stood in the hall looking at Mrs Clayton in disbelief. No, this was not idle gossip and no, there was no mistake. Brother Alf had been called out to Manar this afternoon to remove the body. He had received the telephone call just as Mrs Clayton was about to leave for Hall Bank. Much to Mrs Clayton's regret, she was unable to tell Eleanor anything further and was anxious to get home and extract more details from Alf.

Mr Harriman turned to Eleanor and said: 'I'll talk to you about this development in the morning. I must get on or I'll be late for the meeting.' He said goodnight to Mrs Clayton and departed.

Eleanor followed Mrs Clayton back into the kitchen. 'It's all right, Mrs Clayton, if you have finished organising my dinner you get off home. I can tidy up afterwards.'

'Right you are, Miss Harriman, I've left everything ready,' said Mrs Clayton, cheerfully as she untied her apron. 'I must admit to being curious to find out more from Alf. I'll see you tomorrow then.'

'Good night. I'll telephone Cicely and see if she has heard anything.'

Cicely had not yet heard the news about Mrs Giffard and, after she had expressed surprise and sadness, said: 'What a co-incidence. The Major and his wife are here again.'

'When did they arrive?' asked Eleanor, surprised.

'Late Sunday afternoon. I haven't seen you since Saturday but I assumed you knew. The Major rang first thing on Sunday morning to ask if I had a vacancy. I thought you must have found out something for him. I knew you wouldn't have said anything to me if you had because that's confidential but I thought he must have been coming to see you.'

'No, I didn't know they were coming back to Buxton,' said Eleanor. 'They were intending to go straight to Edinburgh from London.'

'I still don't know if they are connected in any way with Mrs Giffard but if they are perhaps it's lucky they are here,' said Cicely.

Eleanor made no comment. She agreed to telephone Cicely if she heard anything further and they said goodnight.

As she ate her dinner, Eleanor said to Napoleon: 'The Giffards arrived back on Sunday. Mrs Giffard died suddenly on Monday. Is there a connection? The Giffards had returned without warning and Mrs Giffard would not have realised. Otherwise, surely she would have left town again.' Napoleon made no comment so Eleanor continued: 'But she hadn't left town. She had been unable to escape. If she had escaped, would she still be alive? Had the Major been to see her and told her what he knew? Threatened her perhaps? Mrs Giffard certainly had good reason to fear the Major. He could expose her as a liar and a cheat, possibly even a forger but Eleanor found it hard to believe that the Major would resort to harming Mrs Giffard. Did she take her own life rather than face The Park because she thought the truth was about to be revealed? Did she know that the Major had been making enquiries about her? Perhaps someone had seen the Major visiting the Hall Bank office and told Mrs Giffard.' Eleanor paid attention to her dinner for a few minutes, then she said: 'The disgrace of being found out would be unbearable for someone like Mrs Giffard.' Napoleon gazed steadily at her as she spoke but had no answers to give so Eleanor finished her dinner in silence.

It had been a busy day. Eleanor was too tired to think any more about the Giffards and, after clearing away the dinner things, she fed Napoleon, took him for his walk, and went to bed with a book. Her last thought on the subject was that whatever trick Mrs Giffard had used to secure her life interest would now never be known. The truth had gone with her to the grave.

Chapter Thirteen

'It was poison,' announced Mrs Clayton, as she entered the dining room the next morning, teapot in hand. 'Good morning, Miss Harriman.'

'Good morning, Mrs Clayton,' said Eleanor. 'I take it you have this information from your brother.'

'Yes. There's to be a post mortem so the funeral's been held up.'

'And do the police know if Mrs Giffard took the poison herself?'

'According to Alf, no. She didn't. When Alf went to collect the body, Superintendent Johnson was still there. He was searching the room and he told Alf it was because they hadn't been able to find anything where Mrs Giffard was found. Anything that contained poison, I mean.'

'I hope, at least she didn't suffer. Poison is a nasty business.'

'Alf said Mrs Giffard was lying on the floor near the door as if she had been trying to get out, to call for help like, and some of the furniture had been knocked over. So he reckons it might have taken a while.'

'Oh dear,' said Eleanor. 'What a horrible way to die. I didn't particularly like Mrs Giffard but I wouldn't wish that on her. Have the police any idea who might have done this? Or how?'

'Alf says it's out of Superintendent Johnson's hands. Inspector Vardy is on leave this week so there's an inspector coming from Chesterfield.'

'Goodness, Superintendent Johnson won't be very happy

about that.'

'I'll tell you one thing for nothing though….'

James arrived at the dining room door.

'Good morning, James,' said Eleanor.

'Good morning, Miss Eleanor. I'm sorry to interrupt but Major Giffard has just telephoned. He would like to make an appointment for today if that is possible. I said I would speak to you and then telephone him back. What would you like me to tell him?'

'I do need to speak to him as quickly as possible and I was going to arrange an appointment anyway. I can see him at eleven, James, if that is convenient for him.'

'Very good, Miss Eleanor,' said James and disappeared downstairs.

'I'll just get your breakfast,' said Mrs Clayton.

'Mrs Clayton, before you go. Just before James arrived, you were going to tell me something about Mrs Giffard. What was it?'

Mrs Clayton paused and frowned. 'No….It's gone. What were we talking about?'

'Superintendent Johnson not being happy.'

Mrs Clayton stood thinking and then said: 'Oh, yes. It was something our Alf said. When he pulled up at Manar to collect Mrs Giffard he noticed a motor parked further down the street and he was pretty sure it was that Mr Brantlingham.'

'What kind of motor-car was it? Did Alf say? Was it a Crossley, do you know?'

'It might have been but, me, I don't know anything about motor-cars. It was a black one, I think he said.'

'Thank you for remembering that, Mrs Clayton. That is very interesting.'

'Right, now you have your breakfast. It's all ready. If you've got a busy day you need feeding up. Not you Napoleon. All you do is sleep. Is he to have some bacon, or not?'

'Just a small piece, Mrs Clayton, thank you. I'll feed him when I have finished my breakfast.'

When Edwin arrived at the office, he stuck his head around the door of Eleanor's office and said: 'I'm due at the Court in ten minutes. James has just told me the news about Mrs Giffard. Superintendent Johnson will be at Court this morning, do you want to come and see what information we can squeeze out of him?'

Eleanor did not wait for a second invitation. She grabbed her hat and jacket and walked the short distance to the Court with Edwin. When they got there, Edwin said: 'The Superintendent will be prepared to speak about the case in front of you because he knows who you are but I had better do the talking or he might not be too forthcoming.' Edwin asked the Superintendent how the case was going.

'An inspector from Chesterfield is arriving tomorrow, so it's out of my hands,' said the Superintendent. 'There's not a lot to do at the moment because we are still waiting for the post mortem and a toxicology report.'

'So, it's certain she was poisoned?' asked Edwin.

'It seems so,' said Superintendent Johnson. 'Doctor Mackenzie says it was probably belladonna but, at this stage, he can't be certain. She was found near the door of the dining room and some of the furniture had been knocked over, as though she had been staggering around before she collapsed. It's surprising no one heard anything.'

'So, was it suicide?' asked Edwin.

'Dr Mackenzie thinks not.'

Eleanor opened her mouth and Edwin quickly intervened with the question he knew Eleanor wanted to ask: 'Do you know when and how the poison was administered?'

'Well, that's far from certain. According to the doctor, if the poison was administered in food it would have been at breakfast because, as far as we know, she hadn't eaten anything since then. But she didn't die immediately. She left the dining room after breakfast. The housekeeper says the dining room was empty when she went in there at about twelve o'clock but when she returned at about twelve thirty to organise lunch she found Mrs Giffard in there dead.'

Edwin looked at Eleanor. She was frowning and Edwin said: 'Can I just make sure that I have understood you correctly. Mrs Giffard had breakfast and left the dining room and then, after about, what? three hours? returned to the dining room and died there.'

'That's right,' said the Superintendent.

'So it is possible that she was poisoned at some time after breakfast by some other means?'

'Yes. Entirely possible. However, according to Doctor Mackenzie, belladonna can take a while to act so it's not safe to discount breakfast. At this stage, we are not ruling out anything or anybody.'

'And the housekeeper found her?'

'Yes. She telephoned the surgery straightaway but Dr Mackenzie was out seeing a patient and didn't get the message until he got back so he didn't get to Manar until just after… '

'Crown against Hughes' called a loud voice echoing down the corridor. 'Crown against Hughes.'

'Oh, excuse me,' said Superintendent Johnson, 'that's my "break and enter" being called.'

He hurried into Court leaving the sentence unfinished. Edwin went in search of the opponent in his case, and Eleanor went back to the office in a thoughtful mood.

♣♣♣

Punctually at eleven o'clock, Major Giffard arrived at Hall Bank and was brought up to Eleanor's office by James. Napoleon had been banished upstairs.

Major Giffard said: 'Thank you for seeing me at such short notice, Miss Harriman. I received your report last Saturday and it set out the information very clearly.'

'I was sorry to have been the bearer of such sad news about your mother. It must have been a shock for you to read about the manner of her death.'

'Strangely enough, I found the information in your letter comforting. That must sound callous. I didn't mean it to. Naturally, I am sorry for the way in which my mother died but you see I did my grieving for her twenty five years ago and I found the details in the reports of the court case reassuring. It was clear that my mother did care for me and it was not her decision to send me away to school.'

'Yes, it seems that her separation from you affected her profoundly,' said Eleanor.

'The feeling of abandonment that I have had all these years has been laid to rest and that is a great relief. Your letter also answered some questions about my father. At least I know where he went to after Calcutta but I should very much like to know why he disappeared. It seems that the author of that anonymous letter I received had a very good reason for writing to me. When I asked you to make enquiries on my behalf I had no idea where they would lead. I half expected to receive a letter in Edinburgh telling me that the anonymous letter was just a practical joke or a vicious trick and that would be the end of it. I was intending to return directly to Edinburgh but when I received your letter on Saturday and began to understand its implications, I thought it would be better to come here straightaway so that I could discuss your report with you first hand. And, of course, I wanted to ask your advice as to whether it was possible to take any action against Mrs Giffard. Then, your sister told us this morning at breakfast about Mrs Giffard's death and I realised that it had changed everything. I know the cliché is that one should not speak ill of the dead but, in this case, it is difficult not to.'

'I quite agree,' said Eleanor, 'she has had the benefit of a great deal of money to which she was never entitled.'

'So, I should like your advice about what to do next.'

'If you had been here last Friday,' said Eleanor, 'I would have said that the task of recovering your inheritance would not be impossible but that it would be difficult and would involve more than one expensive application to the Court in Ceylon. That is no longer the case. Mrs Giffard's passing has come at a convenient time for you. Now, we simply need to contact the solicitor in Colombo and inform him of your existence and your right to inherit. According to the accounts filed at Court, the very large income which was being paid to Mrs Giffard was profit from your father's tea plantation which has not yet been sold and you will now be entitled to that income and you will also inherit the tea plantation.'

'I am finding it difficult to take all of this in,' said the Major.

'I can understand that,' said Eleanor. 'There is, of course, also the question of whether or not the solicitors in Colombo have been negligent. Mrs Giffard must have lied to them but, even so, it is possible that they failed to make the necessary enquiries which would have allowed them to discover the deception. And there is also the question of what to do about recovering the money wrongly paid to Mrs Giffard since 1914. We would need to commence proceedings against her estate for that. I suspect that a large proportion of that money has gone into Manar and, if that is the case, it will make things much easier. An English court will have jurisdiction and you will be able to commence proceedings here rather than overseas. We will need a copy of Mrs Giffard's Will to find out who the beneficiaries are. As you can see, there is a great deal to be sorted out.'

'Yes. It is all rather daunting. Last week I was just a simple schoolmaster with no experience of anything connected with the law and suddenly I am faced with complicated legal questions and decisions such as these.'

'I appreciate that you need time to think about what we have discussed. Naturally I will not take any action or incur any further expense on your behalf until I have your instructions. We do not have to do anything at all immediately but we cannot wait too long before taking action.'

'That is a relief.'

'There is one thing, however, that I should like to recommend. I should like to telegraph to the solicitors in Colombo and inform them of the situation and of your claim. I could, at the same time, ask what instructions they had from Mrs Giffard when your father died. That would give us a better idea as to how this deception happened and whether or not the solicitors are likely to co-operate with us in sorting things out.'

'I see.'

'If we get a favourable response, we can be confident that they will freeze the accounts and that will give you more time in which to make decisions.'

'Then, yes, by all means telegraph to them as you see fit.'

'I shall ask James to arrange that straightaway. The office in Colombo will be closed now but we could perhaps expect a response by Thursday.'

'Miss Harriman, can I ask one more question? Is it likely that any of this will become public knowledge? Will the police who are investigating Mrs Giffard's death find out about any of this?'

'At the moment, I don't see how it could be relevant. They will, no doubt, look at Mrs Giffard's Will to see who benefits from her death. That is the usual procedure in a case such as this but I think it is very unlikely that you have been named as a beneficiary in her Will so there is no reason for them to need to interview you. There is no reason why the police would make any connection between you and Mrs Giffard. Why do you ask?'

'That is my other reason for wanting to see you as soon as possible. You see, my wife called on Mrs Giffard on the morning she died. Isabel only told me this morning, after your sister told us of Mrs Giffard's death.'

Eleanor was surprised by this information and was silent for a moment while she considered its implications.

'And did your wife tell you why she had been to Manar?' Eleanor hoped the tone in which she asked the question sounded neutral.

'She wanted Mrs Giffard to acknowledge my right to my father's estate.'

'And what was Mrs Giffard's response?'

'My wife didn't see her. She took fright and left the house before Mrs Giffard appeared.'

There was a short pause, Eleanor said as calmly as she could: 'Major Giffard, I think perhaps I should speak to your wife first before giving any further advice. I shall be free at half past four today if that would be convenient. Would you ask her to come and see me, please?'

'Certainly,' said Major Giffard. 'Naturally, I have discussed everything regarding this business with Isabel so you are at liberty to speak freely about this matter with her.'

'Thank you Major. That will make things much easier.'

After the Major had left, Eleanor drafted the telegraph message to be sent to Colombo and asked James to arrange for it to be sent from the Post Office.

Isabel Giffard arrived at half past four and was offered tea and shown into Eleanor's office.

'Thank you for coming to see me, Mrs Giffard. As you know, Major Giffard has to make a decision as to what action to take in relation to his father's estate and recovering his inheritance. He asked me this morning whether or not the police needed to know about his connection with the other Mrs Giffard of Manar. I need to clear up something before I give him any further advice and I think you can help me. I understand that you went to Manar on Monday morning to see the other Mrs Giffard.'

'Yes, that's right.'

'About what time would that have been?'

'At about nine o'clock. Oh, I know that is far too early to be making calls but I wanted to be sure that Mrs Giffard was there and alone.'

'And she agreed to see you? At that time in the morning?'

'Well, I was fully expecting to be told by the maid that she was not at home so on my way to Manar I tried to think of how best to get around that problem. I'm afraid I decided to not to tell the truth.'

'Tell me exactly what happened.'

'The parlour-maid opened the front door as soon as I went up the steps of the porch. I think she must have been in the hall or in the porch because she opened the door immediately. I hadn't even rung the bell. I gave her my card and said I had come to see Mrs Giffard and then I told an untruth. I said that Mrs Giffard was expecting me, which of course was not true. The parlour-maid showed me into the morning room and asked me to wait. She said she thought Mrs Giffard hadn't come down yet and she would go and see.'

'And you sat and waited?'

'Yes, well, no. Not exactly. As soon as I sat down in the morning room, I felt frightened and suddenly I was quite overwhelmed and I just bolted.'

'You mean you left?'

'Yes, I didn't wait for the parlour-maid to come back. I

just rushed to the front door and let myself out. I know it was cowardly but suddenly, sitting alone in that vast room with its expensive furniture and ornaments, I realised that Mrs Giffard would never give any of it up and that she would not care about my husband at all. I realised that it was very silly to have come and I just felt that I couldn't face Mrs Giffard after all.'

'How long were you at Manar?'

'No more than a few minutes.'

'And you were only in the morning room?'

'Yes.'

'None of the other rooms?'

'No,' said Isabel Giffard, sounding surprised.

Eleanor made a note on the paper in front of her and then said: 'Mrs Giffard, I don't mean to be impertinent but may I ask what you hoped to achieve by going to Manar?'

'Well, I thought perhaps if I told Mrs Giffard of our circumstances she would realise how wrong she was in taking what rightfully belongs to my husband. You see, when we received your report I realised what a very great wrong had been done to him. Miss Harriman, I am telling you this in confidence. My husband would feel very awkward if he knew that I had discussed our private life with you.'

'Of course, please tell me only what you want to. I have no wish to pry into your private affairs. I am just concerned about your current position and how best to help you.'

'Thank you. My husband told me that you are a very understanding person and I can see that he was right. My husband has not had an easy life. As I am sure you realise, he had a very lonely childhood. He would never admit it, but being sent away to school as he was, abandoned really, had a terrible effect on him although he hides it well. He has tried all his life to overcome it. This investigation has brought back all those bad feelings associated with the past. And now, he has discovered that he has been cheated of his inheritance as well. Naturally, I was angry, seeing the effect that this discovery has had on him.'

'That is perfectly understandable,' said Eleanor.

'Miss Harriman, I admit that I was very angry and it was that anger which gave me the courage to go to Manar in the first place. These last two years have not been easy for us. He has had to undergo several operations because of his wounds and he also had a mild case of shell shock. He has not been able to return to teaching or do any other kind of work. We have had only his Army pension and his small annuity to live on and it has affected him terribly. He feels that he has let me down, although I tell him that is not the case and try to reassure him. We were managing quite well and things were getting better and then he was offered the teaching position but all of this has…'

Isabel Giffard had struggled to hold back her tears and now stopped, unable to speak. Eleanor waited while she recovered. Isabel Giffard sighed and said: 'Even though you explained that it is possible to challenge the way the money has been paid to Mrs Giffard, I knew that it would be very expensive to do so and we just do not have that sort of money. When we were ignorant of the situation, we were happy. Then to discover that he has been cheated and is powerless to do anything about it, it seems so cruel. I was afraid that it would never be possible for him to get what is rightly his and that the failure would haunt him for the rest of his life. So, I thought that if I went to see Mrs Giffard I could convince her to do the right thing. I intended to tell her that we have found out what she did and to ask her to acknowledge my husband's claim. But, as I sat there in the morning room I realised how powerless I was and how foolish I had been to come.'

'And you didn't tell Major Giffard of your visit to Manar? Until today, that is.'

'No, he was going to the baths for a treatment and I just

said that I was going out for an early morning walk. And then, afterwards, I didn't want to tell him. I thought it would upset him and, anyway, I was ashamed at having been such a coward.'

'The police are bound to find out about your visit to Manar and will want to know the reason.'

Isabel Giffard looked shocked.

'But surely the police don't think....' She paused. 'Surely the police don't need to know anything about the Major's inheritance.'

'I am sure that they don't,' said Eleanor, 'and it is unlikely that they would find out anything from any of the servants at Manar. Also, at the moment, I have no obligation to tell them. I understand that Mrs Giffard died sometime late on Monday morning although I don't yet know the circumstances but the fact that you were at Manar that morning might have some relevance to the enquiries the police are making. You and I cannot withhold information if it is relevant. And I am also afraid that Mrs Giffard's death is going to attract a great deal of publicity and her past might become public knowledge.'

'Oh dear. I really would rather not have this business about the Will made public. This town is so very full of gossips and news spreads very quickly. We do not yet know the full story about Mrs Giffard. She seems to have been a dreadful person and there may have been something in the past, some awful scandal in the family that might affect my husband. I was hoping that all this could be dealt with quietly and that he could claim his inheritance without anyone knowing the truth.'

'Well, there is one person who knows the truth,' said Eleanor. Isabel Giffard began fiddling with the clasp on her handbag. Eleanor continued: 'The writer of the anonymous letter.'

'Oh! Oh, yes, of course.' The fiddling stopped. 'I had

forgotten all about that letter. That was what prompted my husband to come and see you, wasn't it? He was afraid of what that person might know.'

'Well, whoever that anonymous letter writer is, he is possibly still in Buxton. I hope you will not take offence at what I am about to say and I hope you will understand that, as a solicitor, I have to give you this advice.' Eleanor paused. Isabel Giffard nodded her head. 'When I first heard the news about Mrs Giffard at Manar,' continued Eleanor, 'I assumed that we were dealing with a suicide but I have since learned that that is not the case. Until the police find the person responsible, I am afraid that it leaves you in a difficult position.' Isabel Giffard drew in her breath sharply. Eleanor looked at her with concern. 'You see,' she continued, 'her death removes all legal obstacles and enables Major Giffard to inherit the remainder of the estate automatically. It also saves the expense and uncertainty of Court proceedings, an expense which Major Giffard cannot afford. You do understand that the police might regard that as sufficient motive and that I may have to advise you to go to the police and tell them about your visit to Manar?'

'Oh, but that is dreadful. This is such a terrible muddle. Miss Harriman, what should we do?'

'I don't think we need to go to the police just yet, however, I suggest that it might be appropriate for me to find out as much as I can from the servants at Manar about the events of that morning. Then we will have a better idea of what is relevant and what is not.'

'Oh, thank you. Yes, please do that as soon as possible.'

'But you must agree that if I find out something, anything, that makes me think your evidence might be relevant, you will go to the police and tell them that you were there.'

'Yes, certainly.'

♣♣♣

When Isabel Giffard had left, Eleanor looked at her watch and considered whether or not to walk over to Manar to speak to the housekeeper. She decided that she would go tomorrow. Besides, she had to earn her living and there was quite a bit of paper work on other files for fee-paying clients waiting to be done before she could afford the luxury of playing at amateur detective. She went upstairs and retrieved Napoleon from his banishment. He bounded into her office and went immediately to the window. Eleanor followed him and looked out. A Rolls-Royce was taking up a large part of the street in front of their office and, a little way further down Hall Bank, on the opposite side of the street, a chauffeur was propped against the stone wall smoking a cigarette. 'What, in the name of heaven, is Lady Carleton-West doing here?' said Eleanor to Napoleon. 'You had better stay out of sight.' Lady Carleton-West had solicitors in London so it was very unlikely that she had come to Harriman & Talbot on business. It was no use speculating, thought Eleanor, so she closed the door of her office to keep Napoleon out of the way and got on with her work.

Chapter Fourteen

After the office had closed for the day, Mr Harriman and Eleanor were in the sitting room relaxing before dinner.

'Lady Carleton-West came to see me today,' said Mr Harriman.

'Yes, I saw her motor-car in the street. Am I allowed to ask what she wanted?'

'Lady Carleton-West is very concerned about the effect Mrs Giffard's death will have on the town.'

'You mean she is concerned about the effect that it might have on the real estate values of The Park.'

'Now, now. That is probably true but we must give her credit for a higher motive. She thought at first that Mrs Giffard had taken her own life but she has since heard a rumour that someone else administered the poison. Edwin tells me that Superintendent Johnson is treating this as a case of murder. Lady Carleton-West has asked me, well, ordered me actually, to find the guilty person. She is convinced that there is a dangerous killer loose who will strike again. She is also convinced that it is not someone from The Park and she advised me not to waste my time looking there, which is what she thinks the police have been doing, but to consider who, in the town or among the visitors, might be likely to carry out such a crime. She wants the person caught and dealt with so People can get on with their lives.'

'I don't suppose she is prepared to pay you to investigate?'

'Of course not. She believes that it is my duty as coroner to deal with it. For the good of the town, of course. I told her I could make no promises but that I would do what I could.'

'So what are you going to do?'

'Absolutely nothing. I am going to leave it to the police. However, it does rather give us *carte blanche* to snoop around Manar on behalf of the Major.'

'Good, because that is precisely what I am proposing to do next.'

Eleanor brought Mr Harriman up to date with the Giffard matter and Mr Harriman said: 'I think you are right to be concerned, Eleanor. I agree that, at the moment, you have no reason to think that you are under any obligation to tell the police anything about the Major or his affairs but we must be cautious. I am sure that the Major and Isabel Giffard are very pleasant people and upright citizens but we must not blind ourselves to the possibility that Isabel Giffard might know more than she is telling. People often do.'

'Yes. I remember one of the first things you taught me: always assume that there is something your client is not telling you.'

'Yes. It may not be because they have something to hide. It may be simply that they haven't bothered to mention it because they don't think it is relevant. Then, when it comes out in Court under cross-examination, it can be quite damaging. The other side can easily take it out of context and use it to their advantage. I am very glad that the Major made sure that his wife gave us this information right from the start and that is certainly a point in his and Isabel Giffard's favour.'

'Isabel Giffard did tell me something that is a bit worrying though. She said that the Major had suffered from mild shell-shock. I know that can cause people to behave in uncharacteristic ways and to act irrationally. If Mrs Giffard was murdered, I must accept the fact that the Major had the most compelling motive but I still think that it is unlikely to have led to any action on his part or on Isabel Giffard's part,' said Eleanor. 'I realise that, although I like the Giffards very much I must remain objective.'

'Well, anger or frustration have certainly been known to trigger violent action and unpremeditated murder but I think perhaps not in this case. Although it might have taken some time to resolve the Major's claim, there is no doubt that, ultimately, he would have been successful so there was no need for him or his wife to get rid of Mrs Giffard.'

'I know, Father, and I agree. I do think Isabel Giffard has told me everything and I also think she is an unlikely person to have killed someone. But I am conscious of the fact that, at the moment, we do not know the circumstances of Mrs Giffard's death and, therefore, we cannot judge what is relevant and what is not.'

'In a way, it would be better for the Major to have Mrs Giffard alive,' said Mr Harriman, 'so that she could give evidence as to the facts that we need to prove.' The house telephone rang before he could continue.

Eleanor said: 'James has left for the evening' and was just getting up to answer the telephone when Mrs Clayton appeared in the doorway. 'It's Miss Pymble, Miss Harriman. She would like to speak to you. And dinner will be ready in five minutes.'

'Thank you Mrs Clayton. I had forgotten the time and now you mention it, I am very hungry.'

'I'm glad to hear it. What with all these goings on and the hours you work. You need to keep your strength up.'

Mr Harriman winked at his daughter as Mrs Clayton returned to the kitchen. Mrs Clayton's firm conviction that food was the solution to every problem was a source of amusement between them.

As they sat down to dinner, Eleanor said: 'Miss Pymble was telephoning because she wants me to see Ellen, the kitchen maid. The poor girl is in hysterics. Apparently all the Manar servants were interviewed by Superintendent Johnson today. It seems that he thinks the poison might have been administered in the food at breakfast. Ellen is terrified that she will be blamed for Mrs Giffard's death because it was she who prepared the breakfast. After the interview with the police, she sought refuge with the Misses Pymble and is refusing to go back to Manar. Miss Pymble is going to be occupied with the Girl Guides this evening so Miss Felicity is bringing Ellen here after dinner.'

An hour later, Miss Felicity duly arrived accompanied by Ellen. Eleanor went down to let them in and, as she preferred to allow Ellen to tell her story without any outside help or prompting, she suggested firmly to Miss Felicity that there was no need for her to wait as it might take some time. She assured Miss Felicity that she and Napoleon would see Ellen safely home afterwards. Eleanor took Ellen upstairs to the sitting room and gave her a cup of tea and some of Mrs Clayton's irresistible biscuits. Napoleon sat beside Ellen and she stroked his back. Eleanor sat quietly letting Napoleon do his work, reassuring Ellen with his calm presence.

When Ellen had finished two biscuits and started on a third, Eleanor said: 'Now, Ellen, it seems that Mrs Giffard may have been poisoned because of something she ate and Miss Pymble has told me that you are worried in case Superintendent Johnson thinks you are to blame.' Ellen looked as if she was about to cry and Eleanor quickly added: 'Please don't worry. Of course, you are not to blame. I am sure you had nothing at all to do with it but, you see, I think you may be able to help me to find out the truth. Will you try?' Ellen nodded, her mouth full of biscuit. 'Good. Now, first of all, I can understand that you don't want to go back to Manar after what has happened and, in any event, you will need to look for another situation now. I imagine that Superintendent Johnson has told you that you must not leave town.' Ellen nodded again. 'Right. Well, before you arrived here I telephoned my sister and she tells me that she could use your help at Oxford House, at least for the next few weeks until you can find another situation. Would that suit you?'

'Oh, yes please, Miss Harriman,' said Ellen, eagerly, her face a picture of relief and happiness. 'Thank you ever so much. I really would like that. And I know Susan, as works there.'

'Then we must just make sure that Superintendent Johnson knows where you are in case he needs to talk to you again and everything will be fine.'

At the mention of the Superintendent's name, Ellen started to look troubled. Eleanor said: 'Now, I'd like you to tell me about the morning Mrs Giffard died. Will you do that?' Ellen nodded, more vigorously this time. 'First of all, I'd like to know about breakfast. What time did you usually serve breakfast?'

'A quarter after nine.'

'And what do you usually serve?'

'Madam always has, I mean had, a boiled egg and then toast.'

'And who normally prepares breakfast?'

'I do except for the egg. Cook usually does that but she were right busy on Monday morning so she told me to do it. We had dinner for ten that night and only that morning Miss Addison had said Madam was expecting extra for lunch as well. Cook wasn't best pleased because it meant she had a lot to do. And at short notice. We all did.'

'So can you describe to me what you did when you made the breakfast? Try to remember as exactly as you can.'

Ellen frowned in concentration, took another biscuit, and focussed her gaze on the ceiling.

'I put the teapot and things out ready on the kitchen table. Then I put butter into the butter dish and put that on the tray to go into the dining room. Then I got the jam from the pantry and put some in the jam dish and put that on the tray. Then I cut the bread for the toast and got down the saucepan ready to cook the egg. And then I put the tea in the teapot ready to make the tea.'

'And who was in the kitchen while you were doing that?'

'Just me and Cook.'

'What about Hannah, the parlour-maid?'

'Dining room, laying the table.'

'So after you had assembled everything, what happened?'

'Hannah came in for the tray and took it to the dining room.'

'Ellen, I need to get this very clear in my head so can we go through very slowly what happened. Can you remember what was on the tray that Hannah took into the dining room?'

This time Ellen looked at the carpet for inspiration as she concentrated on imagining the tray.

'The cup and saucer and the milk jug. And the plate for the toast. And the butter dish and the jam dish.' She recited this as though it were a lesson she had learnt.

'Anything else?'

'No, the teapot and the egg cup and its plate go in on the second tray. With the toast rack.'

'The sugar bowl?'

'Madame doesn't take sugar. Didn't.'

'So the things that are usually on the first tray would be on the table already when Mrs Giffard went into the dining room?'

'Oh, yes.'

'And then, when Mrs Giffard comes down, Hannah takes the second tray in with the hot food and the tea when it is ready?'

'Yes, only that morning Miss Addison told Hannah to go and clear out one of the rooms in the attic. Something about wanting it for visiting staff. Hannah were right grumpy about it, an' all. She were up there all morning.'

'So Hannah took the first tray into the dining room as usual but not the second tray. Who took the second tray in? The one with the egg and the toast.'

'Miss Addison.' Ellen frowned and there was a pause. Then she said: 'Wait, I've just remembered. I put raspberry jam out but then Miss Addison came into the kitchen and said Madam wanted blackcurrant so I got the jar of black-currant and put some in a dish.'

'Did you get the jar from the pantry?'

'Yes. It was a new jar. I remember because it was the last one in the pantry and I was thinking that it would soon be time to make some new.'

'And is the jar still in the pantry?'

'No. Superintendent Johnson took it away.'

'So, you put some of the blackcurrant jam from the jar into another jam dish and what did you do with that dish?'

'I put it on the tray, the second tray, that is, so it could go in with the hot food.'

'So the blackcurrant jam was on the tray on the kitchen table waiting for you to boil the egg and make the tea and the raspberry jam was already in the dining room?'

Ellen nodded as she bit into her biscuit.

'Now, let me just make sure I've got this right. You and Cook were together in the kitchen most of the morning.'

'Yes.'

'And Hannah was upstairs in the attic. Did she come down to the kitchen at all during the morning?'

'No.'

'Now, I believe that Mrs Giffard wasn't found until lunch-time. Tell me what happened then.'

'Well, Cook said that being as Hannah was busy upstairs I'd have to go and lay the table for lunch as soon as I'd finished peeling the potatoes. And Miss Addison said no, Hannah could do it, and she'd just put the flowers in the dining room and then go and fetch Hannah and that's when she found the mistress. It were awful, Miss Harriman.'

Ellen had been distracted from the emotion of the events at Manar by having to concentrate on the details of the morning's events but now the tears flooded in and she lost control. Napoleon rested his chin on her lap and looked up at her with concern. She sobbed her heart out and hugged Napoleon for comfort. Eleanor waited patiently. When Ellen had released Napoleon and blown her nose, Eleanor said: 'Ellen, this may be very important so can we just go through it one more time to make sure that I have got things right. Miss Addison was in the kitchen most of the morning?'

Ellen thought for a moment and then said: 'Yes, I suppose she was.'

'And so was Cook?'

'Yes.'

'Ellen, you have been a very great help and I don't think there is any need for you to worry. You see, all the time that you were preparing the breakfast, you were not alone in the kitchen. Either Cook was there or Miss Addison was with you and they would have seen what you were doing and would have known if you had put something in Mrs Giffard's food, even supposing you had wanted to.'

'But I didn't want to!' said Ellen, desperately, twisting her handkerchief and looking as if she was about to cry again.

'It's all right, Ellen. I am not accusing you of poisoning Mrs Giffard. I am trying to explain to you that no-one is going to think that you did. Don't you see? You couldn't have done anything without someone seeing you, no-one could, and that means, the police are not going to think that it was your fault. If you told Superintendent Johnson what you have told me, he will know that you had nothing to do with it. So, you have nothing to worry about.'

'You are sure, Miss?'

'Absolutely certain,' said Eleanor. 'Now, Leon and I will

walk you home and then first thing tomorrow morning you can go and see my sister. She will be glad of your help.'

'Thanks ever so, Miss Harriman,' said Ellen, beaming and hugging Napoleon. 'The Misses Pymble said you would help and they were right.'

'Yes,' said Eleanor. 'That is what is remarkable about them. They can usually find a way to help people. Now, come along, and you are not to worry anymore.'

Chapter Fifteen

After breakfast the following morning, Eleanor telephoned her friend and walking companion, Doctor Catherine Balderstone, and arranged to have lunch with her. Eleanor needed a tutorial on poisons. Then she went into her office and, after sorting out her work for the day, went downstairs to say good morning to James.

'While you were on the house telephone, Mr Danebridge telephoned, Miss Eleanor. Would you be free for lunch? He said he would telephone again.'

'Thank him prettily for me, James, but tell him, no, I cannot frivol with him at lunch today as I have another engagement but please tell him that if he is free at six o'clock he can come and walk with me and Napoleon in the Gardens. We shall be pleased to see him.'

'Very good, Miss Eleanor. I shall give Mr Danebridge your message.'

Just after one o'clock, armed with a lunch basket prepared by Mrs Clayton, Eleanor and Napoleon headed to the Gardens where they found Catherine reading the newspaper.

After they had all exchanged greetings, Catherine said: 'So what's this about? Delighted as I am to share lunch with you in the sunshine and fresh air, I feel sure there is what I would call a secondary diagnosis and what you lawyers call an ulterior motive.'

'You're right. Do you want pressed tongue, egg and cress, or ham and tomato to start with?' asked Eleanor as she began unpacking sandwiches from the basket.

'Ham and tomato first for me. Thank you.'

They ate in silence for a minute, supervised by Napoleon, and then Eleanor said: 'I need to know the symptoms of belladonna poisoning.'

'Well, that's a fine topic for lunch, I must say,' joked Catherine. 'Is it safe for me to eat these sandwiches you have so thoughtfully provided?'

Eleanor laughed.

Catherine asked: 'Is this professional interest or idle curiosity?'

'Professional.'

'Soooo! Planning to get rid of someone who hasn't paid your last outrageously high bill? Or just eliminating the opposition's witness?'

Eleanor pulled a face at Catherine. 'Medical student humour can be so tedious.'

They each took a bite of sandwich and the conversation paused while they chewed and Napoleon watched.

'So, belladonna. Tell me about it,' said Eleanor.

'This is about Mrs Giffard, isn't it?' said Catherine.

'Yes,' said Eleanor.

'Right then, what do you want to know?'

'What are the symptoms?'

'Which part of the plant are we talking about?'

'I'm not sure.'

'How was it administered?'

'I don't know that either.'

'Right. I assume that it was not taken voluntarily so whatever part of the plant was used had to be disguised in food or liquid of some kind.'

'Assume that she died after eating or drinking something at breakfast.'

'I see. Well, the symptoms commonly are dry mouth at first, then difficulty swallowing. Then giddiness, racing pulse, shortness of breath. The victim would probably think they were having a heart attack and try to call for help. Then paralysis would set in and breathing would become very difficult. If the victim had been standing up, in the process of trying to call for help, for example, he or she would begin to stagger and then collapse into a coma. Death would follow shortly afterwards.'

'From the little I know so far, that does seem to describe what happened. How long before the symptoms begin to appear?'

'Almost immediately after ingestion of the poison.'

'And how long before the person dies?'

'It's difficult to say exactly. It would depend on the dose and what part of the plant was used and the size and general health of the victim.'

'Doctors make such frustrating witnesses when they give evidence. You're not under oath. Could you make a guess?'

'Sorry, just professional caution. Right, it could be minutes, but probably within a quarter of an hour. However, if I were being cross-examined by defence counsel and it was put to me that it could have been longer, say half of an hour or possibly even longer, I would have to agree.'

'Can I put something to you hypothetically?'

'Go on.'

'If someone administered the poison, and I don't know yet how it was done, is it possible that the victim could have been alive about two and a half hours later?'

'It's possible, yes, but highly unlikely and by then the symptoms certainly would have begun to be apparent.'

'So, the victim would not be sitting in a chair looking perfectly normal, for example?'

'Certainly not. If the victim had not already lost consciousness, he or she certainly would be struggling for breath and possibly hallucinating. So, is this really hypothetical or do you have a suspect?'

'I don't have a suspect but I have a puzzle, an anomaly perhaps.'

'Try me.'

'First hypothesis. Assume that the poison was administered in something served at breakfast and judge the timing of the symptoms from there.'

'Right. What time was breakfast served?'

'About a quarter past nine.'

'Then, if we assume that the victim started on breakfast as soon as it was taken in, she probably should have been showing symptoms by about nine thirty. The dose was large enough to kill her; that is self-evident. So, based on that fact, I would say she would have been dead or at the very least unconscious by about ten thirty or more likely by ten o'clock. And Mrs Giffard was found when?'

'At about twelve thirty.'

'And do you have any information about her condition when she was found?'

'Apparently she was near the door of the dining room and it looked as though she was trying to get to the door to call for help. Some of the furniture, I don't know what exactly, had been knocked over.'

'So, staggering followed by collapse into a coma. That is consistent with it being belladonna. It looks pretty straightforward to me. Eat breakfast, hallucinate, collapse, lapse into coma, and then die. All over by about ten thirty. Where's the puzzle?'

'The housekeeper went into the dining room at about twelve o'clock….'

'And Mrs Giffard was sitting calmly in her chair?' interrupted Catherine.

'No, she wasn't there.'

'And yet, when the housekeeper went into the dining room about a half an hour later, Mrs Giffard was lying dead on the floor near the door?'

'Yes.'

'With furniture knocked over?'

‘Yes.’

‘But half an hour earlier, the dining room was in proper order and the housekeeper noticed nothing out of the ordinary?’

‘As far as I understand it, yes.’

‘In that case, we can rule out breakfast as the source of the poison. If she had been poisoned just after nine fifteen, she is unlikely to have been capable of leaving the dining room at all, let alone leaving it and then staggering back in again at some time between twelve and twelve thirty. I can see why you are puzzled.’

‘But if we rule out breakfast there doesn’t seem to be another opportunity to administer the poison. As far as I know, Mrs Giffard wasn’t served any other food that morning. The only other possibility is medication. Perhaps someone tampered with it, but I have no idea whether she was taking any such thing.’

‘Hmmm,’ said Catherine. ‘Perhaps Mrs Giffard was a secret eater, snacking from the biscuit barrel in her bedroom without the servants knowing.’ She paused to think, then added. ‘Even so, the timing’s not right, not if the dining room was empty at twelve o’clock and she was found there at twelve thirty. And if the poison was administered in medication and not food, Mrs Giffard must have taken the medication at some time between about twelve and twelve thirty, or maybe by eleven thirty but no earlier than that, which means she either took the medication in the dining room, and collapsed where she was found, or she took the medication upstairs and then made her way down to the dining room before collapsing.’

‘But why would she be in the dining room taking medication? Surely she would take it in her bedroom or in the bathroom upstairs. And, even so, what reason could she possibly have had for going to the dining room at that time in the day?’ asked Eleanor.

'Perhaps she left something behind, such as a letter, or was looking for her glasses. Did she wear glasses?'

'There's another thing I don't understand,' said Eleanor, ignoring the glasses question. 'Why was she found near the dining room door?'

'Perhaps she was trying to get out and call for help?'

'Why didn't she just ring for help,' said Eleanor.

'Perhaps the door was closer than the bell-pull?'

'No, she would have been sitting closer to the fireplace than the door. The bell-pull is next to the fireplace. Perhaps it wasn't working.'

'I'm not an expert on bell-pulls, you'll have to ask someone else about that,' said Catherine.

They sat for a while, eating the sandwiches and watching the passers-by. Eleanor was going over in her mind the things that Ellen had told her last night.

'Here's a suggestion,' said Eleanor. 'Suppose the breakfast was poisoned and Mrs Giffard collapsed after about half an hour or so. You said that belladonna poisoning could cause hallucinations. Perhaps she did try to get to the bell-pull and became disorientated and collapsed. When the housekeeper came into the room at twelve o'clock Mrs Giffard was there all the time but the housekeeper didn't see her because Mrs Giffard was lying on the floor on the far side of the dining room table close to the bell-pull and out of sight.'

'It's possible as a working hypothesis. I couldn't rule it out completely. But if, as you said, she was found near the door and some of the furniture had been knocked over, for your hypothesis to work, she would have had to regain consciousness at some time between twelve and twelve thirty and then get up from the far side of the table, stagger around the table to the door, knocking over furniture as she went and collapse a second time near the door. As I said, it's possible.'

'But not probable. I can tell from your tone of voice,' said

Eleanor.

'It's certainly not the best explanation. There is definitely something not right here, isn't there?' Catherine thought for a minute and then added: 'Even if Mrs Giffard wasn't able to call out or reach the bell-pull, there must have been a bit of noise. Furniture being knocked over. It's surprising none of the servants heard anything.'

'Apparently they didn't. At least, Ellen didn't mention any noise but I have to admit that I didn't actually ask her. I must check.'

Eleanor offered Catherine some of the cake which Mrs Clayton had added to the lunch basket.

'Rather,' said Catherine. 'Mrs Clayton's cakes are legendary. I always look out for them on the cake stall at the church fête.'

Eleanor said: 'If Mrs Giffard was poisoned with belladonna, how could someone obtain it in Buxton?'

'It's not such a rare plant,' said Catherine, 'especially around here. It loves abandoned quarries and it's probably lurking unrecognised in quite a few back gardens. And then, of course, there is Mr Wentworth-Streate's well-known collection of rare specimens. I know that he's got a few poisonous plants, including belladonna, and he has everything conveniently labelled for the amateur poisoner. He doesn't keep them locked up either. Dr Mackenzie has spoken to him about it several times.'

'Hmm, and Garroch Brae is only two houses away from Manar. What is the easiest way for a lay person to administer poison?'

'You mean, without having access to fancy distilling equipment so as to create a poisonous liquid?'

'Yes.'

'Well, simply by putting enough of it in food,' said Catherine.

'So, if we ignore all other theories for the moment and

assume that the poison was in the breakfast, how could it have been done?'

'What did breakfast usually consist of?'

'A boiled egg.'

'Difficult,' said Catherine, 'but not impossible. Only with a liquid poison, mind, and that needs the right equipment, so that's unlikely. Let's leave that as a fall back if there is no more obvious way.'

'Tea.'

'Same problem as the egg.'

'Toast.'

'With jam?' asked Catherine.

'Yes, blackcurrant.'

'There you are then,' said Catherine. 'That's how it was done. Nothing easier. The berries of the belladonna plant are black, well, very dark blue. Stick them in some blackcurrant jam and no-one will notice. You'd have to be careful not to crush them because they are red inside, although I suppose if you did crush them and mixed them well with the jam they might not be noticed.'

'So you would need a bit of time to do the mixing?'

'Yes, you couldn't just casually drop them into food in passing.'

'And you could also disguise them in raspberry jam?'

'Yes, it's possible if you crushed them up.'

'And the amount of jam you would put on a piece of toast. Would that be enough to kill you?'

'Could do, yes. But you would need to make sure your victim wasn't found straightaway because if only a small amount of poison was ingested and the victim was found in time, she could be treated and rescued.'

'So it would be important to make sure no-one could hear anything. Cries for help, for example, which would be responded to.'

'Yes, with a small dose the victim would take longer to

collapse so would have more chance to make a noise and attract attention.'

Eleanor thought for a minute or two. She said: 'Ellen, the kitchen maid, said that she got the blackcurrant jam from a new jar, so the poison couldn't have been put in the jar beforehand.'

'No, you wouldn't put it into the jar. You would need quite a few berries if you wanted to kill someone and not just make them very ill. If you mixed them into the jam while it was in the jar you couldn't be certain of getting enough of them out of the jar and into the jam dish. Besides, some of the berries might well get left behind in the jar and you wouldn't want to leave them as evidence. No, the sensible thing would be to mix them with the jam which is already in the dish on the tray.'

'That is the most obvious way that the poison could have been administered,' said Eleanor, 'and Ellen is convinced she will be arrested for murder because she was the one who put the jam out. But I don't see how Ellen could have done it. She was never alone in the kitchen so she had no opportunity to poison the jam. She would have been seen. And what reason could she possibly have had to poison Mrs Giffard?'

'Well, it seems to me that poison in the breakfast is the most plausible theory and blackcurrant jam is the perfect medium for belladonna.'

'But,' objected Eleanor, 'if it was belladonna at breakfast it doesn't get around the fact that Mrs Giffard was still alive two and a half hours later. Of course, it may not have been belladonna at all. Dr Mackenzie told Superintendent Johnson that it was most likely to have been the cause of death but he could not be certain until the post mortem and the tests were completed.'

'Well, Dr Mackenzie would have based his opinion solely on the symptoms that he observed when he examined the body. One can never be certain without the test results. The mystery will be solved when the toxicology report comes back so we will have to wait for that before we have an answer.'

'So the blackcurrant jam might turn out to be a red herring?'

'Black herring,' said Catherine, looking at her watch. 'We'd better get back to work.'

'Thanks for your help, though. I really appreciate it.'

'Thanks for the lunch, at least, thank Mrs Clayton for me. Let me know if you come up with any further information, and mind how you go. Remember, there is a murderer out there. And it might be someone with very little to lose. I don't want to be called in to examine your body.'

Eleanor laughed and the two friends parted at the entrance to the Gardens. As Eleanor and Napoleon walked back to the office, she thought about Manar on the morning Mrs Giffard died. If the poison was in the jam, there was no lack of opportunity and no shortage of suspects. Ellen, the kitchen maid, who put the jam into the dish on both occasions, Hannah, the parlour-maid, who took the first tray into the dining room, the Cook and Miss Addison, the housekeeper, who had both been in the kitchen during the preparation of breakfast, the Major's wife, who had been to the house at the time when the first tray was already in the dining room. Eleanor decided to go to Manar and talk to the housekeeper to see if she could get a clearer picture of the events of that morning and also talk to Hannah to see if she corroborated Isabel Giffard's story. Meanwhile, she had work waiting for her at the office.

At six o'clock Philip called at the office as planned. He and Eleanor, accompanied by Napoleon, strolled in the Gardens and, naturally, the topic of conversation was the death of Mrs Giffard. Eleanor felt that she could safely discuss Mrs Giffard's death as part of the normal town gossip without breaching any confidences on the part of the Major. She did not, however, think it appropriate to tell Philip everything she knew. She joined in a general discussion of the event itself and then Philip entertained her with The Park's opinion.

'The news of Mrs Giffard's death reached my mother on Monday evening. Mrs Hampson was passing Manar on her way back from Burbage and saw Dr Mackenzie's motor-car there. She happened to mention it to Mrs Apthorp later in the afternoon and Mrs Apthorp telephoned Manar to get the details and then contacted as many people as possible but she was disappointed to find that she was not first with the news. Apparently there was to have been a dinner party at Manar on Monday evening and the housekeeper had already rung the guests to tell them that it had been cancelled and, of course, had to explain the reason, which meant that at least seven households had heard the news before Mrs Apthorp got to them. She was most put out.'

Eleanor laughed. 'It amazes me that editors think it worthwhile to publish newspapers in this town. The news is already stale by the time the papers are printed.'

'Especially news as sensational as this. I didn't like Mrs Giffard much, she was irritatingly self-important and not always very kind, but she doesn't deserve to die like that.'

'Well,' said Eleanor, 'somebody thought she did, because this was no random act. Somebody knew something about her that they didn't approve of.'

Eleanor's mind strayed to the Major and the Major's wife as a suspect and quickly moved on to the anonymous letter writer and wondered if he was the murderer. Then she remembered that Mr Brantlingham's motor-car had been seen parked in the street outside Manar. Was there some connection with him, perhaps?

Philip said: 'But to justify killing someone like that, it would have to be something pretty bad. More than just punishing a parvenu or getting rid of a rival for the organising committee of the next charity do.'

'Exactly. If that was a motive for murder, at least half of the population of The Park would be at risk,' said Eleanor.

'It is funny listening to them. Dying in this way diminishes Mrs Giffard in their estimation and it lowers her dreadfully in the social hierarchy. It makes her very undesirable as an acquaintance and People are putting as much distance between themselves and Manar as they possibly can. To hear them you would think they hardly knew Mrs Giffard at all. They have completely forgotten all the dinners they ate at her expense and the bridge and tennis games they played at Manar, although I do know some people who are openly mourning the loss of the best tennis court in town. And I am afraid that there is a rather cruel jest going around. I am almost ashamed to tell you. Instead of being referred to as Mrs Giffard-pronounced-Jiffard it has now become Mrs Giffard-pronounced-dead.'

'That is rather witty though,' said Eleanor. 'And how has Lady Carleton-West taken the news?'

'She is furious. She didn't have much time for Mrs Giffard to begin with and she is congratulating herself that, unlike some, she never once set foot in Manar. And Mrs Giffard was only ever invited to Top Trees when it was unavoidable. Meetings and charity events or with the other ladies for bridge, that kind of thing. Never on her own and never as a dinner guest. Now Lady C. is implying that Mrs Giffard was foisted on her by some of the other ladies and was never really welcome. She is letting it be known that she was convinced right from the start that there was something not "quite quite" about Mrs Giffard, although she is not specifying what. She says that anyone could see that

Mrs Giffard was not really "one of us" and the other ladies should have checked Mrs Giffard's antecedents more thoroughly before introducing her to Lady C. Do you think Mrs Giffard had a shady background? The ladies are certain that she must have been hiding something because well-bred people just do not get murdered, certainly not if they live in The Park. Even my mother, broadminded as she usually is, shares that opinion.'

Eleanor decided not to answer that and, to steer the conversation off centre, she said: 'Well, anyone who saw Lady C. at the Opera House on Saturday would quite believe that someone in The Park could do violent murder. The look Lady C gave Mrs Giffard went she came in late was lethal.'

They walked on in silence for a while.

Philip said: 'I heard that there was an inspector from Chesterfield coming to investigate. Are the police making any progress, do you know?'

'They are waiting for the post mortem and the toxicology report at the moment.'

Eleanor decided not to mention the belladonna. She thought the fewer wild rumours circulating about the town the better and the less likely people would be to tailor their evidence to suit them. Witnesses were notorious for "seeing" or "hearing" what they thought the police or barristers wanted them to see or hear. She said: 'For reasons that I can't disclose, I am going to Manar tomorrow to talk to the housekeeper because I think she might be able to help me with some information I need. I am hoping to talk to Hannah, the parlour-maid, as well.'

Philip said nothing at first, then, after a deep breath, he asked: 'Do you think that is altogether wise? I don't want you to think I am playing the over-protective male stopping you from having fun, but it is difficult to imagine that the killer is a stranger so it is very likely that someone in that house or connected with it killed Mrs Giffard. They might not take kindly to being asked questions by someone other than the police.'

'Yes, I do realise that and I do appreciate your concern, Philip, but people who kill more than once usually stick to the method they know.' Eleanor laughed. 'As long as I don't eat or drink anything while I am there, I should be quite safe.'

'It's all very well for you to make a joke of it but I am being serious,' said Philip. 'I think you should be careful. Will you at least let me go with you? I'll drive you there and I promise to wait outside in the motor-car and not get in the way.'

'Well....'

'Besides,' he added, trying to make light of it and mask his genuine concern, 'you might need a quick getaway.'

Eleanor laughed. 'You've been to the Picture House too often. You're getting wild American ideas.'

'Is that a yes, then?'

'Yes, then.'

'Right ho! I shall be at Hall Bank just before eleven o'clock.'

♣♣♣

Chapter Sixteen

The next morning, Philip arrived at Hall Bank in the Bentley and they drove the short distance to The Park. They turned off Park Road and as they drove up the carriage drive in front of Manar they were surprised to see a green Crossley motor-car parked at the steps leading up to the front door.

'I wonder whose motor-car that is,' said Eleanor.

'It's a Crossley but it's not Brantlingham's. His is black,' said Philip.

'Bother,' said Eleanor, 'if there are visitors, I might not be able to talk to the servants.'

She had barely finished the sentence when a man raced out of the front door and down the steps, and jumped into the Crossley. Hannah, the parlour-maid, quickly followed, shouting at the man to stop and calling: 'Give that back!'

'That is Brantlingham, by Jove!' said Philip. 'He's got a different motor.'

Hannah then noticed Eleanor and Philip and ran towards the Bentley. 'Oh, please Miss Harriman. Mr Danebridge. Stop him! He's taken a letter. It belongs to Madam.'

By now the engine of the Crossley had started and the car sped down the carriage drive to the road. Philip hadn't yet turned off the ignition and immediately began to steer the Bentley down the drive, calling: 'Right you are, Hannah. Don't worry. We'll get it back for you.'

At the end of the carriage drive it was possible to see along the street for quite a way to the left and there was no sign of the Crossley in that direction so Philip turned right and drove the short distance to an intersection. He stopped the car and hesitated. There was no sign of the Crossley, either to the right or the left.

'Blast!' said Philip. 'Sorry. Language. He has several choices of road from here and if we go in the wrong direction we shall lose him completely.'

On their left hand side was a school surrounded by gardens, and one of the gardeners was working close to the side boundary wall.

'Let's ask the gardener,' said Eleanor. 'He might have noticed.' She called out to him and asked if he had seen just a motor-car turning into St John's Road.

'Aye,' said the gardener, 'an' goin' too fast, an' all. 'Ee's gone oop Burbage way.'

Eleanor thanked the gardener, and Philip turned the car on to St John's Road. Then he accelerated hard. They quickly reached Burbage but there was still no sign of the Crossley. At the junction with the Leek Road, there was a maddening wait for some pedestrians and a cart horse which they could not steer around. Philip kept his eyes on the road and edged slowly forward, while Eleanor scanned the road ahead.

'I hope we can get sight of him quickly otherwise we won't know whether he is heading for Leek or Macclesfield.'

'He can't have got too far ahead. We should see him soon.'

They passed Canholes and Eleanor said: 'There he is! Look! On the Macclesfield Road.'

The Crossley had taken the main road to the right and was just disappearing out of sight around a sharp bend.

'We need to catch him before he reaches the Derbyshire Bridge crossing or we won't know which road he's taken from there,' said Philip.

The road twisted and turned back on itself as it climbed

steadily up to the top of the moors. On their right was a deep ravine and on their left the land rose steeply so that, at every bend, their view of the road ahead was obscured. Then the road followed a long arc around to the left, the hillside still blocking their line of sight. They had no idea how far ahead the Crossley was and they could not tell whether they were gaining on it or not. The Bentley had no trouble negotiating the bends so they were travelling quite fast and Philip said, with pride: 'The Crossley won't have performed as well on this stretch so we should be gaining on him now.'

Frustratingly, each time they came around a bend, they could see the road ahead but only as far as the next bend, around which the Crossley had already disappeared. Then the road straightened out and they were on the open moor. They could see ahead to a cross roads where the Derbyshire Bridge road cut across the main road at right angles. The Crossley had kept straight on past that junction. Eleanor said: 'He's staying on this road. He's heading for Macclesfield so he must be intending to go back to Manchester.'

Now the road ahead was relatively straight with only a few gentle bends and there was a long, steady climb to reach the Cat & Fiddle Inn at the summit about three hundred feet higher up. The Crossley was already two thirds of the way up to the top.

Philip said, joyfully: 'Straight road, at last. Hold your hat on, Lella. Let me show you what this old girl can do.'

Philip pressed down on the accelerator and the Bentley responded immediately, surging forward until they had reached sixty miles an hour. Before they reached the summit, Philip slowed to a respectable pace while passing the Inn and then accelerated again. They had reached the top of the moors several hundred feet above the Cheshire Plain. The air was clear and there was an unobstructed view beyond Manchester to the estuary of the Mersey to the north west and across to Snowdonia to the south west. However,

Eleanor and Philip were oblivious to the view and kept their eyes firmly on the road ahead. They were close behind the Crossley now and Brantlingham could have been in no doubt that he was being followed. He was clearly getting anxious because, as they started the descent from the Inn through a series of sharp bends, he took the corners at reckless speed.

Philip said: 'He's going too fast. He obviously doesn't care what damage he does to that motor-car. I suppose one can afford to be reckless if it's not one's own but I'm not prepared to risk my motor that way.'

The Crossley hurtled down the hill and slewed around the next bend. It disappeared out of sight and when they next saw it, it had increased its lead.

'He's getting in front again,' said Eleanor.

'Yes, but he isn't a local,' said Philip, wrenching the steering wheel sharply to the left. 'We'll take the old road. It's quicker.' As they veered off the main road and plunged down into a valley, Eleanor held on to her hat with one hand and gripped the dashboard with the other in order to steady herself.

Philip said: 'We can cut him off up ahead. Let's just hope no-one's moving sheep on this road today.'

'This road will be hidden from view from the main road so he will probably think he has shaken us off,' said Eleanor.

Philip focussed on driving, taking the narrow corners as fast as he dared, and they hurtled towards the bottom of the valley. They passed the Stanley Arms pub and, after making a sharp right hand turn, started to climb back up again to the top of the moor. When they got close to the point where the old road met the new road, Philip said: 'Have a look back will you, Lella. You should be able to see the blighter now. The two roads go parallel here. He might see us, of course, but it will be too late for him to do anything about it.'

'That's if he realises what has happened. He will be expecting us to be behind him' Eleanor looked back and spotted the Crossley. 'Yes, there he is. He's definitely behind us now.'

'Good,' said Philip. 'Now, this is what I want you to do. When we get back to the junction, I'm going to put the motor across the main road so that Brantlingham can't get past. Just before the junction, there's a rise in the road. It will take him by surprise and he'll not be able to see us until he gets almost on top of us. He will have to brake very hard to avoid crashing into us and he'll be going at speed so he won't have much room to stop. As soon as I stop the motor-car I want you to jump out and move to the side of the road well out of the way. That way you will be safe. I'll stay with the car. Understood?' Philip was concentrating hard on taking the sharp bends in the road and he was gripping the steering wheel tightly. He also had his teeth clenched and was looking very determined.

'Absolutely,' said Eleanor. 'But if you stay in the motor-car you will be sitting on the side that he will hit if he is unable to stop. He's not going to have very much control so even if he realises that you are in the motor he may not be able to avoid hitting you. The Bentley will still be in his way whether you are in it or not. So, please Philip. No heroics. Get out of the motor with me when we get there.' Philip did not respond. 'Please.' Still he did not respond. Eleanor said: 'Philip, I know what this is about and I understand. But it's not your fault that you survived the War and others didn't.'

Philip was silent and Eleanor was afraid that she had said too much and made him angry but she knew exactly what was going through his mind. Finally, as they were approaching the point where the two roads joined he said: 'You're an amazing girl, Lella.' He braked sharply and stopped the Bentley at right angles to the main road, blocking the path of Brantlingham's car and yelled: 'Get out now, Lella!' Eleanor did as she was instructed and was relieved to see that Philip also got out of the car and moved to the side of the road.

A few seconds later they heard the sound of the Crossley's engine and then as it came over the rise, they heard the noise of the brakes and watched the Crossley skid and shudder to a halt just inches from Philip's car. Brantlingham sat completely still for a few seconds while he assessed the situation. As soon as he understood what had happened, he opened the car door and ran, heading cross-country over the moors to the north. Eleanor considered giving chase but decided against it. Although she would have been able to move as fast as Brantlingham, probably faster because she understood the topography of the moors, she also realised that she wouldn't be able to hold him down even if she did catch up with him. She could not count on help from Philip and the fact that he could not keep up with her would just make him even more conscious of his disability than he already was. So she said: 'There's no use trying to catch him. Let's look in the motor-car and see what he has taken from Manar.'

There was an envelope lying on the front passenger seat. Philip opened the car door and picked up the envelope. It was addressed to Mrs Giffard and had been sent by post.

'Second class stamp, postmarked Stafford. I suppose he was in Stafford that day selling cars. What shall I do?' asked Philip. 'Open it?'

'Yes,' said Eleanor.

Philip opened the envelope and took out a sheet of paper folded into four. Letters cut from a magazine had been stuck onto the page.

I KnoW YOUr
SeCREcT
DO YoU MiSS
iNDia?

'Blackmail,' said Philip.

'But why would he go back for this?' asked Eleanor. 'What use could it be now that Mrs Giffard is dead?'

'Perhaps he killed Mrs Giffard and went back to remove evidence that might incriminate him?'

'No,' said Eleanor, shaking her head. 'Because if he was blackmailing her she would have been more use to him alive than dead. That makes no sense.'

'Wait a minute,' said Philip. 'Perhaps he wasn't taking the envelope away from Manar at all. Perhaps he was taking it to Manar. Trying to plant evidence that would incriminate someone else.'

'The same objection would apply,' said Eleanor. 'It would still be a case of blackmail with no reason to kill the victim. When was the letter posted?'

'Monday afternoon, three thirty.'

'You wouldn't post a letter to someone you knew was already dead so presumably, on Monday afternoon, he didn't know Mrs Giffard had died that morning and he still thought he could blackmail her,' said Eleanor.

'Or it was a clever trick to make you think he didn't know she was dead or even that he had killed Mrs Giffard and he wanted the police to think that he didn't know she was dead.'

'No, no. That's getting far too complicated. I think the most likely explanation is that he posted this letter not knowing that Mrs Giffard was dead, found out from his cousin what had happened, and came back to retrieve the letter so that his attempts at blackmail wouldn't be discovered by the police.'

'That sounds plausible.'

'As a matter of fact, I happen to know that he has a history of blackmail. A client mentioned that he had encountered Brantlingham engaging in that hobby during the War. I've just remembered something else. How far is it to Stafford?'

'About forty miles I should think.'

'Brantlingham's motor-car was seen in Buxton on Monday afternoon, I would guess at around two thirty. Could he have driven from there and reached Stafford in time to post a letter and have it post marked at three thirty?'

'The way Brantlingham drives anything's possible,' said Philip, 'but it is a bit unlikely. Who says they saw his motor-car? Are they sure it was his?'

'The person thought it was his. Parked near Manar. It was a black one. Oh….'

'Yes,' said Philip. 'This morning we were fooled, remember? We didn't realise it was Brantlingham's motor-car outside Manar because the motor-car was green and we thought he had a black one.'

'He must have managed to sell the black one to someone in Buxton and then got hold of another one, the green one that he was driving today.'

'So perhaps he was in Stafford on Monday and not in Buxton.'

They stood looking out across the moor taking stock of the events of the past half hour and thinking about their next move. The moor was a vast open expanse, no trees, just tufts of grass, low clumps of heather, and peat bog. In the distance, they could see the retreating figure of Brantlingham. He looked back a few times and when he realised he was not being followed slackened his pace.

'I almost feel sorry for him,' said Eleanor. 'If he goes too far away from the road he'll get lost. He won't have any idea where he is.'

'Serve him right,' said Philip with satisfaction. 'It was a bit of luck seeing that gardener chap on St John's Road. But for him we would have had no clue as to which way Brantlingham was headed. We probably would have assumed that he had gone up Long Hill and back to Manchester that way.'

'Hold on,' said Eleanor. 'I've just remembered something.

The gardener. A couple of weeks ago, I needed some information about Mrs Giffard, I can't tell you why, but I had a wild idea that I could get what I needed by talking to the servants. I took Napoleon for a walk past Manar and manoeuvred myself into conversation with Mrs Giffard's gardener. I had forgotten all about it and you talking about the gardener has just jogged my memory. I was about to leave Manar that day when Brantlingham drove up. The gardener complained that the Crossley made a mess of the carriage drive every time it came and I thought that it was unlikely that someone like Brantlingham would be visiting Mrs Giffard at all, let alone more than once. He's not the type that she would have welcomed.'

'He certainly is not. Not a front door visitor at all,' said Philip, shaking his head.

'I thought he must have been trying to sell Mrs Giffard a new motor-car but obviously he was there for other reasons.'

'Perhaps he wasn't visiting Mrs Giffard,' suggested Philip. 'Perhaps he was going around to the back door trying to get useful information out of the servants. Useful for blackmail.'

'That's quite possible. In fact,' said Eleanor, 'you've just reminded me of something else. I saw Brantlingham in the Gardens one Sunday afternoon with two of the maids from The Park probably collecting useful information.'

'Well, it doesn't sound as though he had much to blackmail Mrs Giffard with. Having lived in India is hardly a dirty secret, not one worth paying money to have someone keep quiet about.'

Eleanor said nothing but she was wondering just how much Brantlingham actually did know or had guessed about Mrs Giffard and her previous life. What information did he have that had enabled him to make a connection between her and India?

'Well, I think we have to give this letter to the police and tell them what we know. What about him?' said Eleanor, nodding at the distant figure of Brantlingham still in retreat.

'He can find his own way home. He'll probably head back to the Cat & Fiddle.'

'What about his car?'

'We'll leave it at the Cat & Fiddle and tell them that someone will collect it. When we get back to Buxton we will go straight to the police and they can send out a search party for him if need be.'

'Yes. I think that will be for the best,' agreed Eleanor. 'At least the weather is good and there is no chance of him freezing to death. And then I intend to go back to Manar and speak to the housekeeper as I planned to do some time ago. Thank you for coming along as the protective male, Philip. Instead of saving me from being poisoned, you got me into a motor-car chase. I think my life was in more danger in your motor-car than it would have been at Manar.'

'I like that!' protested Philip. 'It wasn't my idea to go haring off after Brantlingham.'

'Sorry, I'm just teasing. I'm very grateful for your help, really I am. It was fun though, wasn't it,' said Eleanor.

'Rather,' said Philip. 'Jolly good fun, as a matter of fact, and this old girl performed beautifully. Right, well, let's get going. I'll drive Brantlingham's car. You can drive mine, and go steady with her, will you? You're not driving an ambulance now.'

'See you at the Cat & Fiddle.' Eleanor waved confidently as she pressed the starter.

Chapter Seventeen

Eleanor and Philip reported to Superintendent Johnson at the police station. They explained what had happened and handed over the letter which they had taken from Brantlingham's car. Superintendent Johnson looked at them sternly, saying that he would look into the matter, and he asked one of his constables to set about rounding up Brantlingham. He concluded the interview with: 'I suppose you think I should thank you for this information, but I must remind you that it is not appropriate for members of the public to go interfering in police business. Leave it to us in future.'

When they were outside the police station Eleanor said: 'Now we should go back to Manar and see the housekeeper. We will also let Hannah know what has happened.'

Philip laughed. 'You obviously weren't listening to Superintendent Johnson.'

'Yes I was. I'm not interfering in police business. I'm making enquiries on behalf of a client. That is quite a different matter,' said Eleanor decisively.

'I'm not sure that the Superintendent would be able to tell the difference,' said Philip. 'Come on. I'll drive you back there.'

When they arrived at Manar, Philip parked the motor-car outside the front door, pulled out a book from the glove compartment, and settled himself to wait for Eleanor. Hannah answered the door and showed Eleanor into the entrance hall.

'Good afternoon, Hannah. We have rescued the letter for

you but I'm afraid we had to leave it with Superintendent Johnson at the police station. I'd like to speak to Miss Addison now, though, if I may. Will you please let her know I am here?'

'Miss Addison's not here anymore, Miss Harriman. She was only temporary while Mrs Brompton was away at her sister's and Mrs Brompton will be back tomorrow. She finished yesterday. The police told her not to leave Buxton and the agency she's with found her a place in Fairfield for the season. I've got the address if you want it.'

'Thank you, Hannah. As Miss Addison is not here, you might be able to answer a few questions for me.'

'I'll do my best, Miss Harriman, but I don't know much.'

Eleanor began by telling Hannah about the motor-car chase and then asked where the letter had been when Brantlingham had stolen it.

'Here, on the hall table. The police came on Tuesday morning and took away a lot of papers and things but that letter was in the post on Tuesday afternoon. I've just left all the new post on the table because I didn't know what to do with it.'

'That's the best idea. Until the police find Mrs Giffard's next of kin there is nothing you can do except keep things as they were. So when Mr Brantlingham came to the door this morning, what did he say to you?'

'He wanted to know if the police had asked about Madam's post and I said yes they had taken away some letters and things on Tuesday. And he looked a bit put out and then he said could he look at what had come since then because there was a letter for Madam about a new motor-car and he wanted to check if the letter had arrived. So I gave him the post to look through and then he took one of the letters. He just dropped the rest on the floor and he was out the door so quick I couldn't stop him and that's when you arrived.'

'I see. Well, we don't need to worry about Mr Brantlingham for the moment. The police are taking care of him. Hannah, I'd like to ask you about Monday if I may, the day Mrs Giffard died. Where were you that morning?'

'I was upstairs. Miss Addison told me to clear out one of the rooms in the attic because it was needed for visiting servants. She didn't say when they were coming and it was not my place to ask questions but I couldn't see why it had to be done that morning. It was a horrible job too and I was still up there when they found Madam.'

'Do you remember someone coming to the house at about nine o'clock that morning?'

'Oh, yes, the other lady called Mrs Giffard came. It was very early. We never expect front door visitors at that time in the morning. I'd only just sorted the post and I saw that someone was at the door and I....'

'Just a minute, Hannah, I'm not sure I have understood correctly. You can't see through the hall door. It's solid timber. Was it already open?'

'No Miss Harriman. I wasn't in the hall. I was in the porch.'

'Oh, I see. Hannah, this may be very important so can you try to remember every detail and tell me exactly what you did. I need to be sure that I have understood. So you sorted the post. Was that before or after you had taken the breakfast tray from the kitchen into the dining room?'

'Oh, after. I always take the first tray through and check that the dining room is ready and then I come in here and collect the post from the basket on the porch door.'

'So, you sorted the post and...'

'And I took Madam's post into the dining room and left it on the table as I always do and put the bills and things on Miss Addison's desk. Then I came back in here and went into the porch because when I had picked up the post, I'd noticed that one of the potted palms had got knocked over and needed putting to rights.' Eleanor opened the inner hall door and looked at the etched glass panels on the outer door of the porch. Hannah continued: 'Out of the corner of my eye I saw a movement and realised that there was someone coming up the steps to the front door. So, I opened the outer door and the lady asked for Madam and gave me her card. She said she was expected. Madam hadn't said anything about it but with the name being the same I thought she must be a relative or something. It was too early for a morning call so I thought she must have been invited to breakfast. I showed her into the morning room and asked her to wait while I went to tell Madam she had arrived.'

'Was Mrs Giffard in the dining room?'

'No. She hadn't come down yet.'

'Oh, of course, yes. You knew that because you had just been into the dining room with the post. And where was everyone else?'

'Cook and Ellen were in the kitchen.'

Eleanor interrupted with: 'So Cook and Ellen would have heard the front door bell?'

'No, the lady didn't ring the bell because I'd seen her first and let her in. Besides, even if she had rung, Cook and Ellen wouldn't have taken any notice. It's not their place to answer the door.'

'No, of course not,' agreed Eleanor. 'And what about Miss Addison? Where was she?'

'After she told me to clear out the attic she said to Cook she was going to see the gardener because she wanted him to bag the tennis court. Something about Madam was having guests after lunch who might want to use the court. So I suppose she'd gone out to see the gardener.'

'And Mrs Giffard's maid. Where was she?'

'Upstairs.'

'So, if the door-bell didn't ring, no-one in the house would have known that someone had come to the house?'

Hannah thought for a minute. 'No, I don't see how they could know.' She frowned as though she thought this was the wrong answer.

Eleanor felt encouraged by this last answer but didn't comment. She walked across the entrance hall to her right and stood outside the door of the morning room. She said: 'Tell me what happened after you had shown the other Mrs Giffard into the morning room.'

'I went upstairs to tell Madam that her guest had arrived.'

'Which way did you go?'

'Up the back stairs, of course.'

'So, through that door,' said Eleanor, as she crossed the entrance hall and, followed by Hannah, went through the rear door and into the small hall in the servants' quarters on the other side.

'And then up these stairs.'

She pointed to a narrow staircase which led up to the back of the upper floors. She paused for a minute thinking that, in Hannah's absence, Isabel Giffard could easily have left the morning room and gone to the dining room unseen.

'And you went to Mrs Giffard's bedroom?'

'Yes. She said she didn't know what I was talking about, she hadn't invited anybody and when I gave her the lady's card she got very angry. I was rather scared to tell the truth. She looked at me in a dreadful way. Her face was sort of twisted and when she spoke it was like a hissing noise. She told me to "get that woman out of the house immediately" and I was afraid she was going to be violent. I rushed out of the room and came back downstairs. I was wondering whatever I was going to say to the other Mrs Giffard but when I went into the morning room she wasn't there.'

'And then what did you do? Did you look for the other Mrs Giffard?'

'No. I went up to the attic and started clearing out.'

'So, the other Mrs Giffard could have gone into the dining

room?'

'I suppose so. I didn't think about it. I thought she must have let herself out and I went straight upstairs. I didn't want to risk seeing Madam again when she came down for breakfast so I got out of the way as quickly as I could.'

'And you didn't see Mrs Giffard again that morning?'

'Madam, you mean? No, I stayed in the attic to avoid her. I thought if she saw me again I'd get another ticking off for letting the other lady into the house.' Eleanor laughed. Hannah continued: 'I did think it was all a bit rum, though, the other lady calling like that and then disappearing. But it's not my business what folks choose to do. And I can't say that I blame the other lady for not waiting. She certainly would not have been made welcome.'

'And how long do you think you were away from the morning room?' asked Eleanor.

'Hardly at all,' said Hannah. 'I came down those stairs pretty quick after seeing Madam, I can tell you.'

'Have you mentioned to anyone that the younger Mrs Giffard called that morning?'

'No. I didn't let on to Cook or Ellen at the time because I felt a bit of a fool, mistaking her for a guest at breakfast, and I thought they would tease me if they knew. And then, of course, with Madam being found dead and everything, I forgot all about it.'

'And you didn't mention it to Miss Addison?'

'No, she would have told me off for not knowing my job and for making Madam cross.'

'And you didn't mention it to the police either?'

'No. I didn't think to. Was it important?'

'Possibly not but they may ask you about it in due course.' Eleanor paused, then continued: 'Hannah, I haven't asked you about Mrs Giffard's maid. Do you know where she was the morning Mrs Giffard died?'

'Henshaw? She should have been tidying upstairs while

Madam was having breakfast but she was ill that morning.'

'Tell me exactly what happened, please.'

'Well, Henshaw had breakfast with us as usual and then she was taken poorly. She was sick, quite badly and Miss Addison gave her some aspirin and sent her upstairs to her room.'

'And where is her room?'

'Oh, on the top floor. We share.'

'And when did she come down?'

'Not until the afternoon. I went in to see her at about eleven o'clock, just to make sure she didn't need anything but she was sound asleep. In fact, she didn't wake up until mid-afternoon.'

'So when you went up to tell your Mrs Giffard that the other Mrs Giffard was in the morning room, Henshaw wasn't with Mrs Giffard in the bedroom?'

'No, she would normally have been, of course.'

'Hannah, you have been very patient and I have almost finished asking questions. Would you describe for me, please, the routine followed when Mrs Giffard left the dining room after she had finished breakfast?'

'She would ring to let us know she was finished and then go upstairs. Then, when she came down again, she would go into the morning room.'

'So, while she was upstairs, the dining room would be cleared?'

'Yes, that's my job.'

'But you didn't clear that morning because you were upstairs in the attic.'

'Yes. Miss Addison said not to come down. I was to get on with clearing the attic and she would see to the dining room.'

'At what time would Mrs Giffard normally come down again after breakfast and go into the morning room?'

'Generally by about ten fifteen. She would start on her correspondence.'

‘And she would normally stay there until the lunch was served?’

‘Usually, yes.’

‘But you didn’t see her in the morning room on Monday because you were in the attic. Do you know if anyone else saw her?’

‘Well, no. But it would only have been Miss Addison. The others were in the kitchen.’

‘Quite. Well, I think that is all I needed to ask. Now, if you would just give me Miss Addison’s new address, I shall leave you to get on with your work.’

Hannah went into the housekeeper’s room and wrote the address on a piece of paper. She came back into the hall, handed the note to Eleanor and accompanied her to the front door.

‘Hannah, you have been a great help. Thank you,’ said Eleanor.

Philip saw Eleanor coming down the front steps and got out of the car to open the door for her. ‘All done?’ he asked.

‘Yes. I spoke to Hannah and I found out what I wanted to know. I didn’t see Miss Addison though. She has gone to a new position at Fairfield.’

‘So, back to the office?’

Eleanor looked at her watch.

‘Yes, they will be wondering where we have got to. Thank you for your help, Philip. I laughed at you when you insisted on coming but I couldn’t have managed without you.’

‘Any time. You know that.’

Chapter Eighteen

After dinner that evening, Eleanor and Mr Harriman were in the sitting room. Napoleon, from habit, was stretched out on the hearth rug even though there was no fire at this time of year. Mrs Clayton had gone home and they were free to talk about the Giffard matter. Eleanor described the motor-car chase over the moors. Mr Harriman was not altogether pleased about it, but he knew better than to say so. When his daughter was quite young, he recognised that she was gifted and very clever but he also saw that she had a strong character and an independent spirit. He had gradually accepted the fact and tried not to appear over-protective, even though privately he was sometimes concerned for her.

Mr Harriman said: 'Eleanor, you have done very well in this matter. You have found Major Giffard's inheritance for him. He must be very pleased.'

'He is and I am pleased that I have been able to do what the Major asked me to do. And I know that that should be the end of my involvement in this matter…'

'But?'

'I feel that I still do not know the whole truth. I am certain that there is much more to the story that has not been revealed.'

'Such as?'

'Well, the anonymous letter, for one thing. I have no idea who wrote it and the Major would like to know, just as much as I would.'

Mr Harriman smiled and gave a very long drawn out "yes" to which he added: 'So?'

'So, the anonymous letter writer might know something more, something that is helpful to the Major. It could be important in relation to his father's estate or it might tell him something about his family that would help him understand his past. Also, the writer might know something about Mrs Giffard at Manar that would explain why she was killed. The events surrounding her death might somehow be related to the Major's inheritance.'

'I can see that you are not going to be content until you get to the bottom of this,' said Mr Harriman, smiling, 'so let's run through what we have so far and see where it takes us. Perhaps we can unravel a few more strands. Where shall we start?'

Eleanor said: 'Well, when we read the anonymous letter we did not know what was behind it. However, we now know that, in order to have written that letter, the writer must have known that the Major's father was dead. He also knew about the Will, and that the Major was entitled to an inheritance which he had not received. Did the writer's knowledge stop there? Or did he also know that someone else was receiving money from the estate to which they were not entitled? And if so, did he know that it was Mrs Giffard? And why was he interested enough to bother writing the letter? Was it to help the Major or was it to stop Mrs Giffard? Or both? Is he connected with either of them in some way?'

'And,' said Mr Harriman, 'how and where did the letter writer acquire the information? It is the sort of personal information which a mere acquaintance would not normally have.'

'The letter writer must have known the Major's father in Ceylon but it must also be someone who knew that Mr Giffard had a son and heir. Someone who was once in Ceylon and is now in Buxton.'

'Or is in Buxton and has a connection with Ceylon.'

'The only person we know who fits that category is Mrs

Giffard and it certainly wouldn't have been her,' said Eleanor. 'The Major's father obviously started a completely new life when he went to Ceylon and he clearly became very wealthy. He could have supported his son very easily and yet he didn't send for him to join him in Ceylon.'

'Perhaps he was living alone and working very hard and didn't think it was the right sort of home life for a young boy. Perhaps he had only met the second Mrs Giffard towards the end of his life and by then it would have been too late to provide a family home for his son.'

'But he didn't even bother to find out if his son needed money,' said Eleanor. 'Wouldn't it have been natural to at least contact his son to find out?'

'Yes,' said Mr Harriman, 'that would be the natural thing to do. Not contacting anyone, even his son, suggests a strong motive for remaining inconspicuous. Given the great wealth he seems to have generated it must have been difficult to remain unknown, at least in Ceylon. What is also odd, is that Mr Giffard did not claim his pension. There was potentially a large amount of money at stake so it suggests that he had some reason for not revealing himself or his whereabouts to The India Office.'

'Perhaps,' said Eleanor, 'he was so wealthy in Ceylon that he didn't need the extra money.'

'In my experience,' said Mr Harriman, 'people who are rich never think that they have enough money. They are always looking for ways to acquire more. A rich man would not ignore a fat pension without good reason. Nor would his widow, come to that.'

'There is nothing in the newspaper reports to suggest that Mr Giffard was involved in his wife's death or even in any way under suspicion so he would not have been at risk of being dismissed from his civil service job because of her death. He had no need to disappear from India for that reason,' said Eleanor. 'So, why did he leave Calcutta?'

'Perhaps there is more to the death of his wife than we know,' said Mr Harriman.

They sat in silence for a while, contemplating Napoleon who was oblivious to their musings and snoring loudly. Eventually, Eleanor said: 'Is it a co-incidence, do you think, that both of Mr Giffard's wives died of poisoning? Both Mary Rosa Giffard, his first wife, and now Mrs Giffard of Manar?'

'What are you suggesting?'

'Well, should we be looking for similarities, perhaps? Is there a common factor which we have not noticed? Or is there a person who is common to both incidents, a link between the two?'

'Good point,' said Mr Harriman. 'And that link may be the anonymous letter writer. So, we have two deaths by poison, one old and one current. In both cases, the victim is the wife of the Major's father and both victims are called Mary Giffard. In the first case, the motive is said to have been jealousy or rivalry over an affair. We don't know yet what the motive was in the current case.'

'Let's consider the usual motives?' said Eleanor.

'Jealousy, greed, envy, hatred, sudden anger.'

'What about revenge? Could the second killing be revenge for the first?' suggested Eleanor.

'In that case, the most likely person to seek revenge for his mother's death would be the Major so that does not help us.'

'Dear me, no,' agreed Eleanor. 'In any case, even if the motive was revenge why would the Major kill Mrs Giffard? What would be the point? The likely target for revenge would be the person who murdered his mother. And Florence Bryant has been dead for many years.'

'Yes,' said Mr Harriman. 'That makes no sense. What about the Major's wife?'

'Ah, that is something which is troubling me at the moment.'

'What is that?' asked Mr Harriman.

Eleanor said: 'I spoke to Hannah, the parlour-maid, about Isabel Giffard's visit to Manar and the two versions tally but there is still a problem. If the poison was in the food served at breakfast, most probably the jam, Isabel Giffard may have had the opportunity to put it there. I am not saying she did, I am just saying that she could have done it and we do need to take that into account. When Isabel Giffard arrived at Manar, there was a dish of jam already on the dining room table and she probably would have had time to go into the dining room and poison the jam. If she had wanted to, that is.'

'Hmmm. If she had wanted to,' said Mr Harriman. 'It is one thing to want to kill someone and quite another to actually do so. The method chosen required some degree of planning, including getting the poison in advance and prior knowledge of the breakfast routine at Manar and, therefore, suggests premeditation. Isabel Giffard had only arrived back in Buxton the day before and it was late in the afternoon, which does not give her much chance to get hold of the belladonna.'

'I agree. Isabel Giffard admitted to me that she felt very angry towards Mrs Giffard but I think it is more likely that she went to Manar on impulse without any real thought of what she would do when she got there and not because of some pre-arranged plan.'

'It does seem an unlikely sequence, doesn't it? One does not carry around a handful of belladonna berries on the off chance of finding the opportunity to poison someone. And she could not have counted on being left alone while Hannah went to speak to Mrs Giffard.'

'I'm afraid there is another difficulty though,' said Eleanor. 'No-one actually saw Isabel Giffard leave the house so it is possible that, instead of leaving after a few minutes as she says she did, she actually hid somewhere, administered the poison in some other way later on, and then left. But I am at a loss as to how or what the poison could have been.'

'Oh dear,' said Mr Harriman, 'that does complicate things, doesn't it?'

'The fact that she was at Manar that day probably is relevant to the police enquiry and someone is going to have to tell them.'

'Yes, my dear. I think you are right and it is probably better if Isabel Giffard volunteers the information herself. However, criminal law is not our forte so I suggest we consult Edwin tomorrow and get his opinion before we take any further action.'

'That is an excellent idea. Now, there are some other very puzzling aspects to this whole affair which I have not told you about yet. It may not be as straightforward as I have just been suggesting.' Eleanor explained to Mr Harriman the conversation about belladonna poisoning she had had with her friend Catherine and the difficulties arising from the timing of the death.

Mr Harriman said: 'Perhaps we should not take any further action until the medical information is available and we have some facts to work with. Let's see what Edwin has to say, shall we?'

'Yes, that would be best.'

'He's in Court tomorrow so he probably won't be available until late in the afternoon.'

'I'm sure it can wait until then,' said Eleanor. 'I'll take Napoleon for his walk now. I need some exercise after all that talking.'

Hearing the word walk, Napoleon got up, stretched, and started down the stairs before Eleanor could change her mind.

♣♣♣

Chapter Nineteen

On Friday morning, Eleanor and Napoleon went downstairs to say good morning to James. 'Ah, Miss Eleanor, good morning.' James returned Napoleon's greeting with a pat. 'I have two messages for you. Mr Talbot left you this note and, a few minutes ago, the Post Office boy delivered this. I expect it is a response to your telegram to Colombo. I was just going to bring it up to you. Here you are.'

'Thank you, James.' Eleanor went up to her office and opened the telegram, printed as always in capital letters, which read:

TO HARRIMAN AND TALBOT BUXTON +

RE ENQUIRY GIFFARD ESTATE STOP

ADVISE MARRIAGE CERTIFICATE DATED 1887
PROVIDED BY WIDOW STOP
LIFE INTEREST TO WIDOW STOP
ESTATE ADMINISTERED ACCORDINGLY STOP
RE CLAIM BY SON STOP
WILL AWAIT EVIDENCE AS INSTRUCTIONS
FROM WIDOW WERE NO CHILDREN OF
MARRIAGE STOP +

HENRY CHAPMAN

Eleanor had speculated that the solicitors in Colombo had been deceived by Mrs Giffard and whilst her theory remained just that, it was easy enough to contemplate. However, being faced with the reality of the deceit was quite different and Eleanor was shocked. Mrs Giffard had pretended to be the dead wife of Mr Giffard, she had claimed the life interest and prevented the estate from passing to the Major, and she had sought to deprive him of any future interest by lying about his existence. Eleanor found it confronting to think that someone whom she knew had acted in so calculating a manner. She found the level of Mrs Giffard's callousness chilling. When she had first heard about Mrs Giffard's death, Eleanor had felt some compassion for her but now, although she knew it was wrong to feel this way, she began to think that poisoning was nothing more than Mrs Giffard deserved. By her evil acts, she had brought about her own downfall. At least, thought Eleanor, the Colombo solicitors had been deceived by her and had not been negligent and, because of that, would probably be willing to assist the Major in recovering his inheritance. Eleanor then read Edwin's note:

Good morning, Eleanor.

I was at a trustees' meeting last evening and Dr Mackenzie was there. He tells me that the post mortem and toxicology report on Mrs Giffard have revealed the presence of morphine as well as belladonna. I thought you would be interested to know. Must dash. Am due at Court.

See you this afternoon. Edwin.

Eleanor was not sure what the effect of this finding was. She asked herself a string of questions to which she was unable to provide any answers. Was the cause of death morphine poisoning or belladonna poisoning? And if it was morphine, where had that substance come from? Eleanor saw her carefully constructed theory about blackcurrant jam collapsing like a pack of cards. At least, she thought, if it was morphine poisoning, the morphine must have been given after the Major's wife left so I need not worry any more about the fact that she was at Manar. Perhaps that does not need to come out. Or does it? Could death have been caused by a combination of both belladonna and morphine? Were there perhaps two people involved not one? That line of thinking was not going to help the Major's wife. With difficulty, Eleanor turned her mind to her other routine files and worked solidly for a couple of hours until Mrs Clayton brought in her morning tea.

Mrs Clayton said: 'Miss Harriman, you haven't forgotten that it's the tea thing this afternoon at the Crescent Hotel? The one with the fancy name that you gave me and my sister-in-law tickets for.'

'Oh, yes. I had forgotten.'

'I haven't. We're looking forward to it very much. It'll be a right treat.'

'I am pleased. I'm very grateful to you for going, you know. It's not my sort of thing at all and the Misses Pymble wanted as many people to attend as possible. They need to raise funds, you see, and we have to support their efforts but it does take up a lot of one's time. Your going leaves me free to get on with my work.'

'Well, we shall enjoy ourselves all the more knowing that it is for a good cause. Now, you are sure you don't want me to do you dinner? I can easily leave something for you.'

'No thank you, Mrs Clayton. Don't worry. Father and I will dine out. Why don't you go home straight after lunch?'

'Thanks very much, I will, if you don't mind. It'll give me time to get the boys' tea ready before I go.'

'Oh, and I've asked James to give you some money from the petty cash so make sure you see him before you go. There will be donations expected even though most of the money from the tickets is going to the charity. You're just there to enjoy yourselves.'

'Right you are, Miss Harriman, and make sure you have some dinner, mind,' said Mrs Clayton as she departed.

Eleanor worked for the rest of the morning and after lunch took Napoleon for his walk in the Gardens. She had just settled down to work again when Edwin came into her office and said: 'I'm sorry, Eleanor, but you're not going to like this.'

'What?' Eleanor looked up at him and frowned.

'The Inspector from Chesterfield has asked the Major's wife to go to the police station to be interviewed.'

'Oh no. Father and I were discussing last night whether or not we should advise her to go to the police and we were waiting to consult you before we did anything.'

'Well, it looks as though events have overtaken us. The Major had the sense to tell Inspector Renshaw that he wanted a solicitor present and he has made an appointment at the police station for four o'clock this afternoon. I saw Superintendent Johnson at the Court and he gave me the Major's message.'

'Edwin, I know the Major is my client but I am sure you are the best person to sit in on the interview. You are the one who is experienced in criminal law. However, before you go to the police station I had better tell you everything that I know about the day Mrs Giffard died.'

Edwin sat down and listened attentively as Eleanor brought him up to date. They both went back to work and then, at ten minutes to four, Edwin left for the police station.

At five o'clock, Edwin returned to the office and informed Eleanor and Mr Harriman that Isabel Giffard had been arrested. 'At least,' said Edwin, 'I managed to get her bailed. She is distraught, naturally, and the Major has taken her back to Oxford House. Cicely will look after them. The best we can do for them is to keep the arrest as quiet as possible until we can get this mess sorted out and the right person has been locked up.'

'Right,' said Mr Harriman. 'We had better consider what needs to be done and put together a plan.'

Edwin said: 'I told Inspector Renshaw that his case might not be as strong as he thinks and I hinted that there were things he might have overlooked. I suggested that before he goes making an announcement to the press which might have to be retracted, he might want to consider the evidence in a little more detail. He has agreed to give us forty-eight hours. If we can get together enough evidence to convince Inspector Renshaw that Isabel Giffard is not guilty, we can get the charge dropped before it is made public and no-one need ever know.'

'That's excellent,' said Mr Harriman.

'So,' asked Eleanor, 'how did all this come about?'

'Inspector Renshaw interviewed your Mr Brantlingham and he told the Inspector that he had discovered that there was a connection between Mrs Giffard at Manar and Major Giffard.'

'Oh, no,' said Eleanor. 'This is my fault for reporting Brantlingham. I should never have told the police about him.'

'No, Eleanor,' said Edwin. 'You did the right thing. The link between the Giffards was bound to come out one way or another. Brantlingham told the Inspector that there was something Mrs Giffard wanted to hide, although he did not know exactly what, and Brantlingham admitted that he had been trying to blackmail her by pretending to know more than he did. Apparently Brantlingham based his blackmail solely on what he had observed between the Giffards at the Sale of Work and the information he had gleaned from the servants at Manar about Mrs Giffard's sudden absences when she was trying to avoid the other Giffards. He had no idea of the reason for the absences. Apparently his mention of India was just a lucky guess based on the conversation he overheard on Broad Walk when the Colonel talked about a Giffard who had disappeared from there. He seems to have been about as competent at blackmail as he was at selling motor-cars. Anyway, when Inspector Renshaw learned that there was a connection between Mrs Giffard and the Major, he decided he needed more information. So, this morning he questioned Major Giffard, who felt obliged to tell the Inspector about the inheritance. Inspector Renshaw, obviously scenting a possible motive, wanted to know when the Giffards had last been in contact with Mrs Giffard and the Major had to admit that his wife had been to see Mrs Giffard on the morning that she died. The post mortem report and the toxicology report show that there was a significant amount of morphine found as well as belladonna. Dr Mackenzie was Mrs Giffard's treating doctor and he told the Inspector that he had never prescribed any drugs for her which contained morphine. So the Inspector has decided that the cause of death was an excess of morphine and he is satisfied that Mrs Giffard didn't take the dose herself either intentionally or unintentionally.'

'I don't understand,' said Eleanor. 'Is he discounting the belladonna?'

'Apparently, yes. He has convinced himself that Mrs Giffard survived the belladonna and that the morphine was administered later in the morning. That, according to Inspector Renshaw, explains why Mrs Giffard was still alive at twelve o'clock and dead by twelve thirty. The Inspector decided that he was looking for someone with a motive (removal of the person who had stolen the Major's inheritance), the means (access to the supply of morphine which apparently the Major has for pain), and the opportunity (someone who was at Manar at nine o'clock and hid until twelve o'clock when the murder was committed). You see how very neat it is?'

There was a stunned silence.

'I know that getting angry is not going to help one little bit, but I want you to know that I am seething,' said Eleanor.

'I couldn't agree more,' said Mr Harriman.

'Well,' said Edwin. 'At least we have a clear idea of what we are up against. We need to come up with a better solution and some proof.'

'Angry though I am, my brain is still functioning logically,' said Eleanor. 'I think the first thing I should do is go back to Manar and find out if Mrs Giffard was using any medication that contained morphine. Her maid would know that. Has Inspector Renshaw thought to do that, do we know?'

'I did not get the impression that he had even considered it,' said Edwin.

'Good. The second thing I should do is talk to Ellen, the kitchen maid, again about the morning Mrs Giffard died. When I first spoke to her I had no idea what was relevant and what was not so I only got a general idea of what happened. I can do both of those things right away. I'm glad Mrs Clayton isn't here.'

'She knows not to gossip and she is very reliable but, I agree, the fewer people who know about the arrest of Isabel Giffard the better,' said Edwin.

'No, I didn't mean that,' said Eleanor. 'Mrs Clayton is quite safe. There is no question about that. No, it is just that it is going to take me a while to get the information we need so I am going to have to skip dinner. To Mrs Clayton that is a worse offence than being arrested. She would scold me terribly if she were here. She thinks I don't eat enough. And she mustn't find out either because she would blame herself for not being here, having gone off to enjoy herself at The Crescent Hotel. So, you are sworn to secrecy.'

Edwin and Mr Harriman laughed. 'We won't let on,' said Mr Harriman.

'I'll go to Manar now. Could you get James to telephone

Cicely and ask her to keep Ellen with her until I get back? She will miss her tea so could he also ask Cicely to give her something to eat.'

Edwin glanced at Mr Harriman and then said, as casually as he could manage: 'Eleanor, do you mind if I come with you to Manar. While you talk to Mrs Giffard's maid, I'd like to have a snoop around. Unlike you, I have never been graced with an invitation to Manar and it might help me to understand the evidence better if I can get an idea of the layout.'

Eleanor sensed that, for the same reason as previously, her father did not want her to go to Manar alone, but she also realised that the more information Edwin had, the more he would be able to contribute, so she simply said: 'Of course I don't mind. Shall we go in your car? It will be quicker than walking and I don't want to lose any time.'

'While you are doing that I will just stroll down to Oxford House and reassure Cicely. I don't want her thinking she is harbouring a murderer. I'll take Napoleon with me,' said Mr Harriman.

Chapter Twenty

When Eleanor and Edwin arrived at Manar, Hannah opened the door to them and greeted Eleanor. Eleanor introduced Edwin and apologised for calling at such an odd time. She explained that she needed to speak to Miss Henshaw and suggested that she would use the housekeeper's room if that was convenient. Edwin said that there were some questions he would like to ask Hannah so he would wait in the hall until she came back. Hannah showed Eleanor into the housekeeper's room and went to fetch Henshaw.

While she waited, Eleanor looked around the room and then sat down at the desk, wondering why it was taking so long for Hannah to find Henshaw. Miss Addison had left everything very tidy, with the receipt books, order books, cards, envelopes, and other stationery all neatly in pigeon holes, and pens and pencils in holders. Miss Addison was clearly a person to whom organisation was important. She had left a note for Mrs Brompton on the top of the desk and Eleanor sat staring at the note, not reading it but noticing that the handwriting was as neat and tidy as the desk.

Hannah came back 'Sorry, Miss Harriman. It's taken me all this time to persuade Sarah to come down and speak to you. Shall I leave you?'

'Thank you, Hannah. Yes, I think that would be best. Miss Henshaw, please come in and sit down.'

Sarah Henshaw came into the housekeeper's room looking apprehensive. Eleanor judged that she was about twenty. Eleanor introduced herself and said: 'Miss Henshaw,

I have come here to ask you to help me. A person has been accused of poisoning Mrs Giffard. Now, I do not believe for one minute that this person is guilty but I have to be able to prove that and I need your help. Are you willing to answer a few questions for me?' Sarah Henshaw looked doubtful and said nothing. 'I am sure that you would want the right person to be arrested, the person who did poison Mrs Giffard,' said Eleanor. Sarah nodded slowly. 'You see,' continued Eleanor. 'I need to find the evidence to give to the police. I think you may be able to give me the information I need?' Sarah remained silent. 'Miss Henshaw, nothing you tell me about Mrs Giffard can harm her now and it is very important that the police know the truth. I know that, as a lady's maid, you know a great deal about your employer and her private life and it is your job not to repeat what you hear and not to comment to anyone else on what your employer does or says. I know that you would not normally talk to anyone else about her personal affairs but this is very important.' Silence. Eleanor waited.

'But Miss Harriman,' said Sarah, at last. 'I have to earn my own living and I shall have to leave here shortly and look for another situation. There will be no reference for any of us and who will want to employ someone without a reference and worse, someone whose mistress has been poisoned? People will think I didn't look after Madam properly, to have let that happen. And if people find out that, on top of that, I've been gossiping and talking out of turn about Madam's private affairs, especially now she is dead, what will it look like? People will think I don't know how to behave properly, that I don't know my job. No-one will want me and I'll never get another situation. I don't want to end up in the workhouse.'

'Miss Henshaw, I do understand your concerns. I wouldn't ask you these things if it were not for the fact that someone's life is at stake. A person, whom I believe is innocent, has been accused of killing Mrs Giffard. The information you give me may help to clear that person and to find the person who really is guilty. I know that it puts you in a difficult position but if you have any information that will help, I think I can make sure that no-one will ever know that it came from you. Will you trust me to do that?' Eleanor waited.

'Yes, Miss Harriman,' said Sarah.

'Thank you, Miss Henshaw. I only need to ask you a few questions. First of all, did Mrs Giffard take any medicine?' There was a pause.

'Yes,' said Sarah warily.

'How often?'

'Every night.'

'And did Dr Mackenzie prescribe it, do you know?'

'No, Miss. It came from a doctor in Manchester.'

'From Manchester?' said Eleanor with surprise.

'Yes, Miss. The medicine came by post.'

'How often did it come?'

'Regular like. I can't rightly say when.'

'Where did Mrs Giffard keep it? Do you know?'

'In her room. She locked it in the drawer of her dressing table.'

'Is there any still there?'

'I don't know. Madam keeps the key herself.'

'Do you know where Mrs Giffard kept the key?'

'No, Miss.'

'Did you ever see Mrs Giffard take the medicine, Miss Henshaw?'

'No, Miss.'

'Are you sure that she took it every night?'

'I suppose so, Miss. I always had to leave a glass of water on her dressing table for her to drink after she had taken her medicine.'

'And do you know what the medicine was for?'

'No, Miss.'

Eleanor remained silent.

Eventually Sarah said: 'She had trouble sleeping if she didn't take it. Once, she ran out of medicine and she said she hadn't slept at all that night. The new packet hadn't come in the post when it should have and when it came the next day she took some straightaway. She said there was no need to mention it to anyone.'

'Did the police ask you about this medicine?'

'No, Miss.'

'Does anyone else in the house know about it?'

'I don't think so,' said Sarah shaking her head. 'Madam said not to mention it and I never have.'

'Miss Henshaw, you have been very helpful. I can't thank you enough. I think I shall be able to give the police this information without them knowing how I came by it. When the truth comes out and the right person is arrested, the information about the medicine will not be important and probably will be forgotten about so there is no need for you to worry. But I would like you to take me up to Mrs Giffard's bedroom and show me the drawer where the medicine is kept so that I can explain to the police where to look. But before I do that, could I just ask you about your illness on the day Mrs Giffard died? You were ill at breakfast, I believe.'

'Yes, Miss. I started to feel a bit poorly after I had eaten my porridge. Sort of queezy all of a sudden and Miss Addison gave me something to settle my stomach and sent me upstairs to rest for half an hour but I didn't wake up until gone two o'clock, after Madam had been found. I don't know why I slept so long and I don't know anything about what happened that morning.'

'And you were all right again the next day?'

'Well, yes. That afternoon actually, after I woke up.'

'I see. Now, if you would take me up to Mrs Giffard's bedroom, please.'

They went up the servants' stairs and into a large bedroom at the front of the house. It was lavishly and expensively decorated in mushroom coloured silk and velvet, rather fussy and frilled, with an abundance of plump cushions. It was not to Eleanor's taste but she could see that a great deal of money had been spent on the room. Sarah Henshaw went to the dressing table, took a bunch of keys from her pocket, and unlocked a deep drawer on the right hand side. She pulled open the drawer and Eleanor saw that right at the back there was another compartment with a lock, probably intended for jewellery.

'I see. So you and Mrs Giffard both have keys to the drawer itself but only Mrs Giffard had a key to this little compartment inside?'

'That's right.'

'I think we should lock the bedroom door until the police have been able to make another search and if you give me the key to the dressing table drawer I will deliver both keys to the police.'

Eleanor shepherded Sarah out of the room and locked the door. As they were going back down the stairs she asked: 'Does Hannah know about the extra drawer?'

'I don't think so, Miss.'

'Then I think we should not say anything to her about that or about the medicine. It will only complicate things.'

'Very good, Miss.'

When they went into the main hall, Hannah was there talking to Edwin. Eleanor said: 'Hannah, I have locked Mrs Giffard's bedroom door and I have taken the key.'

'Oh, Miss, I'm not sure we should.'

'It's very important, Hannah, and I will take full responsibility. I shall go straight to the police station and give the key to Superintendent Johnson. Thank you both for your help. Mr Talbot and I appreciate it very much.'

Edwin waited until they were in the motor-car and then

said: 'Any luck?'

'I think so. Mrs Giffard was in the habit of taking a small amount of something every night to help her sleep and I very much hope that it was morphine.'

Eleanor told Edwin what she had learnt from Sarah Henshaw. She said: 'I am not certain but I think Mrs Giffard was a mild drug addict. She seems to have been desperate one day when the medicine did not arrive from Manchester.'

Edwin said: 'It does certainly sound like a sleeping drug of some sort. Well done, Eleanor.'

'Did you find out anything useful from Hannah?'

'Yes,' replied Edwin. 'Apparently when Superintendent Johnson was inspecting the dining room he tried the bell-pull and found that it did not work. So even if Mrs Giffard had been able to reach it, she would not have been able to summon help. Co-incidence? Or was the bell deliberately disconnected?'

Eleanor said: 'There is no doubt that this murder was very carefully planned and everything possible was done to ensure that no-one would find Mrs Giffard in time to save her.'

'Yes, it's rather chilling, isn't it? Knowing that there is someone like that in our midst. Where to now?' asked Edwin. 'The police station?'

'I think I would like to pay a call on Dr Mackenzie. Would you like to have the pleasure of taking the keys to Inspector Renshaw and asking him to organise a proper search of Manar?'

'I shall enjoy that,' said Edwin.

Eleanor gave Edwin the keys and explained how to find the locked compartment in the dressing table and added: 'Please don't give Sarah Henshaw away. It really is important to her not to have breached any confidences and I did promise. Can you just leave me at Terrace Road. I can walk up from there and then you can go on to the police station.'

'All right. I'll see you back at the office.'

Eleanor walked up the hill to Dr Mackenzie's surgery. He was the Harriman family's doctor and had known Eleanor for many years. The waiting room was empty because evening surgery had just finished but the receptionist was still on duty and busy with the filing. Eleanor asked to see Dr Mackenzie and was shown into his room almost immediately.

'Good evening, Eleanor,' said the doctor, smiling, 'come in, come in. Are you here to consult me in a private or a professional capacity? If it is a professional visit I should address you formally as Miss Harriman. Whichever it is, you are most welcome.'

'Thank you, Doctor Mackenzie,' said Eleanor, laughing. 'Eleanor, please, although I am here for a professional reason today. I have come to ask for your help.'

'Right, well then, you've time for a cup of tea while you tell me what it is I can do for you?'

'Oh, yes please.'

After he had organised tea, Doctor Mackenzie said: 'Now, what is it that you need?'

'It's about the Giffard case. I don't know whether you are already aware of this or not but this afternoon the police have made an arrest.'

'No,' said Dr Mackenzie. 'I was not aware of that. I must say I am surprised.'

'I should make it clear that the person who has been arrested is a client of ours.'

'Ah, so we are on opposing sides, as it were?'

'Yes, exactly and, of course, I appreciate that there are topics which we cannot discuss. I should also make it clear that I believe that the person who has been arrested is innocent. I think Inspector Renshaw has made a mistake. We have been given forty-eight hours to provide the Inspector with further evidence in order to have our client released and avoid a public announcement of the arrest.'

'Dear me,' said the doctor, 'this is all very dramatic.'

'Yes, and it is making us very anxious indeed but I think you may be able to help. I have some information which I think is relevant and which may establish our client's innocence. I know that Mrs Giffard was your patient but I think I may have discovered something about her medical treatment that you are not aware of. I know you cannot discuss your patient with me so, if you don't mind, I will just tell you what I know. You needn't make any comment, and then I think it will become clear what I would like you to do.'

'Right. You talk and I'll listen,' said the doctor.

'I understand from Edwin Talbot that the toxicology and post mortem reports indicate the presence of both morphine and belladonna and that either is a possible cause of Mrs Giffard's death. Inspector Renshaw is treating the morphine as the cause of death and has made the arrest on that basis.'

'Has he, by Jove!'

'I have established that Mrs Giffard took medicine on a daily basis and it is possible, perhaps highly likely, that the medicine she took contained morphine.'

The doctor's eyebrows went up. 'Indeed.'

'It seems that she used it as a remedy for sleeplessness. It was supplied by a doctor in Manchester which no doubt explains why you were unaware of it. So, I have come here to tell you about the medicine and to ask you to take it into account in considering the reports and the cause of death.'

'I see,' said Dr Mackenzie, looking at Eleanor over the top of his glasses. 'I was under the impression that the police had searched the house and had not found any morphine.'

'The medicine that Mrs Giffard was taking was kept in her bedroom in a locked drawer which is easily overlooked. Apparently Mrs Giffard kept the only key so it must have been with her when she died. If so, it will be among her possessions which the police have. I have been to Manar and I have left the bedroom door locked. Edwin Talbot was with me and has now gone to deliver the key to the police and will ask them to look for the other key. The medicine is probably in a packet and may have the name of a chemist on it, so if it becomes necessary, it might be possible to speak to the chemist or find the prescribing doctor and establish that this medicine was supplied regularly to Mrs Giffard.'

Doctor Mackenzie nodded slowly but made no comment. He was impressed by this confident and articulate young lady and was seeing a completely different side of the person he knew only as a patient with the usual childhood ailments.

'So, you want me to test the medicine and then look at the reports again?'

'Yes.'

'I certainly shall. I see what you are getting at and I understand what you need me to do. I can tell you, Eleanor, without breaching any confidences, that this is an altogether puzzling case. My initial view was that Mrs Giffard had been poisoned with belladonna. The symptoms certainly were consistent with that. However, the fact that she was still alive at twelve o'clock suggests otherwise. On the other hand, it is my opinion, although obviously the Inspector does not share it, that the level of morphine found would not have been sufficient to kill Mrs Giffard or to produce the symptoms which were evident. I know that the Inspector has sought an opinion from a doctor in Chesterfield, who did not see the body. Perhaps it is that doctor's opinion on which he is relying to justify the arrest. But, as far as I am concerned, the cause of death remains unexplained for the moment. What you have just told me is very interesting.'

‘Well,’ said Eleanor, ‘I shall keep looking for a satisfactory explanation.’

‘That’s the spirit. In the meantime, I shall have another look at the morphine issue. I am very glad that you came to see me, Eleanor. Mrs Giffard was my patient and I want the truth for her as much as you want it for your client.’

Dr Mackenzie saw her out of his surgery and Eleanor walked back to the office.

Meanwhile, Edwin had driven to the police station. He decided to deliver the keys to Superintendent Johnson instead of Inspector Renshaw and he described where to look for the locked compartment. Edwin wanted to be sure that there was no break in the chain of evidence which he hoped would save Isabel Giffard so he asked if he could wait while the Superintendent had someone check the late Mrs Giffard’s clothing to see if the key for the compartment was there. Superintendent Johnson agreed and went away to telephone. Eventually, after twenty minutes, the Superintendent returned and assured Edwin that the key had been found. He said that he would send one of his officers to Manar immediately to search the compartment. Fortunately for Sarah Henshaw, Superintendent Johnson’s attention was fully occupied in composing words of reprimand and a suitable punishment for the officer who had searched Manar previously and missed the locked compartment and Edwin had been able to leave the police station before the Superintendent had realised that he had not asked Edwin to explain how he had come by the information about the medicine. Thus, Henshaw’s reputation for discretion remained completely unsullied.

It was seven thirty by the time Eleanor, Edwin and Mr Harriman re-grouped at the office. Eleanor said to Mr

Harriman: 'Is Cicely all right with having Isabel Giffard as a guest still?'

'Absolutely. She was quite indignant at the thought of one of her favourite guests being arrested and it is lucky for Inspector Renshaw that he could not hear her opinion of him. I fully expect him to come out in boils by tomorrow. When I left, Major Giffard was playing draughts with Richard. The Giffards will be quite comfortable with Cicely until we can sort things out.'

'That is a relief,' said Eleanor. 'Now, let's compare notes.'

When everyone had been brought up to date, Edwin said: 'I suppose it is possible that Mrs Giffard took an excessive dose of that medicine either by mistake or deliberately. If it does contain morphine that could be fatal.'

'It is also possible,' said Mr Harriman, 'that someone tampered with the medicine so that she would take a larger dose than usual without realising it. But if that was the case, it would point to Henshaw because it seems that she is the only one who knew about the medicine.'

'But if Henshaw had tampered with the medicine, it is unlikely that she would have told me of its existence when she had no obligation to do so,' said Eleanor. 'Besides, Dr Mackenzie seems to think that the level of morphine present was not sufficient to cause Mrs Giffard's death.'

'I think for the minute at least we should ignore the medicine and simply note its presence. If necessary, we can go back to it when Dr Mackenzie has had time to investigate further,' said Edwin.

'Then, we should concentrate on the breakfast,' said Eleanor. 'We need to know exactly what happened, where the poison might have been, and who might have put it there.'

'Right, so that leaves Ellen,' said Mr Harriman. 'She has agreed to come and she should be here in about half of an hour.'

‘Just time for a cup of tea then,’ said Eleanor, getting up from her chair. ‘Anyone else want one?’

‘Sorry to abandon you, Eleanor, but Ellen will no doubt be more forthcoming without Edwin and me here. We can’t do anything further tonight. I suggest that you get on home Edwin. I’ll go to the Club for some dinner and we can meet again first thing in the morning.’

‘Agreed. I’ll just make myself a sandwich before Ellen arrives,’ said Eleanor, heading for the kitchen followed by Napoleon. ‘I wonder if Mrs Clayton has left any of her biscuits. They managed to loosen Ellen’s tongue last time.’

‘Goodnight, Eleanor,’ said Edwin and he and Mr Harriman went downstairs. As he left he called: ‘I shan’t let on to Mrs Clayton that you only had a sandwich for dinner tonight.’

‘Goodnight, Edwin,’ said Eleanor, sternly.

Chapter Twenty-One

Ellen duly arrived and Eleanor supplied her with tea, biscuits, and Napoleon for moral support. 'Thank you for coming back to see me, Ellen. There are some things that I forgot to ask you about last time, or rather, I didn't ask you because I didn't think they were important but now I think they might be, so will you help me again?' Ellen nodded. 'Now, you told me last time that you usually prepared two trays at breakfast time. The first one contains the china and things like that and the butter and the jam dishes. Last Monday, you put out the raspberry jam from a jar in the pantry and that went into the dining room on the first tray, which Hannah took in.' Ellen munched her biscuit and nodded. 'Then Hannah went up to the attic as instructed by Miss Addison,' said Eleanor. Another nod. 'Then Miss Addison told you that Mrs Giffard wanted blackcurrant jam and you got that from a new jar in the pantry and put it on the second tray to go in with the hot food, that is, the egg and the toast.'

'And the tea,' added Ellen.

Ellen seemed much more confident than she had been last time and Eleanor thought it was probably the result of a few days of being reassured by Cicely. 'And the second tray was in the kitchen waiting ready for when Mrs Giffard came down. Did Mrs Giffard usually say which jam she wanted?'

'No, not usually. We just put out what we had open.'

'Now, you also told me, I think, that Cook was busy with a dinner party and possibly some extra guests for lunch and she asked you to boil the egg that day instead of doing it herself.'

'Yes,' said Ellen. 'That's right. And I'd just put the egg in to cook and that's when the "to do" started.'

'And what was that?'

'Well, the water from the pipe, of course.'

'Tell me about it,' said Eleanor, patiently, hiding her surprise at this information.

'Miss Addison went to turn on the tap, in the kitchen sink, that is, and there was no water. And Cook says how was she supposed to get dinner for ten people with no water? And Miss Addison says for her not to worry she will go and see if the other tap is working and Miss Addison goes into the scullery and tries the tap there and comes back and says that it is working so it must be the kitchen tap that's wrong.' Ellen paused to take a breath. 'Then she says no, the water in the scullery tap might just have been water already in the pipe. And Cook says she doesn't want to risk it, not with having to do dinner for tonight so Miss Addison should get it seen to straightaway. So Miss Addison says we should try the outside tap to make sure the water hasn't been cut off to the house. So Miss Addison tells Cook to go outside and try the tap there and she says to me to go and find Mr Dakin and tell him to come and look at the kitchen tap. So off I goes to look for him.'

'Mr Dakin is the gardener?'

'Yes, an' he were right down on the tennis court.'

'So it took a few minutes for you to find him?'

'A good few minutes, yes.'

'And you came back into the kitchen with him?'

'Yes, and he says who took the tap off? And Miss Addison says never mind that, we've checked that the water supply to the house hasn't been cut off so there must be a problem in the house itself. So Mr Dakin he says he needs to fetch his tools and he goes out to get them from his shed.'

'And while you were outside looking for the gardener,

who went out to check that the water supply to the house had not been affected? Miss Addison or Cook?'

Ellen thought for a minute, then said: 'I'm not sure. They were both in the kitchen when I left and when I came back in with Mr Dakin.'

'So what happened next?'

'Then Cook notices the time and reminds me about breakfast. So I made the tea and put the egg in the egg cup and then Miss Addison takes the tray into the dining room.'

'And was that at the usual time or later?'

'Just after. And that egg must have been hard boiled by the time I got it out of the water and into the egg cup. I said I'd start a fresh one but Miss Addison said there wasn't time.'

'So Miss Addison took the second tray into the dining room and then what happened?'

'Water started spurting all over the place from the kitchen tap. It just started, sudden like, and there was no stopping it. Cook was yelling at me to put a cloth over it and that didn't do much good so then I helped her move the things she had on the table for the dinner so they wouldn't get spoilt and Miss Addison came in and tells me to go and tell the gardener to hurry. The water was going everywhere, all over everything, making a right mess. And just as I was about to go out Mr Dakin comes back in and Miss Addison tells him to go and turn off the water. The tap's in the cellar and the door to the cellar is kept locked and he can't find the key.'

'And who usually has the key?'

'All the keys is kept on a board next to the kitchen door and the cellar key were missing.'

'So somebody had been down into the cellar and had forgotten to put the key back on the board?'

'I suppose so.'

'Do you have any idea who might have been the last to go down to the cellar?'

'Probably me and Cook. Cook had to get some of the things for the dinner and I helped her carry them up.'

'And you don't remember whether Cook put the key back?'

'No, I wasn't really noticing. I remember she locked the door to the cellar, though. Perhaps she forgot and put the key in her pocket. I shouldn't be surprised. She were in a right fluster that morning. She were fine with the ten for dinner because she knew about them last week but Miss Addison had only told her that morning that there might be extra for lunch.'

'And there is a spare key for the cellar?'

'Yes, in a drawer in the housekeeper's room. So Miss Addison had to go and unlock the drawer to get it and she said to Mr Dakin as how she would go down and turn off the water and he was to do what he could in the kitchen meantime. It took a long time to turn off the water and there was Cook shouting about how her ingredients was being ruined and telling Mr Dakin to hurry up and him telling her he can't do nothing till the water's off. Oh, what a "to do" it was.'

'So, eventually, the water was turned off?'

'Yes, but that weren't the end of it, by half. There was still all the water to clear up. I was mopping and mopping and Cook was saying as how the lunch was going to be late and Madam was going to blame her and Mr Dakin was saying he'd like to know who was the silly person who took the top off the tap in the first place and I just kept mopping.'

'So when the water was turned off, Mr Dakin fixed the tap?'

'Yes and when Miss Addison came back into the kitchen she said he was to go back to doing the tennis court and she would go down and turn on the water again and then when she came back she started to help with the clearing up. There was water all over the floor. After the floor was dry, we had to take down all the plates from the rack and dry them and the pots and things on the shelves as well. And the water had got all over the kitchen table and we had to dry that down and sort everything out.'

Ellen stopped and Eleanor nodded encouragement.

'And do you have any idea how long it took to clean up the kitchen?'

'Oh, ages, well probably about....Oh, but I remember. It was twenty minutes past eleven because Cook said just look at the time and we hadn't even started lunch yet.' Eleanor nodded encouragement. 'Well, when the kitchen were back to rights, Cook says as how she is so far behind with things would Miss Addison help with the lunch. And Miss Addison says she will, not because it was her job mind, just to help out, like, but she'd have to do the flowers first.'

'What flowers were they?'

'The flowers to go on the dining room table for lunch and the ones for the sitting room.'

'I see, and where was Miss Addison when she did the flowers.'

'In the scullery. Mr Dakin had left the flowers in the sink ready first thing.'

'And the scullery is next to the kitchen.'

'Yes, you go into the scullery from the kitchen.'

'And there is no other way into the scullery except from the kitchen.' Ellen shook her head. Eleanor waited while Ellen took another biscuit and bit into it. 'Well, next, Miss Addison remembered the breakfast things hadn't been cleared.'

'She remembered that while she was doing the flowers, you mean?'

'I suppose so.'

'What was the usual routine for clearing the dining room?'

'Well, Madam would ring when she was finished breakfast and go upstairs and Hannah would go in and clear.'

'And because of all the fuss with the water in the kitchen, everyone forgot about clearing the dining room. Did Mrs Giffard ring that morning? Can you remember?'

Ellen frowned and sat thinking over that morning's events. 'That's a funny thing, Miss. Now you come to mention it, no, I don't think she did ring. I hadn't thought about it until now. And with Hannah being upstairs in the attic and Madam not ringing, I suppose that's why we forgot about clearing.'

'So, it was Miss Addison who cleared the dining room?'

'Yes, and she said she would clear because Hannah were upstairs and so she comes back with the breakfast things and tells me to wash the pots up and put them away and she goes back to doing the flowers.'

'And had Mrs Giffard eaten her breakfast as usual?'

'Oh, yes.'

'What had been eaten? Can you remember?'

'The egg and the toast. And some of the butter and jam were gone.'

'How many pieces of toast?'

'Three. We always sent in four, just in case, but she only ever ate three.'

'Do you remember which jam had been used?' Ellen looked at the ceiling for inspiration and then shook her head. 'Was there any jam left over?'

Ellen frowned and there was a long pause. Eventually she said: 'I don't know. I honestly can't remember for that particular morning. One lot of breakfast pots is the same as another, isn't it?'

'Yes, I suppose it is. If there was jam left in the dish, what would you usually have done? Put the jam back in the jar? Or thrown it out?'

'Oh, I'd never put it back in the jar. It would go in the scraps bin.'

'And you don't remember putting any jam in the bin?'

'No. Is it important, Miss? Because if it is, I will try to recollect but we were all of a muddle that morning and things are that jumbled up in my head.'

'Don't worry. Just try to remember if you can. Had Mrs Giffard drunk her tea?' Ellen nodded. 'So some of the milk was gone as well.'

'Yes.'

'And I think you told me before that Mrs Giffard didn't take sugar.'

'No, she didn't,' said Ellen and then turned her attention to Napoleon who was looking intently at the plate of biscuits. Eleanor waited.

Ellen said: 'Anyway, the jar wasn't there.'

'What do you mean, Ellen?'

'Well, you said did I put the jam back in the jar but I couldn't have even if I had wanted to because it wasn't there. Not the raspberry. When Superintendent Johnson came, he looked in the pantry and wanted to take the jam away, but there was only the blackcurrant on the shelf.'

Eleanor thought over what Ellen had just told her. Then she asked: 'Do you have any idea what time it was when the dining room was cleared?'

'Ummm, it must have been about twelve o'clock because Mr Dakin had just come in from the garden. He and Pritchard come in for their dinner at twelve and Cook was cross with Mr Dakin wanting to be fed when we were so far behind.'

'Who is Pritchard?'

'Madam's chauffeur.'

'So he came in for dinner too?'

'No, Monday is his day off.'

'I see. And then, at about twelve thirty, Miss Addison took the flowers into the dining room and that is when she found Mrs Giffard?'

'She took the ones into the sitting room first,' corrected Ellen. This was said quite confidently. Ellen was very calm and had obviously forgotten the distressed state she was in on the last occasion. She seemed to remember the events very clearly and was describing what had happened with no attempt at embellishment or exaggeration. Eleanor thought that she would stand up to questioning by the police, particularly after a few more days of Cicely's calming influence.

'Ellen, you have been a tremendous help. The details you have been able to remember are very important. It is also very important not to discuss this with anyone for the moment. Will you remember that?'

'Yes, Miss Harriman,' said Ellen.

'Come along then. Napoleon and I will walk you back to your parents' house. Would you like some biscuits to take home with you? I shall tell Mrs Clayton how much you enjoy her cooking.'

Eleanor took Ellen back to her parents' house in High Street and instead of returning to Hall Bank straightaway, she and Napoleon took the long way home down Terrace Road and past The Crescent. Eleanor needed to think about the events that Ellen had described and she had always found that being outdoors and walking helped information sort itself out in her brain and allowed ideas to form and re-form. When they reached the Turner Memorial Drinking Fountain, Eleanor sat on one of the seats there, enjoying the warm, still air of the evening and reviewing the sequence of events as narrated by Ellen. After a while, Napoleon's attention was attracted by some boys who had arrived at the memorial and were playing about in the water from the fountain. He stretched to the end of his lead trying to join them. Eleanor watched the boys pushing their fingers into the spout, trying to stop the water, and then yelling with delight when the pressure built up and caused the water to spurt all over them. They didn't seem to mind getting wet through. This reminded Eleanor of the scene in the kitchen at Manar. While Napoleon watched the boys, Eleanor continued to think and an idea slowly began to form. Through the fog of information, a shape was faintly visible. Then, the Devonshire Hospital clock struck the hour and broke her train of thought. It also reminded Eleanor that she had missed dinner and she headed back to Hall Bank to make another sandwich.

Chapter Twenty-Two

Eleanor and Napoleon were just finishing their food when Mr Harriman returned from his Club. All three of them went into the sitting room. Mr Harriman asked about the interview with Ellen and so began a discussion which went on long into the night.

'I am certain,' said Eleanor, 'that the idea of Isabel Giffard using morphine to kill Mrs Giffard is preposterous. There is a much better case against her if the poison was belladonna because there is no doubt that she had the opportunity, albeit a brief one, to put poison in the raspberry jam had she wanted to do so. But I think we can safely rule her out.'

'So, how was it done and by whom?' Mr Harriman looked at Eleanor and then smiled. 'You've already worked it out, haven't you?'

'I think I have. But I still need to be able to prove it.'

'Take me through your reasoning then,' said Mr Harriman, 'and we will test your theory. Let's begin with means, shall we?'

'First,' said Eleanor, 'belladonna is not that hard to come by and any textbook on poisons will tell you the correct dosage. In this case, the belladonna was readily available. Mr Wentworth-Streate's plant collection is a likely source and lots of people in Buxton know of its existence. Garroch Brae is also very close to Manar. But, there are plenty of other places around here where it could be obtained. Apparently it is common in disused quarries.'

'Right, I see. So, second requirement,' said Mr Harriman. 'To get the poison into the victim.'

'Food or liquid. In this case, food. Breakfast seems the obvious choice.'

'Although, there is still the question as to why Mrs Giffard was apparently well enough to leave the dining room and then re-enter it almost three hours later before she collapsed.'

'We can put that to one side for the moment because I think I have solved that puzzle.'

'Then,' said Mr Harriman, 'the third requirement is to get the poison into the food without anyone noticing.'

'The obvious place is in the jam served at breakfast. Two kinds of jam were served and it would have been possible to disguise belladonna in either of them but two different people are implicated depending on which jam contained the poison. If it was the raspberry jam, it could have been poisoned in the dining room but probably not in the kitchen, which, leaving aside Isabel Giffard, implicates Hannah. If it was the blackcurrant jam, it must have been poisoned in the kitchen and there are several candidates for that.'

'Do we know which of the two jams Mrs Giffard put on her toast?'

'No,' said Eleanor. 'Ellen couldn't remember what was left and she said that any unused jam would have been thrown out and not put back in the jar so, of course, any remaining evidence would have gone out with the waste bins or been conveniently disposed of down the kitchen sink when Ellen washed up the breakfast dishes. The odd thing is though, the jar of blackcurrant jam was left in the pantry but the jar of raspberry jam has disappeared. I don't know what to make of that.'

Mr Harriman thought for a minute and said: 'Perhaps to make the police think the poison was in the raspberry jam.'

'And the killer is trying to divert attention from the truth? That's possible. If the poison was only in the jam dish and not in the jar, the jar of blackcurrant jam could be safely left on the pantry shelf.'

'Probably neither of the jars contained the poison but by removing the raspberry jam the killer is drawing attention to the dish of raspberry jam which is harmless...'

'…and away from the dish of blackcurrant jam which contains the poison…'

'…in the hope that time will be wasted in investigating the circumstances of preparing the raspberry jam….'

'….which is possibly what has happened. Hannah took the raspberry jam into the dining room and could have poisoned it there but if the raspberry jam is a decoy Hannah is not the poisoner because she was upstairs out of the way when the blackcurrant jam was poisoned and put on the tray.'

'So,' said Mr Harriman, 'if we ignore the raspberry jam for the moment, either the poison was put in the blackcurrant jam when there was no one around or, if there were people around, the poisoner created a diversion to distract their attention.'

'The opportunity to poison Mrs Giffard and make it difficult for us to find the person responsible was very cleverly manufactured. It depended on careful advance planning and the management of a sequence of events that Isabel Giffard could not possibly have engineered. When I tried to make sense of all the information we have about the day Mrs Giffard died, I noticed that several things happened at Manar which were unusual, things which did not follow the usual routine.'

'I see,' said Mr Harriman. 'As Edwin is not here, I shall make notes for his benefit and he can look at them tomorrow.'

'Right then. First, two kinds of jam were served at breakfast instead of the usual one. The second unusual thing that morning was that Mrs Giffard specified which jam she wanted. Usually, she had whatever was sent in. That request created the opportunity for a second jam dish to be prepared. It was left on the kitchen table ready to go into the dining room and, because of the problem with the kitchen tap, various people went in and out of the kitchen without paying any attention to the jam dish. I think that absolves Hannah and the raspberry jam.'

'Number three?'

'Sarah Henshaw was taken ill at breakfast, went to bed, and slept soundly until early afternoon. I think that something was put in her food at breakfast to make her feel sick and that provided the opportunity to give her medicine ostensibly to settle her stomach, but actually to make her sleep. She would normally have been up in Mrs Giffard's bedroom tidying while Mrs Giffard was in the dining room and would have seen Mrs Giffard when she returned to the bedroom after breakfast. However, that day, Henshaw had been put safely out of the way and did not realise that Mrs Giffard had not returned from the dining room.'

'Next thing? Number four.'

'Mrs Giffard didn't ring the bell as she usually did when she had finished breakfast. That was the signal to clear the dining room. Ellen could not recollect Mrs Giffard ringing that morning, which may have been because Mrs Giffard was already dead.'

'Five.'

'Mrs Giffard would usually go down to the morning room after breakfast, where she would be seen by Hannah but Hannah was out of the way in the attic. With both Hannah and Henshaw out of the way in the attic, there was no-one to sound the alarm. There was no-one to notice that Mrs Giffard had not left the dining room, had not returned to her bedroom, and had not gone to the morning room. In fact, Mrs Giffard was not seen alive after nine fifteen when Miss Addison took the second tray into the dining room.'

'It's started to sound very suspicious. Six?'

'Miss Addison went into the dining room three times that morning although it was not part of her normal duty to do so. The first time to take in the second tray with the hot food, normally Hannah's job. The second time to clear the dining room, which Hannah usually did. The third time to take the flowers in for the dining room table before lunch, which also would normally be done by Hannah. And that is the seventh unusual thing. Hannah had been sent to clear a room in the attic although Mrs Giffard had made no mention of anyone coming to stay or of them needing accommodation for their servants.'

'Eight?'

'Mr Dakin was told to bag the tennis court in case there were guests that afternoon who wanted to use the court, even though he had already bagged the court at the end of play on the previous Saturday afternoon and the court had not been used since. Also, the ladies of The Park meet for bridge on Monday afternoons so Mrs Giffard would normally be out at bridge which means it is unlikely that she would have invited extra guests for lunch or invited guests to play tennis at Manar in her absence during the afternoon.'

'All of these unusual events were obviously engineered, they didn't happen by chance,' said Mr Harriman.

'No, they did not. They were all designed to get the various members of staff out of the way and unaware of what was happening to Mrs Giffard. And there is only one person who could have arranged everything.'

'I must congratulate you, Eleanor, on your masterly analysis. And I agree, it does point to one person.'

'Miss Addison. She is the only person who could have arranged everything. But, I have been reluctant to come to that conclusion. For one thing, she seems to be a perfectly ordinary, harmless person. In fact, I rather like her. And for another thing, I cannot for the life of me see what motive she could have for poisoning Mrs Giffard in such a determined manner. She had only been at Manar for a few weeks as a temporary replacement for the regular housekeeper.'

Mr Harriman said: 'There is a lot at stake, Eleanor. Let us make sure that this explanation is the correct one.'

'Right. The second breakfast tray has been prepared and the blackcurrant jam is in the dish on the tray. I need to create a diversion so I go to the kitchen tap and say that there is no water. I go into the scullery and say that the tap in there does have water. Now, that makes no sense. The only explanation is that previously I have turned off the tap in the cellar which regulates the water supply. The kitchen tap really does have no water and I only pretended that the scullery tap did have. No-one could see me in the scullery.'

'So, you turned off the water supply in the cellar before coming into the kitchen?'

'Yes, because as housekeeper I have all the keys and I can come and go anywhere in the house without attracting attention. Now, I need to get everyone out of the kitchen so I send Cook outside to check if the outside tap is working. I send Ellen to find Mr Dakin on the pretext that there is something wrong with the kitchen tap. I have already sent Mr Dakin to the furthest part of the garden so Ellen will take a while to get to him. While Ellen and Cook are outside, I put the belladonna in the dish of blackcurrant jam which is on the breakfast tray. Then I remove the top of the kitchen tap.'

'So Cook comes back and says there is water coming through the outside tap and Ellen comes back with the gardener.'

'Yes. Now, Catherine told me that a person who has been poisoned with belladonna often staggers about before they die so, if I have read the textbook on belladonna poisoning, I know that I need to create a noise which will mask any cries for help or the sound of furniture being knocked over in the dining room. I don't want anyone going to investigate before the poison has had time to work properly because it would be possible to rescue the victim if she is found in time. It seems that Mrs Giffard did stagger about the room, knocking furniture over, and perhaps even calling out for help, and yet none of the six other people in the house heard a sound. It also seems that the bell-pull in the dining room had been disconnected.'

'This really does sound incredibly cold-blooded,' said Mr Harriman.

'I agree, which is why I have been baulking at pointing the finger at Miss Addison but she really is the only one who had the ability to control everything. So, where was I? I have made sure that Henshaw and Hannah are out of earshot. I take the breakfast tray with the egg, toast and tea into the dining room and then, instead of returning to the kitchen, I go down to the cellar and turn the water back on. So, of course, water spurts everywhere because I have removed the top of the kitchen tap. When I get back to the kitchen, there is pandemonium. The water will need to be turned off before the gardener can replace the top of the tap so I delay that as long as possible in order to keep the noise going in the kitchen. I have taken the key of the cellar from the board where it is usually kept and no doubt it is in my pocket. I tell the gardener to go to the cellar to turn off the water. He goes to the board where the keys are kept and finds that the key is missing. I go and get the spare key from my room taking as long as possible without arousing suspicion and return to the kitchen. Cook and Ellen are preoccupied with trying to save the ingredients for lunch and dinner from the water and exclaiming loudly which is the perfect sort of noise to mask any sounds coming from the dining room.'

'Where is the dining room in relation to the kitchen?'

'It is on the left hand side of the building at the back and the kitchen is right across on the opposite side of the building also at the back. Between them is a large rear hall, which is sealed off from the main part of the house. The housekeeper's room, the servants' staircase and the door to the cellar are all there. Now, I don't want to send the gardener down to the cellar to turn off the water because if I let him into the servants' hall he might hear noises from the dining room. So I tell the gardener that I will go down to the cellar and turn off the water. Then I return to the kitchen, the gardener replaces the tap. I send him back to the tennis court and go down to the cellar and turn on the water again.'

'I suppose that these absences from the kitchen might also allow you to look into the dining room and check to see what is happening,' said Mr Harriman.

'Yes, that is possible although the timing would be tight. It is a horrible thought, isn't it? The sheer callousness of it.'

'So, when you are certain Mrs Giffard is dead you need to remove all traces of the poison from the jam dish.'

'Yes,' said Eleanor, 'so I go into the dining room and remove the dishes and I make sure that Ellen washes them immediately. I might even have wiped out the jam dish before I brought it back into the kitchen. It is now about twelve o'clock.'

'The police have created the morphine theory and arrested Isabel Giffard on the basis that Mrs Giffard was still alive at twelve o'clock. But according to your analysis, she was already dead well before then. Which brings us back to the problem we set aside earlier. I can see now, that your theory gets rid of that problem. There is a simple solution. Crystal clear.'

'Ockham's razor,' said Eleanor. 'The less convoluted the explanation, the more likely it is to be the correct one. Miss Addison said that the dining room was empty at twelve o'clock but, in fact, it wasn't. The truth is, Mrs Giffard was dead at twelve o'clock, probably well before then, and had never left the dining room. Catherine is of the opinion that if Mrs Giffard was poisoned at breakfast, she would have suffered symptoms almost immediately and would most likely have collapsed in the dining room within only a few minutes. That would mean she died while all the commotion of the tap was going on in the kitchen. And, of course, everyone believed Miss Addison. She left Mrs Giffard lying on the floor in the dining room, and then, half an hour later, when she took the flowers in, pretended to find Mrs Giffard dead.'

Mr Harriman was silent for a minute and then said: 'I agree with you. There is only one person who could possibly have engineered all of these events and your explanation ties together all the facts we have and gets rid of the timing problem. There are no loose ends. Brilliant analysis, Eleanor, absolutely brilliant.' Mr Harriman smiled at Eleanor and then sat thinking for a moment or two. Then he said: 'But, as you said, what motive could the housekeeper possibly have had?'

'Miss Addison doesn't stand to benefit financially from Mrs Giffard's death, not like the Major does. In that respect, I can see why Inspector Renshaw favours Isabel Giffard.'

They sat in silence for a while. Napoleon got up and stretched. He looked at Eleanor and, after assessing the likelihood of food or a walk, repositioned himself on the hearth rug.

Eleanor said: 'Of course, this may all be an elaborate theory on my part and I may be doing a terrible injustice to Miss Addison. I realise that it all depends on accepting my theory that she lied about the dining room being empty when she went in to clear at twelve o'clock.'

'But if you are wrong and Mrs Giffard did not die until some time between twelve and twelve thirty, where was she after she finished her breakfast?'

'Well,' said Eleanor, 'wherever she was, upstairs or the morning room, neither Henshaw or Hannah were there to see her.'

'This killing was a deliberate and calculated act and it

suggests a killer with a strong motive and no sense of compassion,' said Mr Harriman.

'I agree. So, what is the motive?'

'Well,' said Mr Harriman. 'Motives such as anger, hatred, or jealousy usually provoke an explosive, short term reaction and often are the reason behind unpremeditated killings. For a premeditated killing such as this, it suggests revenge: the desire to pay back suffering or to right a wrong. Perhaps, as you suggested earlier, we need to look back into the past and see if there is some connection between this poisoning and the poisoning of the Major's mother.'

'Well, if the motive was revenge, there aren't many people to choose from. Mr Giffard might have wanted revenge for the loss of his wife, but he is now dead. The Major lost his mother but he has shown very little emotion about that,' said Eleanor.

'However, the only person with a common connection with the two poisonings is Major Giffard.'

'Or his wife. So we have come around full circle.' Eleanor paused and then said slowly: 'There is another possibility though. I have assumed that Miss Addison acted alone and that she wanted Mrs Giffard dead but what if she was merely an accomplice? Or was acting for someone else? Someone who did have a motive to kill Mrs Giffard.'

'I suppose that is a possibility,' said Mr Harriman, 'but who would be a likely accomplice?'

'No-one springs to mind, I have to admit. And it is getting late. I am too tired to think about the Giffards anymore but it has been very useful talking things through like this. I'll take Napoleon out and then I think it is bed time.'

'Goodnight, Eleanor and well done. You have achieved a great deal today and, even if your explanation is not quite right, the information you discovered about the morphine will cause Inspector Renshaw to re-think his position and will certainly help Isabel Giffard. I shall leave my notes on

Edwin's desk and we can talk to him tomorrow.'

'Yes, I shall be interested to hear what he thinks of my theory. Oh gosh! Speaking of tomorrow, I'm supposed to be meeting Mrs Williamson, the wife of Colonel Westerbrook's friend. I had forgotten all about her with the drama about Isabel Giffard. Perhaps Mrs Williamson will be able to shed some light on the past for us.'

'Let's hope so.'

Chapter Twenty-Three

Just before eleven o'clock the following day, Eleanor walked through the majestic entrance of the Buxton Hydropathic Hotel, the finest hotel in town and, at the reception desk, asked for Mrs Williamson. The receptionist checked that Eleanor was expected and a page boy took her up in the lift to the suite of rooms occupied by the Williamsons. She was greeted warmly by Mrs Williamson. Major-General Williamson, thinking that the ladies would prefer to be alone, had tactfully taken himself off to the Crescent to consult the list of visitors in case there was anyone in town whom he knew.

After the formalities of introduction were over, Eleanor and Mrs Williamson settled themselves in the sitting room which had a wonderful view across the Gardens to the moors. Mrs Williamson was a typically self-confident, no nonsense, Army officer's wife and she came straight to the point. 'My husband tells me that you are interested in the Giffard affair. I realise you are probably very busy and have not come to here to listen to me rambling on about our time in India, so don't be afraid to just ask me whatever it is you want to know.'

'Thank you, Mrs Williamson. It's very kind of you to see me at all and I do appreciate it. You see, I have a client who has connections with Calcutta and, in order to help him sort out his affairs, I have found it necessary to investigate the death of Mary Giffard in 1895 and the disappearance of her husband Edward Giffard, the following year. Colonel Westerbrook said that you were in Calcutta at that time and he thought perhaps you knew Captain Bryant's wife and some of the other people involved.'

Mrs Williamson nodded. 'Yes, my dear, that is correct.'

Eleanor continued: 'I have only the newspaper reports of the trial of Florence Bryant to go by, so I am hoping that you will be able to fill in some of the details for me.'

'I shall do my best. I knew Florence Bryant quite well. In those days, my husband was only a lowly captain so naturally I mixed socially with the wives of all the other Captains, including Florence. It was a very sad case. One was used to the London papers giving sensational reports of trials at the Old Bailey but actually knowing someone accused of murder was quite a different thing. I didn't go to the trial but, of course, it was the main topic of conversation for weeks. But I just could not believe that Florence was capable of such a thing, even though she was put on trial for murder.'

'I understand from the newspaper reports that Florence Bryant was sent to a mental asylum and then not long afterwards she died.'

'She took her own life. What happened to Florence was cruel and wicked, utterly wicked. If she did poison Mary Giffard, she was driven to it but I believe she was innocent. I was not able to help her at the time, but later on I learnt things which persuaded me that I was right to believe in her.'

'Mrs Williamson, at this stage of my investigation I have no clear idea as to what facts are relevant and what facts have no bearing on the matter that concerns my client. Would you mind telling me as much as you can remember about these events?'

'Not at all, where shall I start?'

'Well, I would like to stick to the chronological order of events if possible but please interrupt me if something occurs to you out of sequence.'

'Right. Fire away,' said Mrs Williamson.

'I understand that you were all at the hill station at Darjeeling when Mary Giffard was poisoned. Why were the Giffards there and not in Calcutta?'

'Well, the main administration was in Calcutta,' said Mrs Williamson, 'but the heat there was quite unbearable during the summer so, for four months each year, the civil servants decamped to the hill stations. The Governor and his staff went to Simla and the Lieutenant Governor went to his residence at Darjeeling. Mr Giffard was one of the civil servants who regularly accompanied the Lieutenant Governor to Darjeeling so the Giffards went there every year.'

'And did you go to Darjeeling every year?'

'No, no. My husband's regiment was not stationed in Calcutta for very long and it was quite by chance that I was in Darjeeling that year at all. My husband had suffered a bout of enteric fever and he was very ill for some months. He was sent to convalesce at the military hospital at Jelapahar, which is just outside Darjeeling and a family friend of mine, the wife of one of the senior civil servants, was very kind and invited me to stay at her bungalow for the summer so that I would be close to the hospital.'

'And Captain Bryant was in the same regiment as your husband?' Mrs Williamson nodded agreement. 'So the Bryants would not normally have been in Darjeeling either?'

'No. They were only there that year because of Florence. The previous April, Florence's baby was still-born and she was still recovering from the shock. The governess who looked after the Bryant's daughter had suggested to Captain Bryant that it would do Florence good to get away from Calcutta.'

'The governess.' said Eleanor. 'Was that the Miss Hepworth who gave evidence at the trial?'

'Yes, that's right. She had only been with the Bryants for a few months but the previous summer she had been in

Darjeeling as governess to a different family so she knew what the hill station was like and thought it would be of benefit to Florence. Captain Bryant leased a bungalow for the summer and he joined them there for about a month.'

'And you didn't know the Giffards before you went to Darjeeling?'

'No, but the British part of the hill station was only a small settlement and all of the temporary residents lived in the same area. Many of the people had been going there for the summer for years so they all knew each other and new people were always welcomed. We all saw each other daily, at the various clubs and social events, and there were lots of parties.'

'So the civil servants had been in Darjeeling for nearly four months when Mary Giffard was poisoned.'

'Yes, that was in the September and, by then, everyone was getting ready to return to Calcutta. I had already returned the week before so I wasn't in Darjeeling when Mary Giffard died. A couple of weeks before I left there, Florence Bryant invited me to tea. She wanted to ask my advice. She was very upset, poor thing. She said that she had heard a rumour that her husband was having an affair with Mary Giffard and she didn't know what she should do.'

'Do you think the rumour was true?'

'No. Malicious gossip, that's all, and I told Florence it was nonsense. We all went to the same parties and social occasions so, of course, there was plenty of opportunity for people to meet and form alliances during the course of the summer but I certainly had not noticed any sign of such an affair, or even a flirtation. And Captain Bryant was only there for a month, not for the whole of the summer.'

'So you hadn't heard any rumour?'

'No, and I asked Florence where she had got such an idea from but she wouldn't say. After Mary died, the police got hold of the story somehow and according to them, it was the reason for the poisoning and that is why they arrested Florence. They decided that Florence's mental state was already fragile when she found out about the affair. In those days, it was quite common for doctors and people in authority to think that the balance of a woman's mind could be affected by childbirth or, in this case, the loss of a child. It was even thought to cause irrational or violent behaviour. So the police concluded that the rumour about the affair had sent Florence over the edge and she poisoned Mary Giffard out of hatred or revenge, without really understanding what she was doing.'

'Was Florence Bryant suffering from a mental condition, do you think?'

'No. Well, of course, I am not an expert in these matters but I don't believe so. Later perhaps, but not at that time. Mary Giffard was the one being treated for neurasthenia that summer not Florence.'

'And what about the alleged affair?'

'I never saw any evidence of impropriety on the part of Mary Giffard. She just didn't seem the type. In fact, I felt sorry for her. She was clearly very unhappy and very lonely. The previous year, she had been persuaded to send her boy away to boarding school in Scotland. He was five years old and her only child. She bitterly regretted agreeing to let him go. Apparently, her husband had made the decision the previous summer and she hadn't felt able to stand up to him.'

'So she had become ill after her son left?'

'Yes. I think she blamed herself for what had happened and there was no one she could talk to about her feelings. That was why she was being treated for neurasthenia.'

Eleanor was interested to hear this view of the Major's banishment. She was glad that she would be able to give him this information because he would be reassured that his mother had not rejected him. It would be of comfort to him, she was sure.

Mrs Williamson continued: 'The tragedy was that the real story did not come out until much later and by then it was too late to save Florence. I say "the real story" because, in the end none of us ever knew for certain what had actually happened.'

'When you say "us" do you mean the people who were at Darjeeling?' asked Eleanor.

'Yes, and the officers' wives who knew Florence. Naturally, the death of Mary Giffard and the trial of Florence Bryant were the subject of conversation whenever the wives got together. And among the officers for that matter. Believe me, they are just as good at gossip as their wives. There was a lot to talk and then several things which happened after the trial were difficult to explain.'

'So, are you saying that Florence Bryant didn't poison Mrs Giffard?' Mrs Williamson nodded. '…and that Florence Bryant was wrongly convicted?'

'I believe so.'

'But how could that have happened?'

'Because,' said Mrs Williamson, 'there was information which did not come out at the trial which should have and which might have made a difference.'

'How terrible it must have been for Florence to be incarcerated like that if she really was innocent,' said Eleanor. 'It is not at all surprising that she killed herself. You said that none of you really knew what happened but does that mean you have your suspicions?'

'Yes, because of the things that happened after the trial.'

'Are you able to tell me about those things?'

'Certainly. It all happened so long ago that what I have to say can't hurt anyone and maybe it is time the truth came out.'

'It would certainly be better for my client to know the truth. Mrs Williamson, can we start with Mrs Bryant? What happened to her after Mary Giffard died?'

'Well, there was an inquest, of course. That was held in Darjeeling. In those days, the journey between Calcutta and Darjeeling was long and difficult and for the people required to give evidence, it was not worth returning to Calcutta for three weeks and then going back there again for the inquest. So, Florence Bryant and Mr Giffard stayed on. Captain Bryant returned to barracks. Miss Hepworth brought Lilian, that's Florence's daughter, back to the Bryant's quarters at Calcutta and the next day gave notice. The wife of one of the civil servants, Mrs Rawlings, volunteered to look after Lilian. She had also been at Darjeeling for the summer so she had got to know Florence. She didn't have any children of her own and she was glad to do it. In the end, Lilian stayed with her for about seven or eight months. They were in Calcutta at first and then, because Mrs Rawlings had previously arranged to go and stay with her sister in Madras, she took Lilian to Madras with her, which was a blessing because it meant Lilian was out of Calcutta during her mother's trial.'

'And what about Florence?'

'Florence arrived back in Calcutta after the inquest and a few days later was arrested. She was in prison until the trial and then, after the trial, she was sent to the asylum. I did try on several occasions to visit her but every time I was refused permission. And then, of course, she took her own life.'

'Mrs Williamson, if Florence Bryant was not responsible for the death of Mary Giffard, why did she not defend herself?'

'Florence was a very timid and retiring person and not physically robust. She was not at all suited to the life of a soldier's wife. Even if she had been in England with her family for support, she would still have had difficulty adjusting to Army life. Captain Bryant was very ambitious and to get the promotion he wanted he had to take an overseas posting. Poor Florence found India overwhelming, the heat, the crowds, the noise. She was making the effort purely for his sake and she was not coping very well. She was very unhappy and always tired. Also, she was still grieving for the baby she had lost. It was a boy, you see, and there had been a lot of pressure on her to produce an heir. There had been no children since Lilian and Lilian was seven years old. Florence blamed herself for the baby's death and she felt that she had failed. In that frame of mind, she probably thought it perfectly understandable that her husband would find another woman more attractive than she was. I think Florence believed the rumour about the supposed affair. She certainly wouldn't have had the courage to raise the subject with her husband and ask for the truth.'

'So you think that perhaps she felt so unwanted that, after she was arrested, she just gave up?' said Eleanor.

'I think that is very likely. I certainly think she considered that she was to blame for everything that had happened and that she had brought this on herself. Perhaps she felt jealous of Mary Giffard and had wished her dead and then suffered from guilt, thinking it was her fault that Mary Giffard did actually die. Who can possibly know what wild thoughts were going through her mind at the time? Florence was a troubled soul. I only wish I had been able to see her. I might have been able to get the truth from her or at least been some help to her.'

'Why did Captain Bryant not give evidence and deny the affair?'

'The regiment had been posted out of Calcutta by the time of the trial. It was in Sitapor and was about to be deployed to South Africa to fight the Boers. It would have been difficult for the Calcutta lawyers to contact him there. And perhaps he was reluctant to be part of a public spectacle because of the effect it would have on his career. As I said, he was very ambitious.'

'That does seem unfair. But,' said Eleanor slowly,

thinking out loud, 'if the allegation against Florence Bryant was that she poisoned Mary Giffard because of a supposed affair, it would not have mattered whether there actually was an affair or not. The only important thing would have been what Florence herself believed because that is what would have motivated her. In which case, Captain Bryant's evidence probably would have been irrelevant.' Eleanor paused as she thought about this further.

Mrs Williamson said: 'Let me order some tea, my dear.' Mrs Williamson called for room service. As she sat down again she said: 'I can see that we will be some time yet. There is a lot more to talk about than I had realised.'

'Oh, I am sorry to take up your time like this but I do need to get as much detail as possible,' apologised Eleanor.

'I understand completely. I am very happy to be able to help and, of course, as we have been talking things that I had forgotten about are coming back to me.'

Chapter Twenty-Four

After tea had been brought and Mrs Williamson had served it, she said briskly: 'Now where were we?'

'You said earlier that information about the death of Mary Giffard only came out afterwards. After the trial, do you mean?'

'Yes. And not officially. Only in discussions amongst friends and only after Florence Bryant had died and it was too late. I couldn't go to the trial because I was in Sitapur and I am not sure that I would have wanted to even if I had been in Calcutta. Seeing Florence like that and being powerless to do anything to help her would have been most distressing. Because the regiment was going to South Africa I had booked a passage to return to England and my ship was due to sail from Calcutta in May. I went back there for about a fortnight beforehand to pay farewell calls on various friends and that is when I found out more about what had happened. I called on the friend with whom I had stayed in Darjeeling. Naturally we talked about Florence. I am sure that you have noticed that when people talk about something like that, little things which didn't seem important at the time begin to link up and make sense.'

'Exactly,' said Eleanor, 'people contribute separate pieces of information and gradually a complete story forms.'

'Yes. My friend had discovered that there was a liaison going on in Darjeeling during that summer but not between Mary Giffard and Captain Bryant, as we were supposed to believe. It was between Mr Giffard and Miss Hepworth. And, it had probably been going on the previous year, the summer before Mary Giffard died.'

'That would have been 1894?' asked Eleanor.

'Yes. My friend knew nothing about it at the time because she had not been in Darjeeling that year. She had gone back to England to take one of her sons to school but she discovered, talking to people about Florence's trial, that there had been rumours that summer.'

'That would have been before Miss Hepworth was employed by the Bryants, wouldn't it?'

'Yes. At the time, she was employed as governess to another family, of a civil servant who worked in the same office as Mr Giffard. She only went to the Bryants at the beginning of the following year, that is, 1895. When my friend told me about the rumour, it reminded me of something Mary Giffard herself had said to me. Mary and I were talking about how much she missed her son who had been sent away to school. She told me that Mr Giffard had insisted on him going and it was against her wishes. He said he was making the decision on the advice of a governess because a governess, being involved in education, had more experience in these matters than either he or Mary had. The governess had pointed out that it was a long time since Mr Giffard had been in England and he was bound to have forgotten the extent to which life in England was different from life in India. The governess told him that the longer the son stayed in India, the harder it would be for him to adjust to boarding school and her advice was that it would be kinder to send him to school straightaway. It was her opinion that, if it was left any longer, it would be too late.'

'It does seem strange to take advice about one's son from the governess of someone else's children,' said Eleanor.

'Quite. Unless, of course, you know that particular governess very well,' said Mrs Williamson, smiling. 'Well enough to trust her judgment.'

'Well enough to be involved in a liaison with her,' added

Eleanor. 'So, you think that the governess quoted by Mr Giffard was Miss Hepworth?'

'Undoubtedly. And, of course, I wondered if Mr Giffard intended to leave his wife and wanted the son out of the way. I also wondered if Miss Hepworth had engineered Florence Bryant's visit to Darjeeling that summer for her own benefit and not out of concern for Florence.'

'So that she could continue her affair with Mr Giffard?'

'Exactly. Then, when I made another of my leave-taking calls, I received another important piece of information which filled out the story. Mrs Rawlings had returned from Madras by then and Lilian had gone back to England with Captain Bryant. Before Lilian left, Mrs Rawlings had explained to Lilian the different customs in England so that she would be prepared for the change. She explained to Lilian that it was not usual in England to rest in the afternoons. Lilian began talking about the custom in India and she described to Mrs Rawlings how in Darjeeling, she would be taken to her room after lunch by the ayah and put to bed. The ayah was supposed to stay with her but Lilian let out to Mrs Rawlings that the ayah had a young man, one of the other servants, and that when she thought Lilian was asleep she would sneak out into the courtyard to meet him. Lilian quickly realised what was happening and would pretend to go to sleep straightaway and then, as soon as the ayah had left, she would get up and leave her room. At that time of day, the house was deserted because the servants were all in their own quarters, so Lilian was free to wander around the house. At one end of the verandah there were some large pots of bamboo and Lilian made a hiding place amongst them and went there in the afternoons to play with her dolls. Mrs Rawlings discovered that from her hiding place Lilian frequently saw Miss Hepworth leave the house by the side door in hat and gloves, dressed to go out.'

'So you think Miss Hepworth was meeting Mr Giffard

somewhere during the afternoons?' asked Eleanor.

'It seems so,' said Mrs Williamson. 'Unfortunately, Lilian was quite young and not very precise about dates and times so Mrs Rawlings couldn't be sure how long it had been going on.'

'And did Mrs Rawlings tell anyone about this?'

'No. It was too late to save Florence so Mrs Rawlings couldn't see that anything would be achieved by telling someone.'

'And, at the time when the police were investigating the death of Mary Giffard, it would not have occurred to them to question a child.'

'No. Everyone would have assumed that she was in her room all afternoon and had seen nothing. And then, after her mother was arrested, the natural thing was to get Lilian away as quickly as possible so as to prevent her from knowing what was going on. It was not something one could easily explain to a child of that age, or any age for that matter.'

Eleanor said: 'According to the newspaper report of the trial, Miss Hepworth gave evidence that she had not left the Bryant's house on the day Mary Giffard died.'

'Yes and, of course, that may have been the truth,' said Mrs Williamson. 'Mrs Rawlings did not ask Lilian about that particular day because she knew nothing about the evidence given at the trial. She was in Madras at the time.'

'And while you were there in Darjeeling, did you suspect that there was anything between Mr Giffard and Miss Hepworth?'

'No, although I have to admit that I am not the sort of person who is interested in that sort of gossip so I probably don't notice things the way other people do. I can tell you that I hadn't formed a very favourable opinion of Miss Hepworth. She was only about twenty years old. She had no connections and she was obviously the sort who had come to India determined to find a husband. She was always trying to attract attention and I was aware that Mr Giffard took a great deal of notice of her. But then so did all the other gentlemen. She invited their attention and there was a great deal of flirting. At the time, I thought it was no more than that.'

'But you think that the affair was linked to the death of Mary Giffard.'

'Definitely. Because of what I had learnt just before I left Calcutta. Mrs Rawlings and I both agreed that Florence did not poison Mary Giffard. She just would not have been capable of such an act, and we concluded that there was only one other person who could have done so and that was Mr Giffard.'

Eleanor thought: 'Oh dear. The Major's mother was murdered. Will I now have to tell him that his father was the murderer?' She said: 'But, according to the evidence at the trial, Mr Giffard had gone back to his office on the afternoon that Mary Giffard died.'

'He may have said so, yes. But was anyone asked to confirm that? It was most unusual to return to the office in the afternoon.'

'And the story that Miss Hepworth told Florence Bryant about Mary Giffard having an affair with Captain Bryant, what did you make of that?' asked Eleanor.

'I think that it was designed to provide a motive for the poisoning, a reason why Florence would have wanted to kill Mary Giffard. I know it sounds like something from a cheap novel but it is possible that Mr Giffard saw it as a safe way to get rid of his wife with no blame attached to him.'

'Because he preferred Miss Hepworth? It certainly is a plausible theory, and if that is what happened it was a very callous act.'

'Very callous, indeed,' said Mrs Williamson.

'What do you think happened that day?'

'Well, Florence's behaviour was unusual. You see, in

Darjeeling, we didn't make afternoon calls. After lunch, it was usual to stay at home and rest and we wouldn't meet up again until the evening.'

'I see. So the fact that Florence Bryant went to call on Mary Giffard during the afternoon was highly unusual and, therefore, suspicious.'

'Exactly. Also, the explanation that Florence gave for the visit did not make sense and I think that counted against her. If Miss Hepworth had wanted something from Mary Giffard, she should have gone herself, not have asked Florence to go. After all, she was the governess and Florence was her employer. So that was odd, and I thought so at the time.'

'So why do you think Florence went?'

'I think someone probably told her that she would catch her husband there with Mary Giffard, that sort of thing. Sent her a note, perhaps. Someone put her up to it. It is not the sort of thing Florence would have thought of doing herself. She just would not have found the courage.'

'So, you think she was lured there and then made the scapegoat.'

'Yes. Florence said that when she got to the house she found Mary Giffard already dead. I believe Florence was telling the truth. I think she was meant to find Mary Giffard.'

'And you think Mr Giffard set it up intending that Florence Bryant would be blamed for the murder?'

'I certainly think he set it up. I am not sure that he intended Florence to be convicted. It would have been a very dreadful thing to have done. Mr Giffard may have been besotted by the governess but I don't think he was that cruel. I have since wondered whether he thought that Florence was so obviously not the type of person to murder anyone that she would never even be suspected let alone arrested and tried. He may have thought that he was not putting her at risk and perhaps he hoped that no-one would be arrested. Then, after Florence had been arrested, I suppose it was too late. He had to go on with the lie.'

'The report of the inquest suggested that Mary Giffard might have committed suicide. Could it possibly have been suicide?' asked Eleanor. 'Could she have found out about the affair with the governess, perhaps?'

'We all thought that it must have been suicide at first because, of course, it never entered our heads that one amongst us was a murderer. And it is possible that Mr Giffard intended it to look like suicide. But then, at the trial, the Indian servant gave evidence that he had seen Florence and Mary Giffard together in the house that afternoon and that Mary was still alive when Florence got there.'

'Yes, that evidence was pretty damning. But it didn't seem very convincing. It seemed like a story invented well afterwards for the trial. I noticed that the Indian servant was not called at the inquest and later explained that it was because he had been visiting his family for the Diwali festival. I tried to verify that story and I discovered that the date of the Diwali festival varies each year according to the phases of the moon but I was unable to find out when it was held in 1895.'

'It was not until November that year,' said Mrs Williamson. 'I remember because the regiment had to wait for the roads to clear after the festival before it could leave for Sitapor.'

'I see.' There was a pause while Eleanor considered this information. Then she continued: 'Do you know what happened to Miss Hepworth after the trial?'

'No,' said Mrs Williamson. 'She had to remain in Calcutta until the trial but, after she left the Bryant household, we no longer mixed with her socially. I have no idea where she was living then but I do know that a few weeks before the trial, the wife of one of the officers saw her at the P&O booking office and she said that she was booking a passage to return to England as soon as the trial was over. After that, we heard no more news of her.'

'So you think Mr Giffard might have murdered his wife for nothing?'

'Well, there may have been nothing serious between them. It was clear that Miss Hepworth had come to India looking for a good match. She may have only been flirting with Mr Giffard until someone more suitable came along. There was quite an age difference, after all, and Mr Giffard was not particularly handsome or charming and, as a civil servant, he didn't have a particularly important social position. Looked at from her point of view, he was not much of a catch. And besides, it is possible that Miss Hepworth realised that he had killed his wife and had let Florence Bryant be committed to an asylum for life so that he could marry her. Surely, even a person as calculating as Miss Hepworth would be repulsed by someone capable of that.'

'Or very wary at the very least,' laughed Eleanor. 'As the second wife, one would never feel quite easy in the company of such a person.'

'Absolutely,' agreed Mrs Williamson, smiling. 'A veritable Bluebeard.'

'What about Mr Giffard? Do you know what happened to him?'

'After his wife's death, Mr Giffard gave up the house in Calcutta where they had lived and moved into a lodging house in Middleton Row, in the centre of town. Then, the week after the trial concluded, he left his post in the revenue office.'

'Colonel Westerbrook said he thought that Mr Giffard had disappeared,' said Eleanor.

'The Colonel is absolutely correct. That is one of the things which happened after the trial which caused people to wonder. I heard that Mr Giffard was at his office on the Saturday morning as usual and should have returned on the Monday but did not arrive for work.'

'And he gave no explanation?'

'Apparently not. Not even a hint. He hadn't resigned or anything like that. His fellow civil servants expected him to be at his desk on the Monday as usual.'

'And did the police or anyone make enquiries?'

'I was told that enquiries were made at his lodging house and in Calcutta. Mr Giffard had left the lodging house some time on the previous Saturday evening and had not returned. No-one saw him go out and he had not told the owners he was leaving. He left no forwarding address and they did not know where he had gone.'

'So he vanished without any trace?' said Eleanor.

'Effectively, yes. I suppose no-one realised that he had gone until he failed to attend the office on the Monday and by then, he could have been miles away.' Mrs Williamson paused and Eleanor waited in the hope that Mrs Williamson would remember further details. 'Naturally, people thought he might have been set upon in the streets, robbed or killed, but I understand that there was never any report of a body,' she continued. 'And besides, if he had gone out on Saturday evening intending to return and had met with an accident of some kind, all of his things would still have been in his room at the lodging house, wouldn't they? Whereas, there was nothing there. So, you see, he must have been planning to leave Calcutta and had taken all his luggage with him. I thought at the time that his disappearance was quite unusual but if he had murdered his wife, he could have been planning his departure for some time.'

'And I suppose when Florence Bryant was convicted instead of him, he would want to take advantage of that and leave as quickly as possible in case the truth came out. Do you have any thoughts as to where he might have gone?' asked Eleanor.

'No. He must have gone somewhere where he could make a fresh start without anyone knowing who he was. He had no need to work anymore, not with his wife's money, so it was not surprising that he decided to leave the Civil Service,' said Mrs Williamson.

Eleanor's mind flashed back to the probate application and the tea plantation in Ceylon. Was this where the money had come from to purchase the plantation?

'His wife's money?' she asked.

'Yes. Mrs Rawlings told me. She knew Mary Giffard quite well, with both of them being wives of civil servants. Mary Giffard came from a wealthy family who lived in Kenya. They owned coffee plantations. She was the only child and there had been a very generous marriage settlement so I assume the money went to Mr Giffard on her death.'

A motive for the murder of Mary Giffard was appearing and adding strength to Mrs Williamson's theory and Eleanor mentally stored it away for later examination. She turned her attention back to the conversation. 'And what happened to Captain Bryant and his daughter?' she asked.

'I have no idea. We lost touch with Captain Bryant. After the trial, the commanding officer made it plain that he didn't want the husband of a convicted murderer in his regiment. Bad for the reputation of the regiment and morale, that sort of thing. Captain Bryant was ordered to return to barracks in England. He would have had to leave Florence in the asylum and he probably knew that, once he got to England, he would be asked to resign his commission so I suppose that is why he resigned straightaway instead. I don't know what he was planning to do because there would have been no work for him in Calcutta but, then, Florence died and he and his daughter returned to England. I don't know how much Florence knew about what had happened. I always hoped that she didn't know anything. The regiment was the most important thing in Captain Bryant's life and if she had heard that he had been forced to leave because of her she would have been terribly upset. She certainly would have blamed herself for that. I did wonder if perhaps she did find out and that was what drove her to end her own life. Knowing that she was the cause of her husband and daughter being destitute, I mean.'

'Yes. I imagine it would have been dreadful for her if she had known. What happened to Captain Bryant?'

'I don't think Captain Bryant kept in touch with anyone from the regiment after he left India and I never heard of him again.' Mrs Williamson sat thinking. Then she said: 'Oh dear, I haven't thought about Florence for a long time and talking about the murder has reminded me how shocking it all was and how upset we all were at the time.'

'I am sorry to have caused you to revive such painful memories, Mrs Williamson. Thank you very much for seeing me. You have been a tremendous help. I have now got a much clearer picture of what happened and an impression of the people involved. Could I ask one more thing? Can you describe Miss Hepworth for me? What sort of a person was she?'

'Well, Mary Hepworth was very young, probably only twenty-one or two, if that, and very beautiful, strikingly so. Dark hair and eyes. She had a flawless complexion and very even features. She had a heart-shaped face and a widow's peak. It accentuated the shape of her face. In many ways, she was far too elegant for a governess. She had the sort of beauty that the books of advice to housewives counsel against. A governess should be as plain-looking as possible.'

'So as not to put temptation in the way of the gentlemen of the household?' laughed Eleanor.

'Precisely, and I suspect that Miss Hepworth had read those books of advice because she did dress plainly without any frills or flounces, always in grey with black hat and gloves. But it didn't really make much difference. She had a neat figure, quite petite, and she moved very gracefully. She had a charming way of walking and using her parasol, studied of course, which she used to maximum effect, and she danced superbly. And as I said, she had clearly come to India with the intention of snaring a husband and used all her charms for that purpose.'

'Mrs Williamson, can I ask how long you are going to be staying in Buxton?'

'We are booked here for a month.'

'At the moment, I am not at liberty to tell you the identity of my client but I can tell you that he is linked to the events we have been discussing. Sometimes it is best to leave the past buried, but I think that in this case my client would benefit greatly from being able to talk to you about these events. If you can spare the time, that is.'

'By all means bring your client. I look forward to meeting him.'

Eleanor expressed her appreciation again and left the hotel. She walked back to Hall Bank thinking that, until she had uncovered the full truth about this affair, it would be better for the Major not to hear Mrs Williamson's theory about his father.

CHAPTER TWENTY-FIVE

On Saturday, James closed the office at one o'clock and went home to his dinner. Conscious of the time limit imposed by Inspector Renshaw, Eleanor had arranged an appointment for Major Giffard later that afternoon, after the office had closed. Edwin had decided to stay at the office and, before she went home, Mrs Clayton had prepared lunch for the three of them. During lunch, Eleanor relayed to Edwin and Mr Harriman the information she had gained from Mrs Williamson and, when lunch was finished, they moved to the sitting room and discussed the theory which Eleanor had proposed the night before.

'When I consider the sequence of events over the past few weeks,' said Eleanor, 'I realise that each event on its own is unremarkable but when taken together, they do seem to form a chain. And I have been asking myself what started this chain of events? What was the trigger?'

'Well, it cannot be Mrs Giffard and her fraud because she has lived here for some years without incident or comment,' said Mr Harriman. 'The cause must lie in the arrival in the town of someone new and the first new arrival was Major Giffard.'

'Perhaps the chain of events started when the three Giffards met at the Sale of Work?'

'Or perhaps the catalyst was the anonymous letter? said Edwin. 'That certainly set off a chain of enquiries if not events.'

'Perhaps, though, we should see the exposure of Mrs Giffard for fraud and the murder of Mrs Giffard as two separate, unconnected events rather than as part of the one chain,' said Mr Harriman.

'That is a point, I agree,' said Eleanor. 'The work I have been doing for the Major has led to the exposure of Mrs Giffard as an imposter but we would have discovered that anyway whether she was alive or dead because it was the anonymous letter which started that investigation. In that regard, the encounter between the three Giffards at the Sale of Work was irrelevant.'

'And if the death of Mrs Giffard was brought about by revenge, the presence of the Major in Buxton may be immaterial,' said Mr Harriman.

'I wish we could identify the anonymous letter writer because I am sure that would also help sort out this riddle,' said Eleanor.

'Is that chap Brantlingham a candidate, do you think?' asked Edwin.

'Well, he was in the marquee when the three Giffards met but I don't see how he could have known enough about the Major or about the Major's father to have been able to write that letter. Besides, I think it is very unlikely that he would try to help someone recover their inheritance, even supposing that he knew something about it. He is more likely to try to cheat someone out of their inheritance and cause them harm.'

'Yes, he does not seem to be the type to be giving away information for nothing, anonymously or otherwise. If he knew something he would want payment,' said Edwin. 'I shall be interested to learn whether Brantlingham actually managed to get any money out of Mrs Giffard. He does not seem to have been very competent.'

'No, Philip summed him up as a chancer the first time he saw him and he was right. Brantlingham saw an opportunity and decided to follow it up. I think we may safely discount him as the author of the letter,' said Eleanor, 'or as someone even relevant.'

'I agree,' said Edwin. 'The theft of the Major's inheritance has been going on for some time. The writer must surely be someone with a connection to Ceylon otherwise how would they have come by this information?'

'It is possible,' said Mr Harriman, 'that someone heard the story that you have just heard from Mrs Williamson, Eleanor, and made it their business to make some enquiries.'

'It is entirely possible,' said Eleanor. 'There could be any number of ex-Calcutta residents in that category.'

'Well, there may be no connection between the anonymous letter and Mrs Giffard's death but we still have to consider whether or not the two murders are connected. Is this second murder motivated by revenge for the first?' asked Edwin.

'The method was the same and, as I jokingly said to Philip the other day, murderers are known to stick with the same *modus operandi*,' said Eleanor. 'As a result of what I learned from Mrs Williamson, I have added a bit more to my theory as to the second murder. How old would you say Mrs Giffard of Manar was?'

'Late forties?' said Mr Harriman.

'And she was still very attractive,' said Eleanor, 'even allowing for the passage of years. You could see that she must have been quite beautiful in her youth. Mrs Williamson told me that there was a rumour that the Major's father had been involved in an affair with Miss Hepworth, the governess employed by Captain Bryant. Mrs Williamson said that it was her belief that Mr Giffard had poisoned his wife because he planned to marry Miss Hepworth. She thought that nothing had come of it and that Miss Hepworth had returned to England instead of marrying Mr Giffard. I asked Mrs Williamson to describe Miss Hepworth for me. She was about twenty-one or twenty-two, possibly younger. That was twenty-five years ago so that would make her about forty-six or forty-seven now. She had the same colour hair and eyes as Mrs Giffard at Manar but, more importantly, she had a widow's peak. Mrs Giffard had a widow's peak.'

Mr Harriman and Edwin looked at Eleanor and were silent for a while, thinking over what she had said.

'It fits, Eleanor. I have to admit that it fits,' Mr Harriman said slowly. Edwin was nodding his head.

'Miss Hepworth left Calcutta after the trial and everyone thought she was returning to England. Mr Giffard disappeared from Calcutta at the same time. Miss Hepworth could have easily joined him in Ceylon and passed herself off as Mr Giffard's first wife. By co-incidence, her Christian name was Mary so, once in Ceylon, it would have been easy for her to use the first Mary Giffard's documents and pass herself off as her. Away from India, no-one would have been any the wiser.'

'As long as Miss Hepworth didn't meet anyone who had known her in India,' said Edwin.

'So,' said Mr Harriman, 'if Mr Giffard killed his wife it certainly would explain why he disappeared and did not claim his pension. To do so, he would have had to reveal his whereabouts and draw attention to himself. I am loathe to believe it but it is a theory which must be considered.'

'It was difficult enough to have to tell the Major that his mother had been poisoned. It is not going to be easy to tell him that his father was the murderer. I am not going to rush into that conversation,' said Eleanor.

'It does make the Major the obvious suspect for a revenge killing, doesn't it?' said Edwin.

'I think that we cannot rule anything out,' said Mr Harriman, 'but we must remember that until the Major received that anonymous letter he was not aware that he had any reason to seek revenge and even now he does not know the full story. We really do need to identify the writer of that anonymous letter and find out the source of his information.'

'This is very frustrating, isn't it?' said Edwin. 'Apart from what Dr Mackenzie might have to say about the morphine, we really haven't got anything to put to Inspector Renshaw and we only have about twenty-four hours left.'

'Well,' said Mr Harriman, 'I think all that Eleanor can do for the moment is tell the Major what she has learnt from Mrs Williamson and see what he has to say about it.'

'He's due at three thirty,' said Eleanor, looking at her watch. 'I'll just take Napoleon for a walk and clear my head.'

'I'll be off home then but I will keep going over things in case I can see a life-line,' said Edwin.

'Thanks, Edwin. Come on Leon, let's go for a walk and see if we can be a bit less dull in our thinking about this whole affair.'

As they walked, Eleanor thought about the anonymous letter. She thought back to that first interview with Major Giffard and her discussion with him about the clues to the writer's identity. The writer did not want to harm Major Giffard because the message was signed "a well-wisher" so it was safe to conclude that Mrs Giffard was not the author. Eleanor pictured the card on which the message was written. The card and the envelope were of good quality. The sort of quality one would expect of someone who lived in The Park. But when the ladies in The Park had been speculating on Mrs Giffard's absences from Buxton none of them had mentioned that they had any previous knowledge of her or of Major Giffard or even had any connection with India, so it was unlikely that any of them had written the letter. In fact, the only time that anyone had mentioned a connection with India was when Colonel Rathbourne recollected the chap called Giffard who had disappeared in Calcutta.

Eleanor stopped while Leon investigated an interesting scent and then greeted another dog. Eleanor spoke to the owner briefly and they resumed their walk. Eleanor turned her attention back to the anonymous letter and considered the handwriting. She stopped suddenly, causing Napoleon's lead to tighten. Napoleon looked at her reproachfully and sat down to wait. Eleanor realised that she had seen that handwriting recently. At the time, she had been distracted from thinking about it properly. As she thought about it now, she also realised that, at the same place, she had seen a supply of the card and the envelope which had been used.

'How could I have been so slow to make the connection?' she said to Napoleon. 'Oh, how very stupid of me!' Napoleon refrained from comment and maintained a passive expression. 'Isabel Giffard's arrest interrupted the line of enquiry I was following. But it still makes no sense. Come on, Leon, I need to talk this through with father.' Eleanor turned and hurried back in the direction of Hall Bank, Napoleon trotting along by her side. 'I hope there is time before Major Giffard arrives.'

There was no time to talk to Mr Harriman about this new discovery. In his anxiety for his wife, the Major had arrived early for his appointment. Mr Harriman had just invited him to take a seat in Eleanor's office when Eleanor and Napoleon returned. Napoleon bounded eagerly up the stairs scenting the presence of a visitor and burst into the office and greeted the Major before Eleanor could stop him.

'Oh, I am sorry, Major. I didn't realise that you were here. I'll get rid of Napoleon.'

'Not on my account,' said the Major. 'Delighted to make your acquaintance, Napoleon, old chap,' he said, shaking the paw that Napoleon had offered and then stroking the dog's back. 'You seem to have the boundless energy of your namesake.'

Napoleon gave him a soppy look, obviously intending to be friends for life. Eleanor always judged people by the way they treated Napoleon and by his reaction to them and she decided that, motive for revenge or no motive, she was not looking at the murderer of Mrs Giffard. Eleanor sat down at her desk. Napoleon took up a position at the Major's feet. Mr Harriman took the other visitor's chair and waited for Eleanor to begin. She explained to Major Giffard that a possible source of morphine had been found at Manar. She did not go into details, not wanting to breach her promise to Sarah Henshaw. She explained that Dr Mackenzie was going to test Mrs Giffard's medicine and, if it did contain morphine, would have another look at the toxicology report. She told the Major that she hoped that, with this new information, the Inspector might be prepared to release his wife.

'I am certain that my wife did not poison Mrs Giffard,' said Major Giffard, 'but I am extremely grateful to you for providing the proof of her innocence.'

Eleanor said: 'Major, this is not over yet, I'm afraid, and we cannot afford to relax.'

The Major frowned and said: 'But…I thought…'

'I have spent a great deal of time going over the evidence and I think I know who the killer is. As yet, I have no proof and, at the moment, I do not know why Mrs Giffard was killed. If I can understand the motive for the killing, I think that it will shed enough light to allow the police to arrest the correct person. If I am able to do that, your wife will have nothing further to fear. However, until I reach that point your wife is not completely out of danger.'

'But you can't seriously think….' stuttered Major Giffard.

'Major, I have no reason to believe that your wife poisoned Mrs Giffard. In fact, I am convinced that she did not but let me explain to you the difficulty she faces. If the police conclude, as I am sure they will eventually, that the cause of death was poisoning by belladonna and not by morphine, the question still remains as to how that poison was administered.' The Major was about to interrupt with another "but" and Eleanor continued: 'Inspector Renshaw seems determined to suspect your wife and if he moves from the morphine to the belladonna as the cause of death, he may conclude that your wife had the opportunity to put poison in the dish of raspberry jam which was on the dining room table when she arrived at Manar that morning. I am certainly not saying that she did that but, in theory, she could have done so. She was left alone while the parlour-maid was upstairs talking to Mrs Giffard. Unfortunately, judging by his past performance, it is the sort of incorrect inference which Inspector Renshaw is likely to draw.'

The Major remained silent. His shoulders sagged and he stared at the floor in front of him. Then he said: 'Miss Harriman I am enormously grateful for all the work you have done on our behalf and I am loathe to impose on your time further but do you think there is any way of resolving this nightmare?'

'Well, before you arrived I was walking with Leon in the Gardens and I was thinking about the anonymous letter you received. It may be the key to the events which have led to the death of Mrs Giffard. So far, we have not been able to identify its author. However, I think that I now know who wrote that letter.'

Mr Harriman looked surprised but pleased and said nothing.

The Major said: 'Do you, by Jove? Are you at liberty to tell me who it is?'

'At this stage, I think not. What I am proposing is that I should go and see this person to confirm my suspicions and then find out why the letter was sent. I think that the writer knows something about the past which is relevant to the death of Mrs Giffard. I also think that this person may help me to understand the motive for her death and then, as I said, I shall have the proof I need to be able to go to the police.'

'Oh, that is marvellous,' said the Major. 'If you could do that I should be eternally grateful.'

'Then I shall go this evening,' said Eleanor.

The Major was profuse with his thanks and, giving Napoleon a farewell pat, he left the office and was shown out by Mr Harriman.

Eleanor went into the kitchen to make some tea and rifle Mrs Clayton's cake tin. When Mr Harriman returned upstairs they went into the sitting room for further discussion.

'So, Eleanor, what is your idea about the anonymous letter?'

'I am certain that it was sent by Miss Addison and I am very cross with myself for not realising it sooner. When I was at Manar waiting to interview Sarah Henshaw I was sitting in the housekeeper's room, looking at the handwriting on a note which Miss Addison had left for Mrs Brompton, the permanent housekeeper. It was very neat, almost perfectly regular handwriting and quite distinctive. I thought at the time that the handwriting looked familiar but before I had chance to think about it Hannah came back with Sarah and that distracted my attention. It wasn't until I was thinking about it in the Gardens earlier that I remembered what I had seen and made the connection. I also remembered that, in one of the pigeon holes on the housekeeper's desk, there was a bundle of deckle edged white cards and thick white envelopes, just like the ones used for the anonymous letter.'

'I see,' said Mr Harriman.

'But,' continued Eleanor, 'even if I am right about Miss Addison, it still does not make sense. The person who killed Mrs Giffard must have known that her death would be very painful and perhaps intended that it should be so. It suggests someone without compassion. But the person who sent the anonymous letter was someone who cared enough to write it and wanted to help another person, possibly someone she did not even know. How could the writer of the letter and the killer of Mrs Giffard be the same person? Are we looking at Dr Jekyll and Mr Hyde?'

'The judgment of even a normally passive person can be disturbed by the memory of a particularly hurtful incident. People who take justice into their own hands can easily convince themselves that the method of punishment they choose, however harsh, is nothing more than the person who wronged them deserved,' said Mr Harriman. 'But is there any evidence that Miss Addison knew enough about the Major to write that letter? Is there a connection of some sort?'

'I don't know. That is something I'm going to have to find out.'

'The motive for sending the letter was possibly to right a wrong done in the past. Perhaps the motive for this second murder is similar.'

'It certainly all goes back to India and the story that Mrs Williamson was telling me this morning. What I am proposing to do is to go and see Miss Addison and ask her about the anonymous letter. I want to make sure that she is the author and find out what the connection is between her and the Major. I won't mention Mrs Giffard's death or my theory that Miss Addison caused it. I shall pretend that I know nothing about the murder.'

'I don't like the idea of you going to see her, I must admit, but I agree that there seems to be no other way forward. At least take Philip with you.'

'Of course, if it will put your mind at rest. I will telephone to him now.'

'And please remember, Eleanor, that if Miss Addison did kill Mrs Giffard you are dealing with a very clever person. Do not underestimate her intelligence.'

Eleanor went back into her office and spent time going over the new facts, putting them into chronological order, flagging those which were certain and those which were speculation. Nothing had so far shaken her conviction that

Miss Addison was at the centre of all of these events. As to the murder, she realised that every detail had been meticulously planned and it was going to be almost impossible to prove that Miss Addison was guilty. As long as Miss Addison stuck to her story and remained adamant that the dining room was empty when she went in to clear, the identity of the killer was in doubt.

Chapter Twenty-Six

That evening, Philip called for Eleanor and they drove to the address in Fairfield that Hannah had provided. Eleanor walked up the steps to the front door of a large house and rang the bell. A parlour-maid opened the door and Eleanor asked to speak to Miss Addison. She waited in the hall and, a few minutes later, Miss Addison appeared. Suddenly, Eleanor felt overwhelmed by the task in front of her and filled with doubt about the accuracy of her theory. Miss Addison was not a monster. She was a perfectly ordinary person. But then Eleanor remembered Isabel Giffard, also a perfectly ordinary person now wrongly under arrest. She pulled herself together and said: 'Miss Addison, my name is Eleanor Harriman. I am a solicitor and I act for Major Giffard.'

'Yes, I know,' said Miss Addison.

Eleanor was not sure if Miss Addison meant that she knew that Eleanor was a solicitor or that she knew Eleanor acted for Major Giffard. Either way, she was surprised at the response.

'Miss Addison, is there somewhere we could talk. I should like to ask you a few questions if you can spare the time.'

'Certainly, come into my room. We won't be disturbed there. The family is at the theatre.'

She led the way through the door to the servants' quarters and into a room much smaller and less well-appointed than the housekeeper's room at Manar. Eleanor sat in the chair she was offered.

'Now,' said Miss Addison, 'what is this about?'

‘A short time ago, my client, Major Giffard, received an anonymous letter. It advised him to take certain action, and he took that advice. As a result, I have been able to obtain information for him which has been greatly to his advantage.’

‘That is very good news, Miss Harriman,’ said Miss Addison, looking genuinely pleased.

‘Are you acquainted with Major Giffard at all, Miss Addison?’

Miss Addison did not answer. She looked at the floor as though she was unsure of how to respond. Eventually, she said: ‘I know who Major Giffard is.’

Eleanor felt herself standing in front of a brick wall, and she was not sure whether she should try to go round it or climb over it. She said: ‘The letter which he received was handwritten and when I was last at Manar I saw some handwriting that was very like that of the letter. I also saw that there were some of the same cards on which the letter was written and envelopes of the same kind too. It occurred to me, therefore, that the writer of the letter may have been at Manar.’

‘Indeed,’ said Miss Addison.

‘Miss Addison, I believe that the writer of the letter wished the Major well and wanted to help him. The writer wanted him to understand a great wrong which was done to him in the past.’ Miss Addison remained silent. ‘Naturally the Major wishes to express his gratitude to the writer and has asked me to locate that person if at all possible. He knew very little about his family and without the help of that anonymous letter he almost certainly would have remained in ignorance of his true position.’ Still there was no response and Miss Addison continued to look at the floor. ‘Miss Addison, can I ask? Were you ever in India or Ceylon?’

Miss Addison’s head jerked up and she looked straight at Eleanor. ‘Why do you ask that?’

'Because of the content of that letter. You see, I believe that the writer must have known the Major's family or known something about his circumstances. The Major's father disappeared in Calcutta about twenty-five years ago and to have had enough knowledge to write the letter its author must have been in India or Ceylon at some time in the past, or be connected with someone who was.'

'Has Major Giffard been able to secure his entitlement?' Miss Addison looked down at the floor again.

'It will, I think, just be a matter of formalities because there is now no-one to oppose his claim.'

'I assume that you are referring to Mrs Giffard,' said Miss Addison. She was not so calm now and she began fiddling with her necklace. Eleanor recognised it as the one made of jet which she had noticed Miss Addison wearing in the marquee at the Sale of Work. Eleanor remembered her promise to avoid talking about Mrs Giffard but saw that it was impossible to avoid the subject.

'Have the police made any progress, do you know?' she asked, looking straight at Eleanor, her face impassive.

'In relation to the death of Mrs Giffard, you mean?'

'Yes.'

Eleanor sensed that if she was going to achieve her goal she was going to have to turn the mention of Mrs Giffard to her own advantage. She said: 'Well, I can tell you that they have arrested someone.'

Miss Addison was startled and there was a sharp intake of breath. Eleanor saw fear in her face and her hands began to shake. The necklace she had been fiddling with slipped from her neck and fell into her lap. Eleanor was not sure if the clasp had come loose or the necklace had been jerked tight and snapped. Miss Addison caught the necklace and kept it in her hand.

'Oh, but...' Miss Addison stopped and paused. 'Are you able to tell me who has been arrested?' She continued to look with concern at Eleanor and was paying no attention to her hands. She was drawing the necklace through her hands, pausing at intervals to feel one of the larger stones and then moving on to the next one. Eleanor did not answer the question. Instead, she stared at Miss Addison's hands, recalling a description she had read. Miss Addison realised that Eleanor was looking at her hands and she put the necklace in her pocket. But it was too late. It had triggered a memory in Eleanor's brain. She knew exactly why the gesture was familiar. The newspaper report of the trial of Florence Bryant had described Florence holding a jet necklace almost as though it were a rosary. The necklace had been given to Florence Bryant by her husband on the birth of her daughter. Eleanor looked up from Miss Addison's hands to her face and knew that she was looking at Florence Bryant's daughter, Lilian. The daughter whose governess, Miss Hepworth, had been involved with the Major's father. Eleanor's eyes met those of Miss Addison. Eleanor tried to keep her expression as neutral as possible but her brain was racing. To gain time she said: 'Miss Addison, I am sorry to trouble you but could I have a glass of water, please? It is a little hot in here.'

'Of course,' said Miss Addison, standing up and breaking the tension. 'Would you like some tea, perhaps?'

'Thank you. That would be most welcome.'

Miss Addison went to the kitchen to order some tea. Eleanor's brain was now assembling the facts into their proper order and she came to a decision as to how to proceed. Then she remembered joking with Philip about not accepting any food or drink when she went to Manar to interview the servants. In her need to gain time, she had foolishly put herself at Miss Addison's mercy. What if Miss Addison took the opportunity to put something in the water or the tea? Eleanor pulled herself together and tried to look calm and unconcerned.

Miss Addison returned with a glass of water and Eleanor took a cautious sip and then put the glass down. A maid came in with the tea, placed it on a side table, and left. Neither of them touched the tea.

'Miss Addison, you asked me if I knew who had been arrested for the murder of Mrs Giffard. I do know, but I am not at liberty to say.' Miss Addison made no comment. All emotion had been erased from her face. Eleanor did not want to disclose the fact that the Major's wife had been arrested but she had thought of another way of conveying the information. She decided to take a gamble. She continued: 'Are you aware that Major Giffard's wife called at Manar on the morning that Mrs Giffard died?'

Miss Addison looked shocked and the colour drained from her face.

'At what time?' she asked. The question was barely audible.

'At about nine o'clock, just before Mrs Giffard came down to breakfast.'

'I didn't know.'

Eleanor remained silent. It seemed to her that Miss Addison was realising the full implication of this piece of information. They both sat perfectly still.

'You mean she was there in the house?' said Miss Addison eventually.

'Hannah let her in.'

'Why did no-one tell me?' The anquish she was experiencing was evident in her voice. Miss Addison was looking through Eleanor to some other place and she seemed to be asking these questions of someone else. Eleanor thought it better to remain silent and leave Miss Addison to think things through.

'There is no mistake?'

'None,' said Eleanor.

'You are absolutely certain?'

'Yes. I spoke to the Major's wife myself and then I spoke to Hannah.'

'Why did I not hear the bell?'

'The Major's wife didn't ring.'

There was another long silence.

'Do the police think that the Major's wife was involved?' Miss Addison looked at Eleanor. It was clear that she understood the situation.

Eleanor said: 'Yes.'

'They have arrested her?'

Eleanor did not answer immediately. After a pause, she said: 'I believe that the person who has been arrested is innocent.'

Miss Addison suddenly put her hands over her face and bent forward as though in pain. Eleanor waited. She experienced very mixed feelings as she sat there in the silence. Everything was making sense and her theory had been correct. Mrs Giffard had suffered a terrible death at the hands of this woman sitting before her and yet Eleanor was filled with compassion for her. Eleanor knew that she had to be patient and allow Miss Addison time to understand the implications of the information she had just been given. The wrong word now could ruin everything. Minutes passed and Miss Addison did not move. Eleanor was not sure whether Miss Addison was simply reflecting on the past or comparing the past with the current situation. Eventually, Eleanor decided to take a risk and break into those thoughts.

'Miss Addison,' said Eleanor, quietly, 'it may help you to decide what to do now, if I tell you that I know that your mother was falsely accused of the murder of the Major's mother and that she died as a result of that false accusation. I must also tell you that I know what you did at Manar.'

At last, Miss Addison looked up. Her expression was bleak, her face white. 'It's happening again,' was all she said.

Eleanor waited. She hoped that no noises from the other

part of the house would break the silence and distract Miss Addison. Eleanor needed her to come to a decision. 'Miss Addison,' she began but Miss Addison started speaking, almost to herself. She was not looking at Eleanor.

'It's happening all over again. The wrong person is being blamed. Another innocent person is going to suffer. I can't let that happen. Oh, why did she have to come?' She stopped speaking. Eleanor waited. Miss Addison said: 'Why? There was no need. I was taking care of everything.' She was staring blankly at the wall in front of her not focussing on the present but looking back into the past. Eleanor wondered what images she was seeing.

Eventually, Eleanor said: 'Mrs Giffard was your governess, wasn't she?'

Miss Addison looked at Eleanor as though she had forgotten that Eleanor was there. 'Yes,' she said, in a barely audible voice. She did not seem at all surprised that Eleanor should know this.

'Did you know that she was here in Buxton before you took the post at Manar?'

'No.'

'It must have been quite a shock then when you saw who your new employer was?'

There was a long pause and then Miss Addison said: 'She didn't recognise me but I knew straightaway who she was.'

'Yes,' said Eleanor, 'in twenty-five years she had probably not changed a great deal but you would have been quite different.'

'I was only seven years old when she last saw me and my name was different. And besides, when she knew me I lived in a house full of servants. She would not have expected her former charge to be working as a servant.' She spoke the words with bitterness.

Eleanor decided to avoid the trickier subject of Mrs Giffard and concentrate on the anonymous letter. 'Miss

Addison, when you wrote that letter to the Major, you said that all was not as it seemed. May I ask how you knew?'

Miss Addison sighed and almost smiled. 'Not much good has come out of the War,' she said, 'but one thing it has done and that is bring people together. People from very different walks of life who would never normally meet. But for the War, I would never have known about the Major's father.'

'Did you meet someone who knew him?'

Miss Addison said: 'Yes. I was a VAD in France and there was a soldier from the Ceylon Light Infantry on my ward. He was badly wounded and at night he couldn't sleep. I would sit with him whenever I could and he spent a lot of time talking to me about his home and his family in Ceylon. His father was a tea planter. There were terrible riots that year in Ceylon, very violent, and he received a letter from his mother. She was afraid he would hear about the riots and wanted to reassure him that they were all safe. I had to read the letter to him. His mother mentioned a Mr Giffard who had a tea plantation near theirs. He had died the previous year and, because of all the unrest, the widow had decided to leave Ceylon and return to England. His mother wondered if the plantation was going to be sold. I asked the soldier about Mr Giffard and his wife. He wasn't sure but he thought Mr Giffard had bought the plantation some time around 1897. I asked him to describe the Giffards to me. I didn't have much of a recollection of the Major's mother but the description of Mrs Giffard that the soldier gave fitted Miss Hepworth. That is how I knew where she and Mr Giffard had gone and how I knew that the Major's father was dead.'

'But how did you know about the Major's inheritance?'

'I guessed,' said Miss Addison, 'but I didn't know the details. When my mother was arrested I was sent to stay with a lady called Mrs Rawlings. I was with her in Madras for a long time. She was wonderful, very kind and understanding. Her husband was a civil servant in Calcutta. She was the one who told me that my mother had not recovered from her illness and that my father was going to take me back to England. We talked quite a lot about people dying and going to heaven and leaving behind people who would be sad. Mrs Rawlings told me that she knew someone else who had died recently, a lady called Mary, who had left behind a boy who was about my age. His name was Edward Giffard and he had once lived in Calcutta but was now at school in Scotland. Mrs Rawlings said that he would soon be told about his mother and he too would feel sad. I was curious about this boy and asked lots of questions. I felt a bond with him. When I told Mrs Rawlings that I felt sorry for him she said that I needn't do because he was luckier than I was. Unlike me, he would be well provided for because his mother had left him a lot of money and one day, when his father died, he would be very rich. For many months after I left India I missed my mother and also Mrs Rawlings and whenever I felt lonely I used to imagine Edward Giffard all alone at school up there in Scotland and it gave me courage. I felt I knew him. He was my friend.'

'So when you saw Major Giffard at the Sale of Work you realised who he was even though you had never met him?'

'Yes. I overheard his conversation with the other people he was introduced to that afternoon and I realised straightaway who he was. Then, afterwards, when we were clearing up in the marquee, I discovered that one of the maids who was helping at Top Trees worked at Oxford House where the Major was staying and I found out more about him from her. I was surprised to find that he was not rich and that he was going to be employed as a schoolmaster because I knew that his father had died six years ago and, if Mrs Rawlings was right, he should have inherited the money his mother had left him and should not need to work at all. I thought that, somehow, something had gone wrong with his father's Will and I wanted to let him know. I wanted to help him because, without knowing it, he had helped me all those years ago.'

'I see,' said Eleanor, nodding. Having solved the problem of the anonymous letter, Eleanor wasn't sure how to move on to Mrs Giffard's death. She decided that it probably would be easiest if she kept the conversation focussed on the past. She asked: 'When did you find out the truth about your mother?'

Miss Addison did not respond immediately and then she said very slowly: 'Things were kept from me. I knew that something was wrong but I did not understand what it was.' There was a long pause.

Eleanor said: 'I know that you were at the hill station at Darjeeling. Was that the last time you saw your mother?'

'Yes.' There was another long pause and then, when Miss Addison began again, she spoke rapidly as if the flood gates had finally opened. Eleanor had the impression that she had kept everything bottled up inside her for years and she now felt the urgency of telling someone all that she knew.

'I was confused about what had happened to my mother because I kept being told that she was ill but, before we left Darjeeling, Miss Hepworth said my mother had done something very wicked and that she was going to be punished for it for the rest of her life and that I was to forget all about her otherwise I would grow up to be evil just like her.'

'But that is a terrible thing to say to a child,' said Eleanor. 'Even if it had been true which, of course, it was not.'

'I thought my mother had become ill as a punishment for being wicked. Later, when I asked my father, he told me not to ask questions. He never mentioned my mother again and never talked about our life in India. When I was seventeen my father became ill and he knew that there was no cure. He thought I should know the truth and, before he died, he told me that my mother had been tried for murder. He explained that that was why he had changed our name when we returned to England. Addison was his mother's maiden name. He was afraid that people would talk and he didn't want anyone to know that he was related to someone convicted of murder. He said that he did not know whether my mother was guilty or innocent but that she had ruined his life. He explained to me that he had had to leave his regiment because of her and because there had been a scandal. The regiment was his life and he never recovered from the shame and disappointment. He died a broken man.'

Miss Addison paused. Eleanor could not help thinking that Captain Bryant had been a very selfish man. He seemed to find his own thwarted ambition more deserving of sympathy than his wife's wrongful arrest and death.

Miss Addison continued: 'He said that my mother had been sent to an asylum and that she had taken her own life. The day before she died, she had asked one of the nurses to give me a message and the nurse was very kind and wrote to my father. He gave me the nurse's letter which he had kept for me. The nurse said that, the day before she died, my mother had said to her: "Tell my daughter I did not do it. I want her to know that." But my father said that he could not understand why, if my mother was innocent, she had killed herself. He refused to tell me why she had been tried for murder. He said the only thing that I needed to know was that he had been the subject of a scurrilous lie put about in order to blacken his reputation and that it had ruined him.' Miss Addison looked straight at Eleanor. 'Why would he lie? He knew he was dying.' She seemed to be appealing for confirmation.

Eleanor said: 'I think, because of something someone recently told me, that he was telling you the truth. It was a lie, deliberately told although I don't think it was intended to cause harm to your father in the way that it did. It was told for a different purpose. What happened to you after your father died?'

'I had to go into service because my father left me nothing

and I had no means of support. When I read the letter from the nurse I hoped that one day I would be able to find out more about my mother and, perhaps, be able to prove her innocence but I had no idea how to go about it and no money to pay for anyone to investigate. Then, I heard about The India Office and so I wrote to them and asked about the trial and they referred me to the court in India. I wrote to the court and, after a very long delay, I received a letter telling me that a record of evidence was available if I paid the required fee. I had to save the money and then arrange to pay the fee. So it wasn't until about three years after my father's death that I was able to read the facts for myself. I found out why my mother was arrested and ever since I read the report of the trial I have lived with the knowledge that I may have been able to save my mother.'

'But you were only a small child. What could you possibly have done?' asked Eleanor.

'Children notice things without adults realising it, and they may not understand what they see but when they tell what they have seen and adults don't believe them that does not make them liars,' said Miss Addison with conviction.

Eleanor knew that nothing would ease the burden which Miss Addison carried because she had not been able to tell what she knew. Eleanor was afraid that Miss Addison would think that she, Eleanor, did not believe her and then the conversation would stop. She hoped that if she repeated what Mrs Williamson had told her it would give Miss Addison comfort of a kind and encourage her to keep talking. It might even lessen the feeling of guilt if Miss Addison knew that there had been someone else equally powerless to help her mother.

Eleanor said: 'I met someone recently who knew your mother and she was able to tell me something about that time in Darjeeling.' Miss Addison was clearly surprised by this. Eleanor continued: 'She is convinced that your mother was innocent and she too blames herself for not having been able to do anything to save her. She discovered, after it was too late, that Miss Hepworth had been involved in an affair with Mr Giffard, the Major's father. This lady also knows that you had seen Miss Hepworth leaving the bungalow in the afternoons.'

Miss Addison did not respond. Eventually, she said: 'How did she know about that?'

'Mrs Rawlings. Apparently, you told Mrs Rawlings that you had seen Miss Hepworth leave her room and go out of the house in the afternoons when everyone else was resting.'

'Thank you for telling me that,' said Miss Addison. 'I was quite young at the time and memory fades or begins to be interwoven with dreams or things one has been told. Sometimes I almost doubt myself and think I imagined what I saw, but you have reassured me. I was right to do what I did.'

Eleanor assumed that she was referring to the poisoning of Mrs Giffard at Manar but she made no comment. As the opportunity had presented itself, Eleanor decided to ask the question for which she wanted an answer: 'Did Miss Hepworth go out every day?'

'No, not every day.'

'Did you see her go out of the house on the day that Mary Giffard died?'

'Oh, yes.'

'You said that memory fades. You would have been used to seeing Miss Hepworth leave during the afternoons, how can you be sure about the day Mrs Giffard died?'

'That was the day before the party. My party dress was never finished and I was very upset about that. I wanted that dress so much. It had gold embroidery on the bodice. It is odd the things that are important to children, isn't it? And how indifferent they can be to the more important things happening around them.'

Miss Addison was lost in the past again. Eleanor thought how strange it seemed to be sitting here having a normal conversation with a person who was a murderer, someone who would soon be in prison awaiting trial. Life would be very different for Miss Addison from now on. Eleanor thought sadly that this was probably the last time that Miss Addison was ever going to sit and have a normal conversation with anyone. Eleanor decided that there was no need to rush.

'Miss Hepworth lied when she gave evidence at your mother's trial,' said Eleanor, 'because, according to the newspaper report, she said she had not left the house that afternoon.'

'I know,' said Miss Addison.

'But you must not blame yourself for your mother's death. Even if you had told someone about Miss Hepworth that would not have helped to convict Mr Giffard.'

Miss Addison frowned. 'What do you mean?' she asked.

'The Major's father. He killed his wife so he could be with Miss Hepworth.'

'Is that what the Major believes?'

'He doesn't know anything about it yet. The person who told me that your mother was innocent also told me that Mr Giffard had poisoned his wife.'

'That is not true. Please tell the Major. His father may have been a weak man but he was not a killer.'

'How can you be so sure?' asked Eleanor.

'Mr Giffard was at his office all that afternoon.'

'That is what he said at the trial but, like Miss Hepworth, he may have lied.'

'No. The report of the evidence is quite clear. Mr Giffard was in his office when he received the news about his wife and his clerk went back with him to the house. The clerk had been with Mr Giffard all afternoon because they were dealing with some urgent business. Mr Giffard would not have lied about that surely. The police could easily have checked.'

'That's true. Then, if Mr Giffard did not poison his wife, there is only one person who could have had any reason to do so.'

'Yes. Miss Hepworth.'

'Mr Giffard may have known what Miss Hepworth proposed to do,' said Eleanor.

Miss Addison did not respond. Eventually, she said: 'Miss Harriman, whose version do you prefer to believe? Mine or Miss Hepworth's?'

'I think I know enough about this matter to believe you, Miss Addison.' Eleanor had no need to lie for the sake of keeping Miss Addison's confidence and getting to the truth. She believed what she had said.

'Then I shall tell you what else I know about that afternoon when Mary Giffard died and you will understand why I am certain that it was Miss Hepworth who poisoned her. You will no doubt remember the evidence of the Indian servant?'

'Yes. He said that he had seen your mother with Mary Giffard and according to him Mary Giffard was still alive when he saw your mother enter the house. There was not a great deal of information in the newspaper report of the trial but I had the impression that it was his evidence that helped to convict your mother.'

'My mother was a frequent visitor to the Giffard's house and the Indian servant said that he recognised her and that she was wearing a shawl that he had seen her wear before. My mother had a beautiful shawl of a very distinctive pattern. It was her favourite and I remember it very well. I used to drape it around me and dance in the hall in the afternoons when everyone was asleep. On the afternoon that Mary Giffard died, Miss Hepworth went out at usual. I cannot tell you what time that was because time meant nothing to me then. On the other days that I had seen her go out, she was wearing her hat and gloves and carrying her parasol as though she was going out somewhere. But that afternoon she went out without any of those things. She had merely put on a shawl as though she was not going far and the shawl she was wearing was my mother's. It had been left lying on a chair in the hall. Miss Hepworth always wore grey, never anything colourful like that shawl. She wasn't away for very long, not as long as usual, and I saw her return. She took off the shawl and carried it with her into my mother's room. A little while later I saw my mother go out. She was wearing her shawl and she was hurrying.' Miss Addison stopped talking.

Eleanor thought about what she had just been told, then she said: 'When I first read the report about Mary Giffard's death I thought that whoever had killed her had intended it to look like suicide. The coroner certainly considered that explanation. But, adding what you have just told me to what I have recently heard from the lady I mentioned, I think that the intention was always to put the blame on your mother.' She paused and then spoke slowly, thinking as she went. 'So you think that this is what happened that day. Miss Hepworth went across to the Giffards and poisoned Mary Giffard and it was Miss Hepworth that the Indian servant saw wearing the shawl not your mother. Miss Hepworth then came back to your mother and persuaded her to go to the Giffards knowing that when your mother got there she would find Mary Giffard dead.' Miss Addison nodded. Eleanor continued: 'Miss Hepworth said that your mother had gone to return a book and to ask Mary Giffard for some gold thread which she needed to finish your dress. When I read that in the newspaper report, I did not find it very plausible and there is a far more convincing explanation. Your father told you that he had been the subject of a scurrilous lie. Miss Hepworth had asserted that your father was involved in a liaison with Mary Giffard. I think it was a lie invented by Miss Hepworth and told to your mother by her. I believe that Miss Hepworth told your mother that if she went to the Giffard's house that afternoon she would see for herself that the rumour was true. From what you have just told me it seems clear that Miss Hepworth intended that your mother should take the blame for a crime she did not commit.'

'And I could have saved her,' said Miss Addison.

'But you were taken out of the way as quickly as possible and you could not possibly have understood the significance of what you saw so there was no reason for you to tell anyone. Even if you had still been in Calcutta, no-one would have thought to question a seven year old child. And even if anyone had asked you, it would have come down to your evidence against that of the Indian servant.'

'But Kahar did not tell the truth.'

'He must have seen Miss Hepworth not your mother. So he was either lying or mistaken about the identity of the person he saw. Do you think he really did know who it was or did he just recognise the shawl and assume that it was your mother wearing it? Of course, it is possible that he did not see anything at all and merely said what he had been told by someone else to say,' said Eleanor.

'I believe that he saw Miss Hepworth, by accident, and that when Miss Hepworth found out she persuaded him to lie.'

'You mean he asked for payment to remain silent?'

'Yes, or payment to tell a lie.'

'He must have lied at the trial, but…' Eleanor paused and then, continued slowly: 'It did not occur to me before. There must have been an interval of about twenty or thirty minutes between the time when he saw someone giving something to Mary Giffard and the time when he responded to your mother's call for help. During that time, Mary Giffard lay dead on the floor and the person he said he saw had left the house. Why did Kahar not mention that lapse of time? His evidence gives the impression that the two events happened close together. No, I don't think he saw anything. I think he was told what to say.'

'And he lied about not being at the inquest,' added Miss Addison.

'Yes, he did. It was not Diwali for another two months. Perhaps he did see Miss Hepworth kill Mary Giffard and Miss Hepworth got him out of the way until after the inquest hoping for a verdict of suicide and then, when that did not happen and the police continued their investigation, she paid him to lie.'

Miss Addison was not paying attention. Her thoughts had wandered back to India twenty-five years ago and she began to describe a memory. 'There was a place I used to go. In the courtyard of the bungalow at Darjeeling. There was a large tree, a native tree of some kind. It may not have been very large. Everything seems large to a child. I wasn't supposed to climb it so I made sure no-one saw me do it. It had big, thick leaves so I was able to hide there. Sometimes when Miss Hepworth was with my mother and the ladies who came to visit, I would climb the tree and watch the servants doing their work and the people coming and going across the courtyard. One day, I am not sure exactly when but I think it was after Mary Giffard died, I was hiding in the tree and I saw a man come into the courtyard. There was a stone seat in the far corner of the courtyard and he sat down and then leaned backwards and picked up a small packet which was behind the seat and then he left. It meant nothing to me then but I have the clearest recollection of it.'

Eleanor said nothing.

'I wish I had been able to tell what I saw. I could have saved my mother.'

Eleanor sighed, and said: 'Perhaps.'

Eleanor waited to see if Miss Addison would add anything

further but her mind seemed to be still back in India. Eleanor decided to risk moving forward to the present.

She said, quietly: 'The wrong person was accused then and you were unable to help her but it is not too late to save another person who has been wrongly accused.'

Miss Addison did not react at first. She stared at Eleanor and then she nodded slowly.

'You are right, Miss Harriman. You are obviously a very clever person and I have heard people speak very highly of you. I trust you.'

'Then, will you come to the police station with me?' asked Eleanor quietly.

'Mrs Giffard deserved to die. Many lives have been ruined because of her selfishness. It was fate that brought me here.'

Eleanor made no comment. She thought that this was probably as close to a confession as she was ever likely to get. Twenty-five years ago, Miss Hepworth should have hanged for her crime and now, as Mrs Giffard, she had finally paid the price. Although this dreadful act of revenge was inexcusable, Eleanor could understand what had driven Miss Addison to it. Miss Addison still sat motionless and Eleanor was not sure what she would do next. Was she getting ready to run? Or was she going to admit defeat? Eleanor knew that she had to let Miss Addison come to a decision in her own time, but she was also anxious to get Isabel Giffard freed.

Eleanor sat and waited. She tried to imagine what was going through Miss Addison's mind. She had lost a mother when she was only seven years old, just as the Major had. Both of their lives had been shattered by the same person. Even after twenty-five years, the burning desire for revenge had not died down. Or, if it had been dimmed, the flame had been fanned alive again by the fact that, purely by chance, Miss Addison, Major Giffard, and Mrs Giffard were all in the same place at the same time. Eleanor recalled sitting at

Miss Addison's desk in the housekeeper's room at Manar and noticing how tidy everything was and thinking that this was a woman who liked order and preparation. That same dedication to order and preparation had gone into bringing about the death of Mrs Giffard. Every detail of the murder had been carefully planned. The one thing that Miss Addison could not have planned for was the visit of Isabel Giffard and, until today, Miss Addison had been completely unaware of that complicating factor. Also, she had clearly not known about the medicine Mrs Giffard was in the habit of taking, medicine which had caused Isabel Giffard to be accused. In that regard, Sarah Henshaw had been a model servant and Eleanor made a mental note to make sure that she got a proper reference. Eleanor was wondering what else she could say to persuade Miss Addison to go to the police station, when she realised that Miss Addison was speaking.

'She was evil. She thought only of herself. She caused two innocent children to be parted from their mothers. She stole the Major's inheritance so she could live the grand life. That had to be put right.'

'Well, it has been, Miss Addison. Because of the letter you sent to the Major, he will be able to recover his inheritance but it will be a hollow victory for him without his wife.' Eleanor paused to allow this statement to strike home.

Miss Addison remained silent.

Eleanor said: 'You do realise that if the truth about Mrs Giffard is known, the truth about your mother will also be known. People will realise that she was innocent. It is important to achieve that.' Eleanor paused. 'I have a motor-car outside if you wish to go to the police station.' Eleanor held her breath and waited.

'I will come with you,' said Miss Addison, very calmly.

Miss Addison went to the servants' door and Eleanor followed her out and down the path at the side of the house. Philip was sitting patiently in the motor-car and, as the two women approached, he got out and opened the doors for them. To Eleanor's relief he assessed the situation, realised immediately what was happening, and refrained from making any comment other than to say good evening to Miss Addison. They drove to the police station, a sombre, silent party.

Chapter Twenty-Seven

Early the following morning, Edwin accompanied Isabel Giffard to the police station where Superintendent Johnson completed the paper work for her release. The Major went along for moral support. They returned to Hall Bank and Eleanor told them of Miss Addison's arrest and the history of her connection with Mrs Giffard. She did not give them the details of Mrs Giffard's murder, not wanting to prejudice the trial, but she did explain that Miss Addison was the writer of the anonymous letter.

By the end of the day, the news of Miss Addison's arrest had spread through the town and reached The Park. The gossip centred on Miss Addison because Superintendent Johnson had agreed that, for the moment at least, the connection between Mrs Giffard and Major Giffard need not be made public. Miss Addison was removed from Buxton to be held on remand awaiting trial and within a few days she had ceased to be of interest except at the Hall Bank office.

Eleanor, Edwin, and Mr Harriman were relaxing in the sitting room with a pre-dinner sherry reviewing the Giffard case.

Eleanor said: 'It must have been very hard for Miss Addison seeing Mrs Giffard alive and enjoying all that wealth and acting as housekeeper to the person who had brought about her mother's death. Florence Bryant paid with her life for this woman's crime. It must have been intolerable. I know it is wrong but I feel very sorry for Miss Addison and I find it hard to feel anything for Mrs Giffard.'

'That is perfectly understandable,' said Mr Harriman, 'but we must remember that, no matter what wrong was done to Miss Addison's mother, it did not give Miss Addison the right to take another person's life. It is for the law to decide who will be punished and how.'

'I do understand. Miss Addison will be found guilty of murder which means she'll hang,' said Eleanor sadly.

'Yes,' said Edwin. 'Naturally, we shall explore every avenue for the defence, including provocation which would reduce the finding to manslaughter but I am not hopeful. It is a very, very slender straw to be clutching at.'

Eleanor said: 'It is strange to think that all of this was brought about purely by chance. Miss Addison was only at Top Trees for the Sale of Work because she was on loan. Normally, she would have been at Manar and would not have seen the encounter between the three Giffards.'

'And,' said Edwin, 'if it had not been for that chance meeting in the marquee, Miss Addison might never have known that the Major and Mrs Giffard were in Buxton.'

'Exactly,' said Eleanor. 'If Cicely had not told the Major about the Sale of Work, he probably would not have been there at all. And although Mrs Giffard was introduced to the Major and his wife at the Sale of Work, she certainly would never have invited them to Manar so Miss Addison would not have encountered them there.'

'And,' said Edwin, 'it was only by chance that she was sent to Manar as the temporary housekeeper. If someone else had been sent by the agency instead of Miss Addison, Mrs Giffard might still be alive and enjoying Manar as she has done for the past few years.'

'And the Major would have remained in ignorance about his family and his inheritance,' said Eleanor. 'That is at least one good thing that has come out of Miss Addison's actions.'

'There is just one glimmer of hope for Miss Addison,' said Mr Harriman. 'Lady Carleton-West telephoned me today. She has surprised me. She didn't have much time for Mrs Giffard and, having heard Miss Addison's story, she is organising a subscription fund to pay for King's Counsel for Miss Addison's defence. She has also asked if it would be appropriate for her to arrange for Miss Addison's mental state to be assessed at Wye House.'

'Oh, dear,' said Eleanor, 'that would put Miss Addison in the same position that her mother was in. Another case of history repeating itself. Still, it is very good of Lady C to think of it and to help with funds for the defence.'

'And Mrs Williamson has asked to see Miss Addison. Inspector Renshaw has given permission,' said Edwin. 'The Major also wants me to arrange a visit to Miss Addison if possible. He has already written to her to thank her for the anonymous letter but he would like also to thank her in person.'

'I think Miss Addison will be glad of a visit from Mrs Willisamson,' said Eleanor, 'and it will help Mrs Williamson to come to terms with the past too. I am also going to arrange for the Major to meet Mrs Williamson because he will enjoy meeting someone who knew his mother. He will be able to find out a bit more about his family.'

'What is the Major planning to do now?' asked Mr Harriman. 'I assume he wants us to take the necessary steps to recover his inheritance for him.'

'Yes, I have instructions to write to the solicitors in Colombo and explain the situation. The Major has decided to take up the position of schoolmaster for the moment until we see how things lie. He told me that he and his wife have discussed going to Ceylon and taking over the tea plantation but, having spent most of his life in Scotland, he thinks the change of climate and life-style would be too great. We shall wait and see, but the Major has confirmed his booking at Oxford House and he says that, whatever they decide, they definitely will be back next summer. Cicely and Richard are delighted.'

The funeral of Mrs Giffard took place at the Cemetery chapel without a church service. No Will had been found at Manar and a telegram to Mr Chapman, the Colombo solicitor, established that Mrs Giffard had no income and no assets of her own. There was, therefore, no money for funeral expenses. The Major asked Mr Chapman to make an advance in anticipation of his claim being successful but Mr Chapman, naturally cautious and very angry at having already been made a fool of by one person of the name of Giffard was not anxious to repeat the experience and so declined the request. The only alternative, therefore, was a pauper's funeral, arranged by Mrs Clayton's brother, Alf, and an unmarked grave.

Mrs Clayton arrived at Hall Bank with the news. 'Well, that's over. Alf says it was the sorriest affair he's seen and he's arranged a few funerals for unloved people over the years. No relatives. No flowers. Not a soul there except the chaplain. And it was raining. Still,' she added, philosophically, tying on her apron and getting ready to start work, 'you get what you're owed and I suppose that's all you can expect when you lead the sort of life she did.'

Eleanor reflected that if Mrs Giffard had been convicted in 1896 of the murder of Mary Giffard she would have been hanged and buried without ceremony in an unmarked grave inside the walls of a jail. A pauper's funeral, therefore, did not seem unduly harsh or inappropriate.